LOVE AND CHOICES

Miriam McDonald

Her husband forced her to the most difficult choice she would ever have to make. But if marriage meant giving up her whole life for his success, she had to give up the man she once loved more than herself.

Joe McDonald

It had always been just the two of them. Until she wanted to count as an individual. She had helped him to the top. Now she wanted something of her own.

Fletch Harbor

He wanted to love her and be part of her life. But he was so young that if she chose to love him, it could only end badly for one of them.

Howard Veitch

He offered her power at the studio and a shot at big-budget movies. But in choosing to betray her, he underestimated the woman she was.

Andy East

He was now a very rich man, but his feelings for her hadn't changed since they were high school sweethearts. If she chose his love, would he understand how much she had changed?

Other Avon Books by
Neal Travis

CASTLES

Avon Books are available at special quantity discounts for bulk purchases for sales promotions, premiums, fund raising or educational use. Special books, or book excerpts, can also be created to fit specific needs.

For details write or telephone the office of the Director of Special Markets, Avon Books, 959 8th Avenue, New York, New York 10019, 212-262-3361.

NEAL TRAVIS

AVON
PUBLISHERS OF BARD, CAMELOT, DISCUS AND FLARE BOOKS

PALACES is an original publication of Avon Books. This work has never before appeared in book form.

AVON BOOKS
A division of
The Hearst Corporation
959 Eighth Avenue
New York, New York 10019

Copyright © 1983 by Neal Travis
Published by arrangement with the author
Library of Congress Catalog Card Number: 83-90753
ISBN: 0-380-84517-2

All right reserved, which includes the right to reproduce this book or portions thereof in any form whatsoever except as provided by the U. S. Copyright Law. For information address Morton L. Janklow Associates, 598 Madison Avenue, New York, New York 10022

First Avon Printing, August, 1983

AVON TRADEMARK REG. U. S. PAT. OFF. AND IN
OTHER COUNTRIES, MARCA REGISTRADA, HECHO EN
U. S. A.

Printed in the U. S. A.

WFH 10 9 8 7 6 5 4 3 2 1

Palaces

PART ONE

Chapter One

THEY HOARDED THEIR GOOD NEWS, EACH WANTING the other to tell first. Miriam and Joe opened a bottle of champagne, sipping the cold wine and catching glimpses of river traffic that went with the East Fifties apartment. They hugged each other, and hugs led to caresses and they made love on the rug knowing that the draperies were open to the early evening light and the people in the highrise across the street. Finally, giddy, Miriam insisted Joe tell.

"Give," she said, grinning at him lying on the floor, spent and naked, wine running down his chest and mingling with the sweat. "What did Penton say?"

Joe McDonald sat up slowly, refilled his glass and reached out to Miriam. She sat down on the floor beside him and drank from his glass. The sun reflected into their big living room from the windows across the way, lighting the two of them with a reddish-gold glow. The long, awful New York winter was over. Miriam had never in her life felt more filled up.

"Mr. Penton," Joe said, slowly, "thinks the outline is, and I quote, 'a sure-fire, number one best seller.' He says all I have to do is put in a couple of extra chapters on the Los Angeles scene and maybe a bit of Midwest color, and we've got a national hit." He drank some more and fondled Miriam's breasts under her blue sweatshirt. "And Mr. Penton says when I've done that he will give me the first third of the advance." He stopped talking for a moment. "The advance is 265,000 dollars."

She began to cry. All the years of prodding, of boosting up Joe's ego. Now Joe McDonald was going to be a famous writer and they were going to live happily ever after.

"I thought he was going to reject the book," Joe continued. "We had lunch in the Rose Room, at the Algonquin, and he was bullshitting on about all the great writers who'd drunk there. Being so nice about what a good columnist I was, but kind of hinting that I was a newspaperman and the fucking ghosts in the Algonquin were *writers*. So I was prepared for the let-down. Then, just as the waiter brought coffee he said, 'How would 265,000 dollars suit you for the advance?' All I could think was that's an odd figure. Why not something round, like two fifty or three hundred? And then it started to sink in. Oh, shit, honey, I thought I was going to break down and cry. The book is going to happen, and you got me to do it."

Joe had spent the afternoon dazed and drinking, but even so, he was aroused and they made love again on the rug. He was still deep inside her when she told him her own triumph.

"Mike Benedict finally got the money for his movie," Miriam said. "Not enough to finish it, but enough to start." She ran her hands up and down his bare back and felt the goose bumps. The sun had gone and the room was growing cold. "Put something on, darling," she said. "We can't have the famous writer catching cold." She felt him slip out of her and they lay side by side, staring up at the ceiling. "He can't pay me much, and most of that will have to be deferred, but he wants me to be the assistant director."

Joe held her to him.

"Assistant to Benedict! Anyone would pay for the chance to work with a director like him. I'm so proud of you! You've worked so hard for this. You're going to kill 'em. I knew you'd make it."

"It's all so much at once," Miriam said. "We're too lucky. You get your book. I get my movie. I'm almost scared, Joe. Is there some price we're going to have to pay?"

He held her tight and stroked her back.

"We have paid it," he said. "All those years in all those towns, you following me from one shitty newspaper to another, nowhere to call home, no way to have kids . . . we paid our dues. Now we're going to enjoy it."

He stood up and, naked, waved at the old man across the way whose binoculars glinted.

"Show's over, fella," Joe said happily. He reached down and helped Miriam up. "I blew away the whole afternoon. God knows what I'm going to put in tomorrow's column. I'll have to be everywhere tonight. And all I want to do is stay home with you and celebrate. You better come on the rounds with me. The shape I'm in, I need someone to guide me. Actually, there're a couple of okay parties, and then we can stop by Elaine's. Sinatra's in town. He'll be there. I can always get a line out of him."

"I can't, Joe," she said. "I've got to start working on schedules for Mike. The money's so tight, we can't waste a day."

He shrugged. "All right. I'll face the glitterati on my own, drink Perrier, and conceal my joy. Don't wait up, though. It's going to take all night to put a column together."

Joe went off to shower and dress and Miriam checked the refrigerator to see if there was something for her own dinner. It was often like this: She didn't care that much for the endless round of party-going that comprised Joe's job. At least tonight she had a job of *her* own.

She fixed a tuna salad sandwich, put on a pot of coffee, and lit the fire in the living room. Joe came in, fresh and glowing from his shower, elegant in a soft blue tweed suit but looking boyish and excited. He seemed to be bouncing on his toes.

"Sure you won't come with me?" he asked. "We could make it a celebration instead of just another night of digging up gossip for the voyeur readers of the *Globe*."

"I'd love to, darling," she said. "But I've got to get to work on the figures, start calling people. You know what Mike's like—best underground filmmaker in the business, but the worst businessman. I'm going to have to be virtually the producer as well as assistant director."

"You want me to give him a plug in the column tomorrow?" Joe asked. "It might bring some more money in."

"Thanks, but it's too early for that yet," Miriam said. "You've done so much for Mike already. He's very grateful. Ever since you started writing him up, the industry has been taking him seriously." She frowned. "I'm not sure that isn't why he's hired me as AD."

He kissed her and laughed. "Honey, you got the job on merit. You know no one works harder than you, no one's learned more about the business in such a short time as you. The only thing I did was introduce you to Mike Benedict. After that, you were on your own with just talent going for you."

"And the fact that I can afford to work cheap, thanks to a successful husband," she said. She hugged him. "I do appreciate what you're letting me do, Joe," she said. "A lot of men would demand their wives stay home, wash their socks, warm their beds. But you've put up with all the mad hours and hopeless projects I've been involved in. I love you so."

"I love you, too," he said. "It's I who owe you. All the jobs you had to give up, all the moving, the nights waiting up while I worked the lobster shift. If I have to give up a little tender loving care at home for the sake of your career, you earned it."

"I don't want you to have to give up anything, Joe," she said. "I just want us to go on being happy and in love. Don't let your success—or mine, if success ever comes—do anything to us."

"It won't, darling," he said. "We're too smart to let anything come between us." He glanced at his watch. "But right now my deadline looms and I've got to hit the streets. A good gossip columnist is never found in his own living room after the sun goes down."

She kissed him good-by and went back to the fire and the script of Benedict's movie. It was so good, the closest thing to commercial work Mike had ever attempted. A simple story of three friends growing up in Manhattan. Almost none of the dark symbolism serious critics had praised in his past low-budget efforts but which had kept the audiences away in droves. She made notes on a yellow legal pad as she read: location pointers, sound and light problems, permits and permissions that would be required. She felt wonderful, in control but easy with it, the warmth of the fire on her.

Film. Movies, they'd called them when she was a child. Her father took home movies of birthdays, end-of-summer picnics, Christmas, everything.

"Dadsi!" She had never called him anything else, though Deborah always said, "Dad."

"Dadsi, you didn't get Mother in the kitchen."

He took the same scenes every year, pictures of what he called his princesses in their palace, unwrapping gifts he arranged by height, wrapped for maximum color. Deborah hugging an endless series of dolls, Pete the hound racing across the yard, skidding in the snow.

"Dadsi, you forgot Pete. And the tree, did you get it? Maybe you better film the living room again."

Eight years old; her father's AD. He held all their lives. Odd, but she'd never looked at the home movies since her father's death of a heart attack five years ago. No curiosity. She had helped him make his movies: It was enough that she had helped, enough to have made sure, year after year, that he left nothing out. She didn't need to see what he'd filmed. What could she possibly not know?

Odd, too, she thought, that viewing rushes or a finished film she'd worked on didn't have much impact on her even now. She pretty much knew what any shot would look like, and what went on during filming. Preproduction was all she cared for. Playing it out on the screen seemed an afterthought.

When the phone rang she cursed and went into the hall to answer it.

"Hey, big shot! You don't call your friends anymore, now that you're working?" Claudia Dennis, her best friend in New York, the one who shared all the frustrations of trying to break into the low-budget film business.

"I was going to, tonight," Miriam said. "You were the first person I wanted to tell, after Joe."

"You ought to know our business by now, kid," Claudia said. "One of us gets a job; we all know instantly. But, shit, AD to Mike Benedict is really something. I hear he's even going to pay you."

"Well, kind of," Miriam said. "Nothing like scale, of course, and the hours are going to be awful and we've only got about half the budget so far. But, yes, he's paying me."

"And does this epic run to a semiprofessional cast and crew?" Claudia demanded. "I mean, what's in it for me?"

"You, of course, are going to do the sound," Miriam said triumphantly. "Mike thinks you did great work on that children's documentary and he jumped at your name when I put it up."

"I bet," Claudia said. "He knows I come cheap. But just how cheap?"

"Seventy-five a day, no penalties?" Miriam said.

"Shit, I could make more than that just hiring out my Nagra," Claudia said. "But this sounds like more fun. I'll take it, of course. And thanks, Miriam. I won't let you down."

"We won't let each other down," Miriam said. "Not after all we've been through. We'll show everybody."

"You want to come over to my slum and open a bottle of wine to celebrate?" Claudia said. "Or, better, I come to you. Thank God Joe doesn't think three bottles of Raspberry Ripple make up a cellar."

"I forgot to tell you about Joe!" Miriam said. "They've bought his novel. Big, *big* money. He's made it! Can you believe it? All in the same day, I get a movie and Joe gets a book."

"Oh, Miriam, I couldn't be happier for you both," Claudia said, abandoning her usual cynicism. "Tell Joe congratulations from me. He deserves it. You've both worked so hard. Well," she added, "I guess you two are having a cozy celebration tonight."

"No," Miriam said. "I'm here alone. Joe's out doing his rounds for the column."

"The column?" Claudia said. "Isn't Joe going to tell the *Globe* to shove it now?"

Petite, blond Claudia, pretty even after a day grubbing in a tenement studio, never failed to shock her friend with blunt talk. *Foul mouth*, Miriam could hear her mother saying.

"Oh, no," she said now. "Joe loves that column. It took him years to get it and, well, you know . . . Joe's very loyal. He'd never quit; the *Globe* is like his best friend."

"We'll see about that." Claudia laughed her bubbling laugh. "I don't know anybody who kept working once he got published—not if he could help it, anyhow. So, are we getting together tonight to celebrate or have you got something more wonderful to do?"

"I have to block out the script tonight. Lunch tomorrow? My treat, and we'll go someplace gorgeous because, once we start on this film, we'll both be living on cat food."

Miriam went back to the fire and the script, but it was hard to keep her mind on the job. Claudia always reminded her of school, awful graduate school where Claudia had been her one salvation, her only friend.

The university had boasted the best film school on the East Coast and Miriam had had no trouble getting in, but it took only two weeks to see that she didn't fit in and would never feel comfortable there. These were *kids* she was learning with. Worse, it was kids she was learning *from*, the instructors all looking like her kid cousins. She felt old and slow and out of it every time she sat down for a lecture, every time she watched some whiz pick up the rudiments of camera work, heard students talk about technical matters. Everyone seemed to be speaking Japanese.

She'd had no choice but to stick it out, but the decent grades meant little. All she cared about was having the master's and being able to make a film. That the other students were gracious only made things gloomier: They were *trying* to be nice. It galled her, depressed her, and every night she hurried home to the comfort of Joe. Without his comfort, she wouldn't have gotten through school, that she knew.

She and Joe were so lucky. This big, comfortable co-op, the downpayment coming from a magazine series he had sold a few years ago. The comforts they could afford. Their marriage, still warm and trusting after ten years. They'd come a long way from Madison, Wisconsin. Surely Joe had come a long way from clumsy young reporter on a small paper to top New York columnist. And now she, too, was set to make her mark.

Something had been nagging at her all evening, though: What if she didn't have this film? What if they were celebrating only Joe's book, nothing for her? What if she didn't get another film after this job?

She stared into the fire, purple and orange, and chewed on the ends of her mousy brown hair. Used to be mousy, she reminded herself, now streaked a little blond. She was what men called a lovely woman. She was married to a successful man. She had her own . . . *thing*, she guessed they still called it, because it wasn't a career, not yet. She cast her memory back over the eight places they had lived in before this one, the towns they'd spent just enough time in to get Joe established in a job before they found him something better, elsewhere, and moved on, never having been a real part of the town they were leaving without regret.

What, she wondered, if it would always be that way? What if the one thing she had ever passionately wanted didn't happen for her? Could she live as just Mrs. Joe McDonald? What, in fact, if one success was all their marriage was going to have?

All the things they had planned together, way back then. She smiled.

"The good life," he had promised when they

were married. "We'll be where it's all happening. You'll meet famous people, live in fabulous cities. Because I'm good at what I do, and writing brings power, money, friends in high places. We'll travel all over the world, stay in royal palaces, go to the races with the Aga Khan."

She remembered laughing, snuggling next to him on the old divan in Joe's crummy apartment across the street from the Madison newspaper office. The palaces seemed too far away for the eager young man. But it hadn't mattered to Miriam. They would have their own palace, built on the foundation of their love.

It had taken a long time, but they were now dwellers in a Manhattan castle. The fire burned down and Miriam kept working.

He tried not to wake her but he stumbled against the bed as he was taking off his pants. It was almost dawn.

"Sorry," Joe whispered, sliding in beside her. "Things got out of hand. I phoned in the column and then I spilled my news to everyone and we closed Elaine's." His speech was slurred. "Everyone was so damn happy for me." He snuggled against her. "I didn't know I had so many friends."

Miriam, half asleep, felt Joe pressing against her, nuzzling the nape of her neck, moving his lips down to caress her nipples through her light cotton nightgown. It felt so good, lying there feigning sleep while he moved farther down her body, gently pushing up the gown and parting her legs. She shivered at the roughness of his cheeks between her thighs and then his tongue was there, probing. She was still pretending sleep when he entered her. He felt enormous, rock hard, thrusting deep within her. She kept herself still, languid, as if feeling these beautiful sensations were happening to another body.

He was quickening, and at last Miriam abandoned the pretence of sleep and came with him in a climax that went on and on until their bodies molded into one. Then he lay beside her and they held each other until she felt him drift into sleep.

"Three times in twelve hours," she whispered. "Success is good for you." She giggled and kissed him and they both slept, oblivious to the sounds of the wakening city below their window.

"It'll mean some changes," Claudia said. "All for the best, I hope. Don't you two let the money screw you up. You're about the last happy couple I know."

They were lunching in Le Cirque, elegant and expensive, surrounded by the beautiful, successful people who all had that look of belonging, having made it in Manhattan. Miriam had been to the restaurant before but always with Joe, tagging along as a welcome but inessential guest.

"It won't change us." She smiled. "It will just make a good thing better. Maybe it'll mean a new car, renting a place in the Hamptons for the summer. It just means I won't feel so guilty about not bringing in any real money while I'm trying to get established."

"You've got nothing to feel guilty about," Claudia said firmly. "Every time you got a good job, Joe moved on. If you'd stayed put instead of rushing off with Joe, you'd be a physicist or something by now. What about the research job in Chicago? You always said that would have led to something that mattered. And Miami and so on."

"I know," Miriam said. "And don't get me wrong. It's Joe who feels guilty for costing me whatever chances I had. But if we'd stayed put somewhere, I'd never have gotten into films. Now I can concentrate on being damn good at it without worrying about immediate returns."

"Don't say so too loudly." Claudia laughed. "They're all screwing us already, with the excuse of giving us experience. If they know you're an almost-rich girl, they'll be demanding *you* pay *them*. Anyway, tell me all about Benedict. It sounds like the best chance either of us has had so far."

They talked about the film through lunch, both unabashedly thrilled at being involved in a project with some remote chance of being seen by people other than underground film buffs. They both knew it would be an arduous process, horrendous hours and relentless corner-cutting, of constant strain to do it cheaper. But it was a chance to get a screen credit someone might see and remember. It might mean another job, another step to becoming professional filmmakers. It was their break. They were gleeful.

Miriam spent what was left of the afternoon working out of Mike Benedict's makeshift production office on lower Broadway. Benedict, as she had expected, was more than willing to turn all the preproduction work over to her. Of the four low-budget films he had made, three had been exhibited at festivals and one had been reviewed (savagely) by the *New York Times*. None had earned back its modest production cost. But he believed in himself, he had stamina, and he still had a few backers with faith in him.

"You look after crew and locations," Mike told her that afternoon. "I'm still trying to fix the script and get Firestone for the lead. Marcia Thomas will do the female lead for a deferral. Her show folded last week. Howard owes me and he'll take the second lead for not much more than zip. But Firestone's holding out for money. He's got himself an agent now! For Christ's sake, some people would rather earn scale on 'General Hospital' than work on a film like this."

"Some of them have bills to pay, Mike," Miriam said reasonably.

"Bills can wait. Art can't," he snapped.

From anyone else it would have sounded idiotic, but Miriam knew how seriously Benedict meant it. She had met him at the New Directors' Festival, through Joe, six months before.

"I feel sorry for the poor bastard," Joe had said. "He used to make a bundle directing commercials and gave it all up for underground stuff. He lives in a rathole, starves, lost his wife, lost all his old friends—to make movies hardly anyone will ever see."

Miriam had gotten to see all Benedict's small body of work and was thrilled. His first films were technically flawed, showing the problems of shooting on less than six-figure budgets, but they had a quirky realism that most of the multimillion-dollar Hollywood pictures lacked. In the months she had known him, while he was frantically hustling money for the new film and she was getting occasional assignments on commercials, Benedict had taught her a great deal about movies. High ideals didn't get in the way of a wry sense of humor and a gentle self-depreciation. He would be tough to work with, but he would always be inspiring.

"How much do you still need?" she asked. "This hundred thousand—is it all firm?"

"About half of it." He shrugged. "The rest is iffy, but once we get rolling it'll probably come through. Then we need about another fifty grand to finish. Don't worry. I'll raise it."

She met Joe at Grady's, the bar where the *Globe* staff hung out. He was still celebrating, happy as a kid and only a little drunk.

"You better come on the rounds with me tonight," he said. "I need a legman. They had to cut about a third of the column I phoned in last night. It was junk. What the hell, though. Soon I won't need the *Globe* and their fucking column."

She was shocked.

"Joe, you love doing that column. The book won't change that. I know you're all excited about the book, but you love newspaper work. Please, don't even think about throwing it all away. You're a little punch-drunk these days. Remember that."

He shrugged and grinned. "I guess you're right. It's just I don't see how I'm going to find time to finish the book while I'm working the hours the column takes."

"Use some vacation time," Miriam said. "They owe you a couple of months. You could finish it in that time, couldn't you? Take the summer."

"Yeah, I guess so, if we get out of town," he said. He waved his hand around the crowded bar.

"I'd have to be away from the usual distractions, away from Manhattan. Otherwise, I'd be hanging out every night, even without the column." He thought a moment. "It's not a bad idea. We always wanted to take a summer place in the Hamptons. We could rent a place out at Bridgehampton, away from the social scene, and I could work twelve hours a day and still hit the beach. Christ, Bridgehampton's full of writers—people to talk to when I run dry. Let's do it!"

She got caught up in his excitement.

"Yes," she said, "a little cottage near the beach, nothing fancy, with no room for guests. You writing in the attic while I'm downstairs." She paused. "There's one thing, though. Mike's film. It should be in full swing during summer. Who'd look after you out on the island if I was in town filming? I know all about those grass widows in the Hamptons over summer."

He laughed. "We'll worry about that if it happens. Benedict never starts a movie on time. He'll still be screwing around next fall."

Chapter Two

SHE FOUND THEM THE BEACH COTTAGE, A CONVERTED two-hundred-year-old stable half a mile from the beach and, as Joe noted, less than two miles from Bobby Van's saloon—where all the writers of the colony did their drinking. The cottage was quaint and tiny, just a kitchen and living room downstairs and two small bedrooms upstairs, one of which, facing out over the potato fields, would be perfect for Joe's study.

The rent was reasonable, and they decided to take the cottage from May 1, using it on weekends until Joe's long vacation. She found an old scrubbed pine table in a Bridgehampton junk shop and installed it in Joe's room and he began the arduous task of turning an outline into a book. He grumbled a lot each Sunday night, driving back into Manhattan, but Miriam always joked him out of his bad humor, reminding him of all the time he'd have for her and the book during July and August.

Except that late in June everything came together for Mike Benedict. He had his finished script, the actors ready, the crew assembled, and, most importantly, the backers with all the promised money.

It was astonishing, Miriam told Joe, just after they had made love in the sun-speckled bedroom of the cottage. It was a beautiful early-summer Sunday afternoon and the room was washed in a green glow from the surrounding woods and fields.

"Oh, shit!" he said. "I knew everything was going too well. Can't you put it off? This is going to wreck the whole summer."

"Joe, darling," she said gently. "Mike's not going to delay his film because an untried assistant director has a husband waiting in a cottage in the Hamptons."

"Okay then," he said. "What about dropping out of the film?"

"I can't, honey," she said. "You know how much this means to me. It's the best chance I'm going to get for some time, a credit on a Mike Benedict film. I'm sorry. I can't bear the thought of us being apart. But I've got to go ahead with this."

"Maybe I can put off my vacation," Joe said. He started to sound desperate. "Except that I've promised my publisher a first draft in September. Oh, Christ!"

"We'll be okay, darling," she said. "I'll be working around the clock, six days a week. You'll be out here with no distractions, also working around the clock. It's only for a few weeks. If we get finished on schedule, we can have the last two weeks together."

"Mike Benedict has never finished a picture on schedule," he said, miserable. "Look, I don't know if I can function without you. I need you!"

"You're a big boy now," she said, trying to tease him out of his misery. "You know how to broil a steak, and there are a dozen good restaurants within two miles of here. You'll be all right."

"I'm not thinking about food," he snapped. "I want you with me, encouraging me. You know I'd never have started this damn book without you pushing me. I don't know if I can finish it without you."

"You can," she said firmly. "We'll talk on the phone every day and I'll have one day off every week—even Benedict can't work more than six days. It'll work out."

It did.

Even if Joe had been in Manhattan, Miriam would have scarcely seen him during the hectic days of production. She was working sixteen hours a day, loving it but going home exhausted after each day. She called Joe twice a day, during meal breaks. He sounded tired but confident that the book was coming along well. Her first day off, Joe drove into Manhattan, they made love, ate in Chinatown, and Miriam nodded off at the table. After that they decided to wait for a two-day break for their next reunion. With only one day off, all Miriam wanted was to sleep.

Joe established a good working routine, writing from eight AM until noon, breaking for lunch and a swim, then working from about three until eight. Then he would walk to Bobby Van's, eat there and spend an hour or two at the bar with some of the local writers. He knew a lot of people in Bridgehampton that summer, and there was always someone to talk to, someone who knew the joys and frustrations of writing.

Joe had been around authors for a couple of years but it was only now, in joining their ranks, that he began to realize what a peculiar breed they were.

"You have to be a bit crazy," Ron Spellman told him one night in Van's. "When the words are coming easy, you work around the clock. When you get the dries, you might as well recognize it and go get drunk for a couple of days." Spellman was into his fourth book and this summer he was suffering the dries as never before. "I think I'm lucky if I get one finished paragraph a day," he complained. "So here I am, propping up Bobby's bar hours on end, the deadline getting closer. Still," he said, "it could be worse: If I'd stayed in Manhattan after the first book came out, I'd still be working on the second book. You've got to watch that. You can easily waste a couple of years sitting in Manhattan bars with other-writers talking about the last book you did and the one you're going to do next."

"But don't you miss it?" Joe asked. He had known Spellman slightly in the old days, when the novelist was editor of *Planet* magazine. "Don't you miss all the intrigue, the gossip, the friendship, the bullshit?"

"Of course," Ron said. "That's the *point*. I moved out here to the potato fields to get myself away from that scene because I enjoyed it too much! It gets in the way of your writing. Look," he said, "everyone writing his first book has to be working at some other job. But if that first book works, you have to give up everything else and go full tilt on the next, giving it your best shot. You got a shitload of money up front, Joe. If this book hits, you'll get another shitload. And you should quit the *Globe* the day you sign your new contract. Writing a column—you can always go back to that. But you only get one big shot in the book business. It better be your best."

Over the weeks, as the pages mounted, Joe

found himself more and more in agreement with Spellman. He was working hard and well and when he did relax and go drinking it was only for a little while. If he'd stayed in town, the partying would have been all night. He missed Miriam terribly and looked forward to their daily calls. But he knew it was better like this. He had no responsibility to anyone but himself and his book. She was happy, fulfilled with her film as he was with his novel.

Except that, after three weeks apart, and despite the excitement the emerging novel was giving him, Joe was sexually bursting. The beach and streets of Bridgehampton, the bars, the restaurants, all seemed caldrons of sexuality. The teen-age girls in their tight, tiny shorts, the topless young matrons toasting on the beach, reading steamy books and contemplating affairs while their husbands worked the four-day summer weeks in the city, the literary groupies who hung around Van's at night.

Joe had been unfaithful to Miriam only six times in their ten years of marriage. And never seriously. Only on the few occasions when his job had taken him away for more than a couple of nights, when passing intimacy with some other traveler stranded in a motel was better than a lonely drinking jag.

But in the heat of the Hamptons summer and the elation of the work he was achieving, Joe seemed to have a perpetual hard-on.

PALACES

"I'm horny as a toad," he told Ron one night in Van's. "It's funny. I love my wife and I wish she was with me but, hell, I need to get laid."

" 'Course you do," Ron said. "Everyone does. You can take the new celibacy and shove it. You and me, old buddy, we're of an age that just missed out on all the fun the new generation's having. If we fuck around, we feel guilty. If we don't, we end up with our balls in a knot. You're going to feel bad whatever you do, so you might as well feel bad doing something that feels good."

Joe blearily considered Ron's dopey wisdom. After all, it was Miriam's choice she wasn't here with him. He wouldn't even be thinking about making it with someone else if she was with him.

"You figure it would help my creativity?" he asked Ron.

"It surely wouldn't harm it," Ron said.

"Where do I start?" Joe asked.

"Here's as good a place as any," Ron said, waving at Van's crowded tables. "Look at 'em, all those ladies who like to fuck writers and only want you to sign your book for them. Shit, you're years younger than me, in good shape, lots of promise, even if your first book hasn't come out yet. Partake of the Bridgehampton Banquet." He gulped another rum and tonic. "But if you want a classier fuck, come along to Sheila Davie's the day after tomorrow. That's the literary mafiosi party of the season. You're on Sheila's list, aren't you?"

He was. Every writer, would-be writer, socialite and pretender on the island was invited to Sheila Davie's annual party in Easthampton. He hadn't planned to go but, hell, the work was coming so well he could afford a little fun.

The party was held in an old laundry which had been converted into a trendy restaurant. Joe and Ron arrived an hour after starting time, having fortified themselves with a few drinks at Van's. The party was in full swing.

It could have been any of the big parties he covered in Manhattan for the *Globe*, except for the clothes. Everyone was in his best casual gear. The silk shirts gleamed and the cotton ducks sparkled. The original occupants of the building would have been proud.

"Wall-to-wall pussy," Ron bellowed as they pushed through the crowd to the bar. "And most of the guys here are gay so you've got no competition." Ron didn't care who heard him. He was big and burly and, anyway, he was expected to be rude: He was a successful writer.

Sheila Davie descended on them instantly.

"Ronny, Joe," she cried, kissing both. "Welcome to my summer salon. *Everyone's* here. Isn't it marvelous? You two get something to eat at once. You writers need nourishing. I hear you're a summer bachelor, Joe," she said. "I must have you over to the house for dinner, make sure you get something hot." Winking at him, she wafted off into the crowd.

"Don't go unless you're an exhibitionist," Ron said. "Sheila's old man gets his kicks watching other guys fuck her. He—and the whole scene—have made old Sheila a bit nuts. She'll do anything to feel she's part of the arts. Her 'summer salon'! Poor bitch, we all just use her."

The drinking and the gossip flowed easily. Sheila knew how to provide for the guests she so eagerly courted: Fresh shrimp and oysters, bowls of caviar, smoked salmon, and quiches came flooding from the kitchen. The food was matched by French champagne, burgundy, good liquor, and icy imported beers lavishly dispensed.

Joe stuck with Heineken, pacing himself. All around him were people who hadn't bothered. Two very famous writers exchanged ineffectual punches, the only injury sustained when the taller of the two combatants slipped on a shrimp and cut his head on a crystal salad bowl. No one took much notice of the scuffle. The pair had been punching each other out at parties for years.

It was the year cocaine came out into the open and it was abundant. Joe wasn't really into coke, and smilingly declined proffered hits.

"You're absolutely right. Never touch that street

shit," Devon Bond said. "They're cutting it with soap powder. You want a good toot, stick with me. I've got some ninety-two pure, straight up from Bogata."

Joe knew Devon Bond casually. She was a giver of fund-raising parties for worthy causes and powerful politicians. She aspired to political power herself, was in her late thirties, and was a very, very rich widow. He'd never paid much attention to Devon in the city; she was out of his class. But now, out here on the island, with an almost-completed book, he felt her equal. She was beautiful in a strong, commanding way, almost intimidating. She was about as tall as Joe, dark skinned and big boned, and she carried herself with an air of certainty, probably from the knowledge that she could buy anything she wanted. She was so unlike his small, slim, gently pretty Miriam, Joe thought. For a second he felt an intense loneliness and considered slipping out of the party and heading back to Bridgehampton. But there was no one waiting for him there.

"I hear great things from your publisher about the novel," Devon said. "I always had you picked out to do something special. You look too smart to spend your life writing garbage for the *Globe*."

"You've always been happy enough to get a plug in the *Globe*," Joe said. It rankled when this crowd disparaged what he did. "Christ, half this room relies on the columns to keep their names known."

"Don't be touchy." Devon laughed. "I just mean you're destined for bigger things." She hooked her arm in his and pressed against him. The touch of her and the generous glimpse he got of her perfect breasts made him shiver. She grinned. "I'm leaving soon," she said. "The governor's having a little party in Southampton. Would you like to come?"

"Sure." Joe grinned. Ron was nowhere in sight and the party was down to the hard-core drinkers, the desperate ones.

But even if it had been the greatest party in the world, Joe would have gone with Devon. He was hungry for sex, certainly, but there was something more. She had the aura of power and riches, a knowingness.

The Rolls Royce and her careful chauffeur took the bumps out of the Montauk Highway and they glided through the night down to Southampton and the governor's party. It was a dull affair, the governor in one of his surly moods, the same tired old wheelers and dealers paying court to him. Everyone gave the impression of wanting to be somewhere else as soon as possible. No one seemed at all surprised when Devon Bond swept into the party with Joe on her arm. It was as if he belonged among these rich and powerful people.

But he knew he was accepted only because he was with Devon, just as it was his by-line, not himself, that made him acceptable at other important parties. They stayed only forty-five minutes, then back into the Rolls for the short ride to Devon's Gin Lane "cottage."

He'd been in the Gin Lane house once before, when Jerry Rich owned it and it was the scene of some wild show-biz parties. Devon had dressed the place up well. Instead of Jerry Rich's jean-clad gofers, there were a black-tied butler and starched maids. Devon spoke with the butler while Joe stood in the big entrance hall. Then she turned to him and took his hand.

"Lobster, salad and champagne on the terrace," she said. "You don't mind if we keep it simple? It's been a long, hot day." She pressed against him as they walked up the broad stairs and out onto the terrace which overlooked a long dark lawn rolling down to the Atlantic.

The day's filming had gone badly. Robby Firestone, the lead, had blown take after take. Mike was in an awful mood, and Miriam, closest to him, suffered most. The whole cast and crew were unsettled, skittish. It was a hot August Saturday night and they were stuck in this shabby studio on the Lower East Side.

"The only reason we don't get mugged leaving

here," Claudia had said the night before, "is we look as down and out as any of the locals."

They finally wrapped at ten o'clock and Miriam found Robby Firestone beside her as she was packing her gear. He was an interesting actor, conventionally handsome, several strong Off-Broadway productions behind him, a safe and comfortable career in commercial television spurned because he believed in film and in people like Mike Benedict who were trying to make films they cared about.

"Christ, I was awful today," Firestone said. "I just tried to talk to Mike and he told me to fuck off. Look, will you have dinner with me tonight? Talk things through, see if we can find why I'm having so much trouble with this scene?"

She wanted to say yes. As on every film set, except the ones where everyone knew from the start the project was a failure, they had all become family. Robby particularly attracted her. He was nice looking, talented, and he hadn't sold out. If they went to dinner, it would lead to bed. The thought of a warm, friendly body beside her was almost overwhelmingly attractive. But she had never cheated on Joe and she never would.

"I'm sorry, Robby," she said, "but I'm bushed. I'm going home, open a can of beans, and fall into bed. Don't worry about today—everyone's tired. We'll all sleep tomorrow and get it right on Monday."

When she got home she called Joe in Bridgehampton and was neither surprised, nor upset he didn't answer: It was, for normal people, early Saturday night, and he'd be out having a few beers with the boys. She was glad for him.

The vast bedroom looked out over the ocean. Devon commanded the room as if it were a ship and she the captain.

"Take a shower in there," she said, directing him to the left. "You'll find robes and razors and whatever you need. Then come back to me and we'll fuck like crazy."

He did exactly as he was told. Things were out of his control, and Joe was enjoying the sensation. Through supper she had played with him, teasing and flattering, hinting at the delights awaiting them. In the shower he had a massive erection and was glad he had restricted his drinking all day.

Devon was waiting for him, sitting up in the big bed with a fresh bottle of champagne and a vial of coke beside her. She was wearing something light blue and transparent and he could see her nipples erect through the filmy thing.

"You look sweet, like fresh-baked bread," she said. "Come in with me." He dropped the robe and slid between the crisp sheets. She stroked his damp hair and handed him the coke. "Have some," she said. "Like I told you, it's ninety-two pure. You're going to love this."

He took two snorts from a little gold spoon. There was an immediate rush. This indeed was not street shit. The drug made him feel strong and wise and enduring, packed with energy, sybaritic. He felt his cock grow even stronger as Devon's smooth fingers found it.

"Lie back," she said. "I'm going to blow you like you never had it before. Then we'll do some more coke, drink a little champagne, and play."

And that was the way it was. She made him come, then brought him back to come again. She fed him cocaine, which gave him perpetual virility, and cold champagne for the dryness in his throat. She used every part of her body to satisfy him until, finally, she left him drained.

Then it was her turn.

"In the bureau drawer," she said huskily, "you'll find some ropes and stuff. What you do is, you tie me to the four corners of this bed and you take the whip that's also in the drawer and you punish me. Hard. I'll tell you when to stop. And you keep saying, 'Bad little girl, this is for your own good.' " She looked at his confused face. "Joe, have some more coke and relax. This is my thing. It's a game, but when we start playing it's got to be for real. See?"

He took two more spoons of cocaine and a swig

of champagne. Sure, he nodded, he saw. She spread-eagled herself face down on the bed and Joe found the silken ropes and tied her limbs to the bedposts. He flexed the leather whip, staring at it, and she looked around at him, her face pressed against the pillow. Her lips were moist and her eyes hungry. She gave a tiny nod and turned away. Joe raised the whip and aimed at her trembling buttocks, so firm and brown, no bikini line. He flexed the whip again and prepared to strike.

And then he started to laugh. He couldn't help it or stop it. The laughter built and built on itself. He dropped the whip and collapsed on the bed beside Devon. The coke and champagne and all the sex he'd had gave him a feeling of well-being, of wisdom. He leaned over and patted Devon gently on her bottom.

"You're a funny lady," he said, laughing. "There's no way you really want me to hurt you."

She glared at him, real hate in her eyes.

"You fucking hick," she said. "You are so far out of your depth. Get out of this house—now. Go back to your fucking wife, or wherever you get your fucking provincial rocks off." She was crying, tears of anger and frustration. "Go! Now!"

He scrambled into his clothes and fled the mansion, up the sweeping gravel drive to Gin Lane. He had to walk a mile to find a phone to call a cab and he took it back to Van's, which stayed open very late. Ron Spellman was there, swaying a little but still in command. Joe sat beside him and, as if describing an odd dream, told him. Spellman seemed bored by it all and, when Joe had finished, grunted.

"If you *had* tanned her ass," he said, "the next step is she asks you to piss on her. That's the stage where I bowed out. Poor silly bitch."

Suddenly Joe was worried. Who would untie Devon?

Ron shrugged. "The butler does it."

They wrapped the picture only a few days late and Miriam was able to spend the last week of Joe's vacation with him in Bridgehampton. The book was finished. The publisher loved it. Mike's film had a lot of postproduction to be done, but it could wait a little while. They had a wonderful week together, loving and close and certain everything in their lives was going to be great from that time on.

Chapter Three

"THEY'RE TAKING THE BOOK SERIOUSLY," JOE TOLD her. "A first print of seventy thousand, promotion budget of more than a hundred grand . . ."

"A hundred thousand just to promote one book?" Miriam said. "Hell, I could make a whole movie for that."

Joe grinned. "It doesn't seem fair, does it? Still, that's what it takes to make a best seller these days. Launching parties, author's tour, advertising."

Miriam had been trying not to let her career frustrations show during the lead-up to Joe's publication. Everything was going right with the book. It was the lead title in the spring catalog, advance notices were great, and Joe's publisher was pressing him to sign for another novel.

"It *is* unfair," Joe said again and again.

They had completed Mike Benedict's picture just as the book was being readied for publication, and the contrast in the handling of the two projects could not have been greater. Benedict's film ran four days in a Village art house, was sketchily reviewed, seen by three hundred and twenty-two people—not including family and friends, who got in free—and then vanished. Since then she'd had a few days' work on commercials and a documentary. The rest of her time was devoted to Joe's big event. The *Globe* column took so much of his time, Miriam did most of the liaison with his publisher, checking galleys and cover copy, the cover itself, the picture of Joe for the jacket.

"I'll get my turn," Miriam said, kissing him. "Let's just enjoy what's happening to you right now. Now, have you worked out your list for the party?"

"They said we could have forty of our own friends," Joe said. "It's going to be hard to keep it to that. At least I haven't got any family to worry about."

"You don't have to worry about mine," Miriam said. "Mom won't leave Wisconsin and Deborah can't get away right now, either. Maybe if the tour takes us anywhere near Madison we can get together with them."

"They're still setting up the tour," Joe said. "But it looks like the full bit—forty cities in twenty-five days. They didn't buck at all when I said I wanted you to come along. I've heard about these authors' tours. Real nightmares. I said I couldn't make it without you along to guide me."

"Is the *Globe* still unhappy?" Miriam asked.

"Of course," he said. "And they're going to bitch more when we get back from the tour and I ask for three months' leave of absence to get the new novel started. But I'll worry about that when I come to it. I've got 'em over a barrel, anyway. They know I don't need their fifty thousand a year anymore."

She looked at him quickly. It wasn't that he had grown arrogant; just that he didn't seem to care about his column anymore. This book was all that mattered to Joe now. It saddened her. He was such a good journalist, and they had enjoyed good times in the newspaper business. She didn't like to see Joe turning his back so easily on what had been his love for so long.

"It's only a matter of time," Joe said. "I can't do justice to either job if I'm doing both at once."

"Let's wait and see," Miriam said quickly. "I know the book's going to be a great success, but there's no need to do anything drastic about the column yet."

They staged the publication party at Tavern on the Green. Joe had called in favors to get a respectable number of stars and media personalities there, and the party got good coverage.

The tour was hell. Endless "Good Morning Winetka" television shows, Joe sandwiched between teams of gymnasts and dog handlers; then whisked away to talk radio; then to a book-signing at a chain store; then the race to the airport. Pittsburgh, Cleveland, and Detroit in one day. Rubber chicken dinners with earnest fiction-appreciation societies. Final drinks in nearly empty hotel bars, their only companions other solitary travelers out selling their wares to the great American public.

"I didn't realize it would be so horrendous," Joe said to Miriam on one of the few nights they weren't booked. They were lying in bed in the best motel in Grand Rapids, eating overdone room-service hamburgers, drinking Scotch and tapwater and waiting for Joe to come on the late night news. "I'm sorry I dragged you along," he said. "I should have spared you. But thank God you did come with me. I'd have freaked out long ago without you."

"It's all been worth it," Miriam said. "It sells books and we're lucky all these people want to talk to you! Don't worry about me. I'm here to look after you. That's what it's about."

She hugged him and they moved together. They hadn't had the time or the energy to make love in more than a week. Miriam felt him against her, big and hard, and she guided his hand over her. She was ready for him at once and he entered her deeply. She could just see over his shoulder to the television set. His interview came on.

"Tell us, Mr. McDonald," the blonde with the teeth was saying, "what Jackie Kennedy's *really* like?"

She looked at the image of her husband on the TV screen, struggling to frame a new answer to a question he'd been asked two dozen times already, and she began to giggle. Joe started to laugh too, and they came together in waves of passion and great good humor.

Joe's agent called them in Los Angeles. The book was going on the *New York Times* best-seller list at number eight. He had a $400,000 offer for Joe's next work and advised him to sign.

They celebrated at the Beverly Hills Hotel with Bloody Marys beside the pool.

"That's it, then," Joe said. "The *Times*'s list was all I was waiting for. I'm writing the *Globe* today and quitting." He raised his hand before she could protest. "I know, darling. But this is a decision I have to make on my own. I can't go on with the column and do justice to the books. And I also know . . ." He ordered two more drinks from the waiter before announcing, "I can't write in Manhattan."

"So what I want to do," he said, grinning and proud, about to bestow his gift on her, "is this. Remember when we were working in Miami and we used to go down to Key West? How much we loved it? Well, last month I called old Rory Market and asked him to find us a place there. A place to buy. He should have something for us to look at when we get finished with this tour."

Stunned, she slumped back in her deck chair.

"It's going to be so great for us," Joe said. "I'll be able to work on the new book without worrying about who's feeling up which celebrity under the table at Elaine's. We'll have time together. Fucking in the sun, drinking coconut cocktails under the stars, catching fish off the dock. We'll get a little boat, learn sailing. And a sports car. Life is going to be a ball from now on." He took her hand. "I owe you so much, darling. All the years you've given to me and asked nothing for yourself. We'll get down there and relax and live the good life. And, maybe, if you want, we could think about having a kid. Miriam?"

He was still holding her hand. She looked across at him. He was so eager for her approval, a little boy bringing home a terrific report card. The anger rose in her but she would not spoil his moment. She drank deeply and waited for the emotion to subside.

"Joe," she said very carefully, "you're the only

one who knows whether you can write and do the column at the same time. And, yes, we both loved Key West. There's just one problem: What happens to me? Look, I know my career hasn't been too brilliant so far, but darling, I'm on the edge of making it. I've done my time. I've paid my dues, and soon, if I stick with it, I'll be a real director." She waved around the pool. "Joe, *I* could be bringing *you* here one of these days." She laughed. "Okay, it'll be a long time before I get an Oscar nomination. But it could damn well be, and I'm going to try and make it happen."

"I'm sorry, darling," Joe said. "I wasn't thinking clearly, I guess. Of course you'll continue with your films. We'll keep the place in New York, so you've got a base to work from. And I'm not giving up the city, not totally. I'd still want to come to Manhattan every month or so, to see everyone and keep a sense of what's going on. No, you go on making films and we'll work it out. Hell, you've only worked about three months out of the last twelve, anyway."

"Don't rub it in," she said. He squeezed her hand and she knew he hadn't meant the remark to sound that way. He was just a little clumsy sometimes.

Back in New York, all their friends applauded the idea of the move to Key West. Everyone would miss Joe and Miriam, but they'd all visit, and Joe was right to get out of the city. Everyone envied them. Everyone except Claudia.

"It won't work," she said, keeping her voice down. They were having a drink in Steve's Place, a little downtown bar near Claudia's sixth-floor walk-up in Chelsea. Miriam liked Steve's Place: It was so unlike the glamorous places Joe usually took her. At Steve's, most of the drinkers were young, broke, and struggling, but nevertheless supremely confident.

"How's Joe going to cope with you away on location for six or eight weeks?" Claudia continued. "Or spending three or four days on a commercial when he wants you to give a party for Jimmy Buffett or whatever? I know you, Miriam, and I know you're going to be torn apart by guilt if you're not playing your part as loving wife and supporter of the great writer. Honey, you might as well face up to it now. Forget about this damned business. Go with Joe, enjoy yourself, get fat on Pina Coladas and babies. Don't take any risks or you'll get hurt."

"You don't know me that well, Claudia," Miriam said. "I damn well can cope with two roles. I'm not going to let Joe down, but I'm not going to let me down, either. We're two grown people who love each other, Joe and I. If and when I start getting a lot of work, Joe will be right with me."

"Bullshit," Claudia said. It was as close as they ever came to a real quarrel. "I'm sorry," Claudia said. "I've got faith in both of you, and I want it all to work. Anyway, it's none of my business."

"Yes, it is," Miriam said. "You're the best friend I've got and you and I have been through so much together. You know how much giving up would cost me. *You* wouldn't just turn away from it."

"Don't be too sure, kid." Claudia laughed. "So far no one rich enough has asked me to give it all up for him. I don't know how I'd react. Maybe I'd take the easy life."

"You wouldn't," Miriam said flatly. "And I won't. It means too much to me. I can't give it up."

Miriam loved Claudia. Her friend was warm, honest, generous, and she cared about Miriam and worried about her marriage. But why, Miriam asked herself, did she always have to explain everything to Claudia? Wasn't a real friend somebody who knew things without being told? It was as though Claudia loved Miriam without being close to her. In fact, the only person who seemed really to feel for her was Joe. Joe understood in ways nobody else ever had. Joe: he was all she had. Maybe he was all she would ever have.

Miriam stalled the move from New York as long as she could. Joe had a month's notice to work out, which helped, and then there was a round of farewell parties. She grabbed at any work offering, desperate to add to her experience and reputation before heading south. She was afraid that, when it was known she was living in Key West, the phone would never ring.

"There's a new series of Foot Haven commercials coming up," Claudia told her. "I'm booming for the soundman, Bob Gardner, again. Why don't you call Karl Bennett and see if you can be AD."

Miriam laughed. "Forget it! Ace director Bennett made it very clear if I ever want to be his AD again, I've got to sleep with him."

"I know that," Claudia said. "That's how Rosie with the big boobs got to do the last Foot Haven series. But Rosie's sleeping with bigger sharks now and Bennett's got to have an AD. Call him."

"No way," said Miriam. "I want work, but not that badly."

In the end Bennett called *her*. He sounded sheepish and she was instantly on the alert.

"I'm sorry about what . . . happened . . . Miriam," he said. "I was only kidding around and it got out of hand. I really want to work with you again. I'll make it worth your while. More responsibility and I'll pay you over scale."

She couldn't believe the change in him but, for $165 a day, she was willing to trust him. And as soon as she got on the set she knew who had made Karl Bennett toe the line.

"Miriam, my little Miriam," Solly Behn boomed.

"Welcome back." The owner of the Foot Haven chain was a little, fat, bald man in his seventies. He had gotten very rich by paying attention to every detail of his vast operation, and he took particular notice of the production of his commercials. He was always on the set. He hugged her with genuine affection.

"What's wrong with you?" he said. "You look so thin. Your husband the famous writer doesn't feed you? You come to our place and Momma Behn will feed you her chicken soup." He patted her hand. "It's good to have you working with us again," he said. "This schmuck here"—Karl reddened but said nothing—"thought you didn't want to work for me any longer. Said you didn't need old Solly's money anymore. But I told him, 'Karl, you get Miriam. No more of those girls with the big bazooms who don't know a take from their tush.' So here you are!"

Miriam smiled back at him.

"You know I'd never get too big to work for you, Solly," she said. "Foot Haven's about the nicest assignment Claudia and I ever worked on. I'm just sorry I missed out on the last series." She glanced at Bennett, who looked embarrassed.

The commercials were fun to make. This time they were using the New York Islanders to promote the joys of Solly's shoes. It was a holiday atmosphere. The hockey players clowned around and muffed their lines, messed up take after take and tried to make dates with Miriam and Claudia. Bennett was a good commercial director, for all his other faults, and they captured the exuberance of the team.

"I love it," Solly said on the final day. "You're all wonderful. But if you boys don't play hockey better than you act, you'll never win the Stanley Cup."

Rory Market had several Key West houses for them to inspect and they flew down to Miami when Joe had finished with the *Globe*. They rented a convertible and drove out on the causeway, over the blue sea and through the bustling, vibrantly colored settlements along the Keys.

"Christ, it's beautiful," Joe said as the sun and salt air caressed them. "Who'd ever want to live in the city when they can have all this?"

She smiled across at him. It *was* beautiful here, unspoiled despite the tourists; romantic, tropical, exotic. And, she told herself, it was only two and a half hours from Manhattan. Maybe they could make this arrangement work. She looked at Joe, his hair blowing in the wind. He looked so excited, so happy, the cares of Manhattan falling from him.

They were staying in the Hibiscus Inn in Key West, a gracious old hotel dressed up for the burgeoning tourist trade. They drank rum punch on the balcony of their room in the early evening, looking out through the tall palms to the sea. The trade wind moved gently through the trees, and little green lizards scurried around, keeping away the insects.

She felt a delicious languor coming over her: It would be so easy to just lie back and enjoy all this with the man she loved. She held Joe's hand and they sat there in silence until it was quite dark. Then they went down to dinner.

If the Keys hadn't changed physically in the four years since their last visit, the tempo of the place had. The restaurant crowd was much younger than before, and more hyped up. They dressed in old jeans and T-shirts but they had expensive tastes. It was a caviar and French champagne clientele now instead of conch stew and cold beer.

"It's the drug money," Joe said as they watched the parade of costly foods and wines pass their table. "Florida's greatest growth industry is running grass and coke up from South America. Kids in their twenties making millions of dollars, all in cash. They want to spend it."

After dinner they strolled down to the Moonglow, a seaside shack that sold fresh shrimp and cold beer. Miriam saw three Rolls Royces and a couple of Mercedes. The Moonglow hadn't changed—still the thatched roof, rattan floor, and sagging cane furniture. But there was disco music, and the young crowd on the tiny dance floor was high on something more potent than rum. Joe was enjoying himself but Miriam thought they could as well be in some New York disco.

Rory Market arrived from Miami the next morning. Joe had gotten to know him well in the days on the *Miami Herald*. Rory was a Cajun who'd drifted down into Florida from Louisiana and stayed because there was nowhere farther to drift. He was shaped like a barrel and he dressed like a seaman. He hugged them both.

"Welcome home," he said. "But you're gonna find it's changed a lot—all for the worse. These drug punks have pushed the prices way up. It's not like the Keys we used to know. Everyone's running something these days—drugs or Haitians or guns to Cuba. There's too much money around. I operate just about the only clean charter business out of Miami now, and I tell you it's hard to find anyone who just wants to go fishing."

"It doesn't look too different to me," Joe said. "I still figure it's one of the last great places to live in America."

"It's fine if you keep your nose clean, stay away from the smart guys," Rory said. "I'm okay. I'm an old guy now and no one bothers me and I mind my own business. But you get tempted: They tell you, a quarter of a million in cash if you lend us your boat for two days to run over to Colombia. Or, a thousand dollars a head to ship in a load of Haitians. Just don't fall for it. Sure, everyone's making a fortune and the feds never catch anyone and, if they do, you'll get a bond as a first offender. But these people kill each other. All these nice young college boys, making a fast buck and thinking they're Errol Fucking Flynn because they're breaking the drug laws, they wake up too late—when some Cuban with a machine gun takes their shipment and offs 'em and feeds 'em to the alligators out in the swamp.''

Joe laughed.

"I don't need to mess with that stuff, Rory," he said. "Didn't you know, I cracked it big at last? I'm a writer now, man."

"You better be a damn successful one, you want to live down here," Rory said. "You'll see what I mean when I take you around the places I got picked out for you."

The third house he showed them was perfect, a simple white wooden cottage with a broad screened porch running around three sides. Inside it was run-down, funky, but it could be fixed up easily. There was a scruffy lawn out front, running down to their own dock. They both loved it.

"Yeah," Rory said, "it's the pick of them and even it isn't much good. I guess you'll smarten it up, honey. There's nothing else to do down here but decorate or fry your brains in the sun. They want fifteen hundred a month for this." He spat. "Time before, when you were here, it would've been three, four hundred. But at least you can have a long lease, three years or so."

"We'll take it," Joe said. "It's the place I was dreaming about." He looked eagerly at Miriam. "It *is* okay, darling, isn't it? I can write in that big front room while you swing in the hammock on the porch. There's plenty of room for guests, kids. We could fix the place up real well."

Miriam nodded. It *was* a romantic cottage, and it could be made a joy; sunny days and tropical nights with Joe, happy ever after. She'd still have her work every now and then. She didn't have to drop out altogether.

"I love it," she said.

They sealed it over beers with the owner in a dockside bar. The owner was an old Florida cracker and, like Rory, he didn't fancy the way things were going.

"Glad to rent to a nice young couple like you," he said. "Don't look like coked-out hippies, or smugglers, and I guess you ain't queer. Fuckin' queers, ruinin' the place. The old days, we'd have run them out of town. Still get a beatin' if they don't stick to their own bars. But, Christ, they're so accepted down here now, there's even a gay Chamber of Commerce. Queers and drugs have ruined this place."

"It's not that bad," Rory said when they parted from their new landlord. "He's right about the drugs, but the gays don't hurt anyone. They're good for business and they keep coming back. There is some resentment—that writer who got the shit kicked out of him last fall, but he *was* running around in a dress—but if it came to a choice between the faggots and the druggies, I'd take the fags every time."

Their lease was from the first of the following month and they flew back to New York filled with plans for the place. Miriam meant to spend the time ordering fabrics and furniture but, on the second day home, she got a job call.

"Soft porn," Roger Neil insisted. "I'm getting out of the X-rated stuff. I want to be legit. I'll pay you top dollars to direct it. One and a half weeks' shooting. Five grand, okay?"

"The five's okay, Roger," she said. "But *you* going straight? I don't believe it."

"Nobody does," he said, sounding hurt. "But, shit, I'm a good producer. I bring things in on time and on budget. Why the hell shouldn't I do a regular movie? I've got to be better at it than some of the clowns running around these days."

"But one and a half weeks," she said. "What kind of movie are you going to shoot in one and a half weeks? It's got to be another of your hard-core jobs. Listen, I don't care what you shoot and who goes to see it, I don't care that feminists picket your shows. But I'm trying to make a name for myself in the straight end of this business and the last thing I need is director's credit on a raincoat pic."

"I told you, soft porn, R-rated stuff," he said. "And it's the biggest money you ever earned. Come on, Miriam, it can't hurt."

"Why me?" Miriam insisted. She had met Roger Neil half a dozen times, at parties and previews. He was one of the classier porn producers: His films had a sense of style and some humor. He had offered her work once before and she had turned him down, not from any revulsion over his films but because she didn't need the money and knew a porn movie credit could hurt her all the way down the line.

"Because you're a good young director," he said. And then, disarmingly, "And because my own guy just walked out on me. I've got everyone booked for this shoot, play or pay, and I've got to start it Monday. I told you already, it's not hardcore. Tits and ass, sure, but I'm shooting for the drive-in circuit instead of the raincoats. Do it. It'll be fun."

She held the telephone and thought. It was the biggest fee she'd ever been offered; she would be the director; it was only ten or twelve days' work. God, it would pay for fixing up the Key West place. And it did sound like fun.

"You're sure you're not conning me, Roger?" she said. "If you're not, I'll give you my best and—even on a quickie like this—we'll make it work."

"Darling," he said, "would I lie to you? Softcore, I promise. Come around to my office first thing tomorrow and we'll work out all the details."

He hadn't exactly lied to her, as it turned out. But one of his major backers suddenly said he wouldn't proceed unless they shot the film as an X-rater.

"Do it anyway," Claudia said. "It's all experience. Just close your eyes and think of the money. I don't think it'll hurt you."

They shot the film in a West Side motel which contained all the sets Roger needed. There was a rooftop swimming pool, several suites, and a bar. The film was something to do with three suburban couples who come to Manhattan for a weekend of wife-swapping.

The couples themselves, the stars of the picture, were surprisingly young and nice looking.

"That's the key to it," Roger explained. "Girl-next-door types the audience can relate to. Keep the story simple, a few laughs, and a come-shot every ten minutes."

She didn't have to ask what a come-shot was.

There was no time wasted. They started straight into sixteen-hour days and shot the film in sequence, which at least made it easier for Miriam to keep track of the rudimentary script.

The leading man, Stud Collins, looked like a college football player and was, as Roger proudly pointed out, hung like a horse.

"How does he keep it up?" Miriam asked Roger after she had filmed Stud servicing each of the girls in the space of two hours.

"He's a legend in the business," Roger said. "But even *he* has problems sometimes. So we send him off to the dressing room with Mabel. That's Mabel over there in the corner."

A quiet little woman sat off the set, knitting. Miriam had thought she must be someone's relative, allowed on the set to watch the filming on condition she kept very quiet.

"Mabel's the 'fluffer,' " Roger said. "Best in the business. I use her on all my pictures. The star can't get it up, Mabel takes him away and fluffs him up. She ought to be a sex therapist, but I pay her more than any clinic could. That mouth of hers could rouse a eunuch."

At first Miriam was embarrassed by the activity going on around her. Everyone, particularly the girls, seemed too young and clean-cut to be in this business. But they had all done it many times before and moved through the picture with cool professionalism.

"The big scene today," Roger explained during a break, "is where little Audrey here gets it on with all three of the guys at once." He called Audrey over. She was a young and pretty blonde, wearing a demure gingham dress. She looked like any young matron shopping at the A & P. "Lift your dress up, honey," Roger said. She hoisted her skirt to the waist, above the obligatory stockings and suspender belt. "No, no, no!" Roger said. "Black panties are out! Go put on some white ones. You're supposed to be the timid member of the group, almost virginal."

"Yes, Mr. Neil," Audrey said, and went off to change the offending garment.

"You've got to keep your eye on things like that," Roger said. "White or red are turn-ons; black panties are sleazy. I've been thinking about pastels. Understated, you know? But they might be a little bland on screen. What do you think, Miriam?"

It wasn't the kind of problem Miriam, thus far in her career, had had to cope with. But she tried to give the question full consideration.

"I think white says what you want it to say, Roger," she said.

"Good," he said. "It's details that make the difference between a good film and a bad one. You've got to know what your audience likes. Now, when we're filming Audrey's orgy, you've got to get close-ups from all angles: front, back, and top. They like long, lingering shots. Explicit. But for the lesbian stuff, you can pull back a bit, gauzy shots, not so much detail."

They shot the orgy scene and Miriam felt herself growing more flustered. On the one hand, the actors approached the scene like it was all in a day's work. On the other hand, there they all were, on a huge bed making love. Four young bodies, thrusting and moaning, coming together in incredible configurations. It wasn't a turn-on for Miriam, it was . . . she heard herself giggling.

"Cut!" she heard Roger yell. "I know this is your first porn pic, Miriam, but you have just committed the cardinal sin in this business.

"You must never, never laugh," Roger said. "This is a deadly serious business. You laugh, then the actors are going to start laughing and we've ruined the mood. Compose yourself and we'll try again. Sorry, gang," he said to the actors, who had flopped back on the bed. "Let's take it again."

She found herself sitting by Stud Collins during the meal break.

"It *is* a bit of a laugh," Stud said. "But Roger's right. The audience takes it all very seriously. As it is, with the number of gags Roger puts in his movies, he's skirting the line. Some of the distributors want him to play it dead straight. That's what I like about Roger. He has standards. No rape scenes, a proper plot, nice-looking people. He's the best in the business."

"You've been in . . . the business a long time, then?" Miriam asked.

"This is my sixteenth picture," Stud said proudly. "They put my name above the titles, sometimes. It beats driving a truck, which is what I was doing before I got into pictures. And I'm a real celebrity in the gay clubs."

"You're gay?" Miriam asked.

"Of course," Stud said.

Later she talked with blond Audrey.

"I almost made it as a model," the girl said. "But I am kind of short and too stacked. This is my fourth movie but I don't know how many more they'll want me for. Unless you're a star, like Spelvins or Chambers, they prefer new faces."

"Don't you feel . . . used?" Miriam asked.

"I did at first," Audrey said. "And I'd die if my parents ever found out what I'm doing. But, look, this pays well and it's easy once you get over your hang-ups. What else am I going to do? Be a secretary, making coffee and letting the boss feel me up?"

They finished the movie on time and Miriam got paid on the spot, declining screen credit as director. Roger was hurt. He thought it would be a nice gimmick to bill the picture as the first hard-core from a woman director.

"You could give a press conference," he suggested. "It would get the picture a lot of publicity."

In the end they agreed on a *nom de plume* for director.

"You should have taken the credit," Claudia said. They were having a drink in Steve's Place the day after shooting finished. "There's nothing to be ashamed about directing a porn movie. Some of the best directors got started that way. How did you come through it all, anyhow?"

"In the end, it was just another job," Miriam said. "At first it seemed so exploitive. But they're all free and all adults: No one pressured them into doing it. I know pornography is demeaning to women; at the same time, I feel they're entitled to make a living the best way they can. For me, the whole project was kind of desensitizing. All those orgasms, all those naked bodies—it certainly wasn't a turn-on. Thank God we were working such long hours I hardly saw Joe. I don't think I could have made love without either crying or laughing."

Angela Leonard, one of the regulars in their group at Steve's Place, had been listening.

"You shouldn't have done it," she said. "It's wrong for a woman to be involved in the exploitation of other women."

"That's fine for you to say, Angela," Claudia snapped. "You've got your nice safe job on Wall Street. Miriam and I are just breaking into our careers. We've got to take whatever's offered."

PALACES

Miriam didn't want a fight.

"I won't do another one," she said quickly, and they dropped the subject.

They made the move to Key West at the end of the month, Miriam insisting on using what Joe called her porn money on the house. The purchases she made for it arrived a couple of days after they did.

They spent a fevered two weeks painting and primping the little house, installing furniture and glassware, turning the place into a comfortable, simple but very pretty, oceanside home. Joe bought an old wooden sailboat, a sturdy, unfashionable thirty-two footer, to moor at the end of their dock. The *Miami Herald* came down to interview them for the Style section and they were presented in the article as just about the happiest, luckiest young couple in Florida. When Miriam read about them she wondered why she didn't feel ecstatic. They had everything, at least in the Style section.

Chapter Four

IT HAPPENED GRADUALLY. MIRIAM STARTED GETTING A lot of work: commercials, industrials, a documentary. She commuted from Key West for a few months, but she and Joe admitted it was stupid to work for three days, fly to the Keys for three more, then return to New York for the next job.

"It's best this way, really," Miriam told Claudia. "While the work is flowing I stay up here in the apartment and Joe can push ahead with the new book, without interruptions. Then, as soon as the job scene quiets down again, I'll take a good long break down there with him."

"Knock wood it never quiets down," Claudia said.

That season in New York had an abundance of work for both of them. Hollywood-on-the-Hudson was booming and all the young filmmakers were finally getting a chance to show what they could do.

"It will fall off," Miriam said. "It's always boom or bust in this business. All you can do is grab whatever's going while it's going. God, I've had forty days in the past two months. I'm actually keeping myself."

Claudia looked at her across the table.

"Is that what's in the back of your mind?" she asked. "Keeping yourself?"

"Hell, no," Miriam said. She tried to explain. "I don't mean to be independent of Joe, but if I can't make a living in films, I won't feel I've succeeded. Joe understands."

"I hope he does," Claudia said. "The periods you spend together are getting further and further apart. You haven't seen each other for—six weeks? Is that right?"

"Well, yes," Miriam said. "He's going to take a break next week and come up and see me. Even if I'm working, I'll make a lot of time for us."

"I think you better," Claudia said. "I can't see Joe liking sitting in Key West alone for months. You've got to face it, Miriam. He's down there in lotus-land, surrounded by all those pretty little hippies all looking to get laid—especially by a bestselling writer. You don't think he's not tempted? He wouldn't be human if he weren't."

Miriam looked miserable.

"I try not to think about it," she said finally. "I know Joe's got his needs and I know there's plenty of women around to satisfy them. But it's my choice to be here instead of with him, and if that means Joe's going to fool around a little, then I just don't want to know about it."

"What about *your* needs?" Claudia insisted. "Don't tell me you don't sometimes think of having a little affair during all those weeks apart."

"Oh, come on," Miriam said. "I'm here to work, not fool around. And when would I get time for an affair, even if I wanted one?"

"We don't work all the time," Claudia said. "And I know all about loneliness, what it can do to you, particularly in a big city. You've had Joe all these years and you haven't had the need to play. But, Christ, once you start living alone the way I do, you find there are times when any warm body is welcome. I've slept with some real creeps, just because they were alive. Just so I wouldn't wake up alone in the middle of the night, in my crummy apartment. Alone again."

"Sure I get lonely," Miriam said. "But it's the price I have to pay for doing this thing. I'm not about to start bed-hopping."

When Joe did appear for their reunion it didn't go quite as planned. She was working only days, so time was no real problem. The problem was Joe. He actually seemed to have changed. He looked good, all trim and tanned, but there was a brittleness to him. He was tense, snappish, so unlike . . . unlike *Joe*. He was critical of everything in the city. It was all phony. He sneered at her friends and put down his own just as harshly. He didn't say it, but he implied that her job was just a hobby. It was time she grew up and stopped playing.

It all came to a head his third night in town. He was drinking too much and using a lot of cocaine. They were in Elaine's, a large happy bunch of writers and actors and sports stars. Everyone was pleased to see Joe back and wanted to hear about his progress. She could feel how hyped up Joe was and suddenly she was afraid. He made regular trips to the bathroom, she knew he was coking up.

At first it was just a little kidding. He took on a couple of his old columnist friends about their jobs and needled a writer they both admired for not working harder. Watching him perform, she knew he was exercising a cruel streak, an aspect she hadn't seen before.

Late in the evening an actor they liked came and sat at their big table. The actor put his arm around Miriam and squeezed her.

"You're nuts, Joe," the actor said. "Dropping out of the world's greatest city to live with a bunch of beach bums. And leaving a treasure like our lovely Miriam here to fend for herself. You're taking a big risk."

"No risk," Joe said grimly. "No risk at all. This city, this restaurant, is filled only by deadbeats, impotents, and faggots. Like you."

There was utter silence. Then the actor casually tossed his glass of burgundy in Joe's face.

"This city," he said, "was doing fine before you came back and it's not missing you at all. I believe you need more than one book to your credit before you can set up as a critic of the city. And us."

The wine dripped down Joe's face and onto his white silk shirt. Then he lunged across the table at the actor. The table collapsed. Glasses and bottles smashed to the floor. Someone screamed.

The fight was short and not particularly vicious. The actor was older, shorter and fatter than Joe, but he handled himself well and bloodied Joe's nose before the waiters could get to them. Except that she was so angry, Miriam would have cried for Joe, standing there bloody and humiliated. He spun around and headed out the door to Second Avenue.

Miriam hurried after him but he was already in a Yellow Cab and he slammed the door on her and sped off into the night. She went wearily back inside, signed the check and got her coat. She didn't look at anyone. She couldn't. All she wanted was to be at home.

Joe wasn't in the apartment. She stayed awake as long as she could but there was no message from him. She figured he'd gone to one of the after-hours bars. There was nothing she could do and she was so tired. She slept.

The phone woke her at nine AM.

"I'm calling from Miami," Joe said. "I spent the rest of the night in La Guardia and took the first flight down here." He sounded exhausted and despondent and beaten. "I couldn't get the blood out of my shirt," he said. "So I had to buy a T-shirt from the gift shop. It said 'I Love New York.' Miriam, I hate the fucking city. It'll destroy me if I stay there. Can't you see what it does to me?"

She was going to say coke and booze were the problems, not the city, but it wasn't the time.

"Please, Miriam," he said. "Please give it all up and come live with me. I'll make it all right for you. You don't need a career. You don't need to live in the city."

"Joe, please try to understand," she said. "I need some time to test myself. A year is all I ask. I feel terrible leaving you alone like this, and I miss you every minute we're apart. But this is something I've got to do."

Even as she said it, she knew it was not all true. She did miss Joe. She missed him in her bed, missed him on sunny Sunday mornings, missed him across a table. But she didn't miss him every minute. There were long periods when she was working and confident when she didn't think of Joe at all.

He sighed. "We'll try it your way. We'll be all grown up and modern about this. You do your thing up there and I'll do mine here." He laughed bitterly. "Most husbands I know would give anything for a situation like this.

"You work hard—and be careful," he said. "They'll all be after you now, you know. All our so-called friends will be trying to get you into bed, because we've parted."

"But Joe," she cried, "we *haven't* parted. This is just a temporary thing. Nothing's changed between you and me." She was sobbing into the telephone. "We can make it work. Just give me time. And understanding."

"I'll try," he said. "I'll try. But I won't show my face in New York again for a long while. You'll have to come down here, to our house. Between jobs. We'll try."

He hung up.

It worked for a while. All they had done was to make formal what had been going on for the past few months anyway. They called each other regularly. He said the new book was coming along fine. She entertained him with stories of her successes and disappointments. Sometimes he sounded distant, almost bored. Often he complained of how lonely he was. Couldn't she for God's sake take a break and come down for a while? The worst call came the night she had just gotten her best job. He listened to her news in silence. And then he started.

"That's fucking great for you, honey," he said. It didn't sound like her Joe, so bitter and accusing. "But you are my wife and you're leaving me here, stranded, on my own. Well, fuck it! Fuck it all! I've been a good boy all this time, letting you have your head, hoping you'd come to your senses. I've had it, Miriam, had it. I'm sick of this. There are wall-to-wall girls here who would be very happy to fuck me. You know what I'm going to do when I hang up? I'm going to a bar and I'm going to pick up some tall, blond college girl with a suntan and I'm going to bring her home and I'm going to *fuck her all night*."

"You do whatever you have to do, Joe," she said. She was weary and, for whatever reason, she felt nothing at all. "We'll talk it all out later on."

It was a big job, half a million budget, practically a real commercial movie. It had a good chance of being picked up for distribution by one of the majors. Ralph Shannon, the star, was going to make his debut as a director, directing himself, which was why there was so much interest in the project.

"Why me?" Miriam had asked when Shannon called her to be his AD. "I'd think you'd want an experienced old pro to back you on your first directing job."

"That's just what I don't want," Shannon said. "I've starred in a dozen movies turned out by the old pros and now I want to do something fresh. I've checked around and they all say you're the best of the new talent. We'll make some mistakes, but we'll make the film my way. That was my stipulation when I raised the money."

Even with a half million for the shoot, they had to cut a lot of corners. Many of the young filmmakers Miriam had worked with before were hired, because they were willing to go below scale in order to get this experience.

"One of these days," Claudia said, "someone is going to offer us jobs that carry real money, pay penalties after ten hours, and have a goddamned caterer to feed us. We've got to be crazy, Miriam."

"It'll come." Miriam smiled. She liked sitting in Claudia's apartment. It felt good. "I'm on a hundred and ten a day. You're getting ninety. It's a hell of a lot better than what we were doing this time last year. And think of the experience. Ralph's just handed me the job of location scout, on top of everything else. All I've got to do is find us some nice little hotel in Manhattan that won't mind having a crew and cast messing up their guests for the next six weeks. I can't offer them any money, just the great publicity it will be for the hotel. Some chance!"

"What about the film?" Claudia asked. "You think Ralph can do it?"

"It's a good script," she said. "I'll have your copy for you tomorrow. Basically an *Unmarried Woman* kind of thing. Bonnie Vine plays a woman who runs this hotel, her man leaves her, she has an affair with one of the guests, played by Ralph. Some good mature sex scenes, nice dialogue, sad-happy ending. It ought to work. What worries me is there's so little experience at the top. Ralph's a great actor, we know that, but he's never directed. He's raised the money from friends and a few small businessmen who think it sounds like an easy way into the movie business. There's no producer, as such, and I'm just scared things will get out of hand. With a cast of ten and a crew of thirty it's going to be hard to stretch the money over the schedule, and if we go over schedule there's no back-up money."

Claudia laughed. "*You* should be the producer," she said. "Worrying about finishing before we've even started. You want some more wine?"

Miriam nodded and Claudia went to the tiny room that served as her kitchen. Miriam watched her friend move around the small walk-up and marveled again at how well she coped with a precarious existence. Claudia was small, blond, and pretty. She was also tough, brave, and determined. The cheap apartment in the crummy neighborhood didn't bother her. She had beaten off two muggers and now the people in the area treated her as one of their own. She lived alone, had no steady boyfriend, no money, but Claudia seemed to be leading a much richer life than Miriam was.

They ate and drank all evening in a nearly hilarious state, laughing about anything that came up. They looked drunk, but they weren't. Miriam was reacting to the separation from Joe, and Claudia was going right along with her, trying to keep her friend aloft. After she had made coffee, she asked, "How's it going with Joe?"

"Not good," Miriam said. "We haven't talked for a few days. The last time, he was bitter and nasty. Said he was going out to get laid."

"I hate to say I told you so," Claudia said. She patted Miriam's hand. "Don't let it get to you. It won't hurt anyone if Joe has a bit of a fling while you're working. You can't really blame him, I suppose."

"I don't," she said. "That's the funny thing. I can't get too upset. I just don't want to know about it. But it's not like just an affair. It's as if he's trying to blackmail me into rushing to his side. It's all so complicated. I love him as much as ever but I won't be forced into giving this up. It's my turn to do something for myself now. But I don't know how high a price I'm going to have to pay—or how much I'm prepared to pay."

"You may not have to pay any price," Claudia said. "Maybe Joe will come around. He'll get bored with living down there. You'll start getting big pictures, set in good locations. God, his trade is portable, he could tag along with you."

"I wish I could believe that," Miriam said. "But you know what film sets are like. One big, exclusive family. I've seen it when someone in the cast or crew brings a wife or whatever on location. It's all right for a couple of days, then they start getting in the way. And they feel shunned because everyone else is part of the process. I can't see Joe being a hanger-on."

"Just try and put it out of your mind while we're doing this picture," Claudia said. "You're going to have more than enough to worry about."

Miriam did try, throwing all she had into preproduction work, knowing it was vital to have everything ready the day crew and cast came on the payroll. Faulty preproduction and the lack of a finished shooting script had ruined more movies than bad acting or directing.

The principal location, the hotel, was proving to be what she had expected—a headache. No one wanted the disruption of a movie.

She had been laughed at by a dozen hotel managers by the time she found the place on lower Park

Avenue. It was a faded but pretty little hotel well off the tourist route. It could really have been the hotel described in the script. Expecting another refusal, she went in and asked the desk clerk for the manager, preparing her well-worn sales pitch.

The manager came out of a small office in the back, blinking behind his spectacles as if unaccustomed to light. He was tall, shambling, and just a little unkempt. It was instant flashback to high school in Madison, to awkward embraces in the back of his beat-up Chevy.

"Andy! Andy East," she gasped. "What on earth are *you* doing here?"

His eyes lit up and he hurried around the check-in desk to her.

"Miriam," he said, wrapping her in his arms and kissing her on both cheeks. "It's so great to see you. Eleven years!" He clutched her hand. "Come sit down in the bar for a while. Okay?"

They settled in the little bar off the lobby and their excitement subsided, replaced with sudden shyness. They were both thinking of the Chevy. They had been so close, before Joe came on the scene and swept her away.

"How's Joe?" Andy finally asked. "I read something about his book, and of course I used to see his column in the *Globe*."

"Oh, Joe's fine," she said. "Actually, he's living down in Key West while he finishes his new book.

But if you knew we were in town, and you were here, why didn't you get in touch?"

He fiddled with his glass and sent ice tumbling across the table. As gawky as ever. She smiled.

"I didn't want to," he said. "I don't play the good loser too well. I'm still mad at Joe for moving in on us. The fact that you're still together and still in love does nothing for my wounded pride."

She laughed. "We were just a couple of kids then, Andy," she said. She took his hand. "But, gee, it's great to see you. I've thought about you so much. I went home, two or three years ago, and asked about you, but I heard you'd gone to Chicago."

"I've thought about you a lot, too," he said. "What it might have been like for us."

Miriam found herself blushing as she remembered those two years of high school courtship. The drive-in intimacies, the curtailed passion, the fear of going "all the way"—the frantic desire to do so. If Joe hadn't come along when he did—the dashing, sophisticated reporter—she would have given her virginity to Andy, she knew that and had known it then. Joe McDonald had reaped the benefits of the steamy frustrations she and Andy had built up. It all seemed a lifetime ago now, sitting across a table from Andy East.

"So what brings you to the Hotel Bancroft?" he

PALACES

asked. The question snagged her mood. She explained, telling him about her career, this job.

"It's a real long shot," she said, "and it's not something I'd ask an old friend to do, so we'll forget it."

"Have I seen anything you've done?" he asked.

"Not unless you frequent midnight showings at art houses, or watch budget commercials on all-night TV," she said. "But this one is my biggest chance so far."

She told him a lot about her struggle to make a career for herself. He listened closely, sometimes smiling his shy smile.

"I hate to admit it," he said, "but I misjudged Joe. It sounds like he's been trying to help you."

"Oh, yes, Joe's been a treasure," Miriam said. "He's made it all possible for me. I owe him an awful lot."

"Anyway," Andy said, "if you want to use the hotel, it's yours. There's only a handful of guests right now and we're going to shut down soon for a complete face-lift. You make a good film here and it could rub off on us as great publicity."

"I told you," she said. "I couldn't do it to a friend. A stranger I'd try and con into believing the disruption wouldn't be too bad. But you don't know what it's like, having a film crew tramping through the place all hours of the day and night.

Any guests you have aren't going to like it. I don't think it would please your owners, Andy."

Andy looked down at the table.

"Um, actually I, ah, own the place," he said. "So you see, there's no one else to worry about. I'd be very happy for you to make your picture here. It could only help me."

"You *own* it?" she said. "Wow! I thought you were just the manager. That's a pretty big scene for a boy from Madison, owning a Park Avenue hotel."

"It's no big deal," he said. "I got my M.B.A. in Chicago and thought about a life in business. It seemed so boring. Then my dad died and left me some money. I went off to Paris for a while and drifted into a hotel management school. I got this idea I could run a small European-style hotel in New York, something the other end of the scale from the Hilton. I bought this place cheap, but so far my great idea hasn't paid off. The mass still prefers the Hilton. You and your film people couldn't do me any harm. The place could use a little life."

"If you're serious, Andy, I promise you we'll keep the disruption to a minimum," she said. "And I'll get the Hotel Bancroft sign in every frame." She laughed. "I'm not trying to snow you, now. It just might rub off as good publicity."

"At least it'll be fun," Andy said. "There's only one condition. You have dinner with me."

PALACES

"Instantly accepted," Miriam said. "Us old Wisconsians have got to stick together in the big city."

"How about tonight?" he asked. "I know a nice little place in the Village. You like Northern Italian food?"

They had dinner together four times in the weeks they were filming in the Bancroft. Miriam loved the feeling of being with an old and trusted friend. Andy was a welcome break from the increasing chaos of the film.

"I'm realizing my worst fears," she told Andy one night. "The whole production is out of control. Ralph the actor is fighting Ralph the director all the time. He's throwing out the script, ordering retake after retake. Some of it is great but we've spent so much money already. And all we've got so far is the hotel scenes. We've still got to shoot a week in the subway and a week up in Westchester."

"Surely you started with enough money to finish?" Andy said. "You didn't go into it with an open-ended budget? That wouldn't be businesslike."

"Businesslike?" She laughed. "This isn't a business, it's a massive ego trip. Ralph's like a lot of people in film. He promises his backers the world, swears he'll finish on time and on budget, then starts playing around with the script, doing take after take, trying for perfection. The idea is, when you come up short you've got your investors over a barrel. Either they come up with more money to finish the picture or their whole investment is lost."

"And you think Ralph's heading that way?" Andy asked.

"I'm sure of it," she said. "I don't know what's going to happen."

"It sounds tough," he said. "You've taken on a big responsibility. I think you're really brave."

"I'm not brave," Miriam said. "I'm scared. I feel out of my depth. And very alone. That's why it's so good to have you."

"What does Joe say?" Andy asked hastily. "Do you talk it over with him?"

"Joe? Joe doesn't say anything." She was close to tears. "Joe wants this film to be a disaster. He wants me to give up my 'hobby' and go hold his hand in Key West. Joe wants a mommy-wife and mommy-wives don't go off on their own careers."

Andy was bewildered. "But you said Joe was right behind you in all this."

"I lied," she said, amending, "Well, he was, once." She felt sad and bitter as all the frustrations of the past months welled up. "Things between Joe and me are a real mess. It's not working. I feel so guilty, like it's all my fault. And I suppose it is. But, Andy, is it so unreasonable to want to do something for myself?" She cried in earnest then and

Andy was shocked and embarrassed. He could hardly pat her hand. Quickly, he poured her another glass of wine.

"I don't know," he said. "I'm the last person you can ask for an unbiased opinion. Because . . . you know, you must know how I feel about you."

"Please don't say that. Just be my friend," Miriam begged. "It's a friend I need right now, nothing more."

It got worse. They started filming in the subway, gruesome work down under the streets in the dirt and noise and darkness, surrounded by derelicts and muggers. They all knew the picture was falling apart, but Ralph was more autocratic, more demanding than ever. He screamed at everyone and Miriam was his special target.

"I knew I should have gone with a professional," he yelled when they failed yet again to capture a key scene on the subway platform. "Must I do everything myself? Is that the only way we'll get it right?"

Miriam took the abuse bravely but the crew resented it. They were all sick of Ralph's posturing and contemptuous of the panic he generated as the movie plunged deeper and deeper into trouble.

"Please, Ralph," said Claudia. "Would you just decide on your mark and then work from it? It's hard enough getting sound down here without not knowing where you're going to be standing."

"Don't you teach me my craft!" Ralph hollered, the sound echoing off the subway walls. "I've done this a dozen times. And now I'm reduced to working with a bunch of amateurs. Women. Tomorrow, I swear, I'm going out to hire a professional crew."

"Yeah, but you'd have to pay 'em, Ralph," Claudia said. She was standing nose-to-nose with him. The bag ladies and the winos came inching out of the shadows. It looked more exciting than the film they'd watched being shot.

"You think I can't raise all the money I need?" Ralph demanded. "Even after you bunch of amateurs have done your best to sabotage my picture? I'll show you!"

Miriam moved in quickly.

"Let's just wrap for the night, Ralph," she said. "We'll look at the rushes and see what we can patch together. We've probably got what we need and we'll find it in the cutting room."

She was filled with despair and numb with exhaustion when she got home and she desperately needed someone to talk with. Joe. Dear Joe who loved her. He would console her.

At first he was happy to hear from her, and concerned because she sounded so tired and strained.

But his annoyance rose as she spilled out her troubles. Finally he snapped.

"Stop whining," he said. "You're doing *your* thing at *our* expense. Why don't you just stop fooling around, get on a plane, and get down here where you belong. Forget this film bullshit. You're never going to get anywhere."

"I am, Joe. I am going to get somewhere." She was icy calm by then. "Whether it's this film, or the next, or the next. I am not going to quit."

"You better think about it, Miriam," Joe said. "I've had it. I've been very patient, but not for much longer." He hung up on her and she fell into her empty bed, wondering what had brought them to this stage.

At last, they got out of the subway. The footage wasn't great but, with a skillful edit, it would be passable. Ralph stopped screaming and began to function almost normally, but they all could see he was stretched to breaking point. He didn't talk to anyone but plunged into the remaining Westchester scenes as if racing against time.

Joe had taken to phoning Miriam in the middle of the night, wild calls, pleading calls. First he wanted a divorce, then he wanted to fly to her side. He threatened and cajoled, pleaded for understanding, sneered at her. He sounded drunk most of the time and claimed his work had gone to hell because she wasn't there. Finally she couldn't take it anymore.

"Joe," she said, "I've somehow got to finish this film. Everyone is depending on me. Ralph's burned out and the money's almost gone. If production shuts down, none of these people are going to get paid. And all our reputations will be shot to pieces. I can't cope with your tantrums while I'm coping with this. I'll come down and talk it all out with you when we're finished, but for now I'm not taking your calls anymore. If you call again, you'll only get the answering machine."

She stuck to her ultimatum, covering her head with a pillow whenever she heard the answering machine click on. Joe's rantings permeated the pillow, so she turned down the volume.

No one had been paid for two weeks, but they pushed ahead on Ralph's promise that he was arranging fresh money. But on the night before the final day's shoot, the production accountant came to Miriam. The accountant was a nice, quiet, little old man. Ralph had brought him out of retirement.

"I shouldn't tell you this," he whispered. "But I can't see you all let down. There isn't any fresh money. There never was. Ralph intends to wrap the film tomorrow and let you all just hope for your salaries."

Miriam organized a series of discreet meetings with the cast and crew. They were devastated. No

PALACES

one could afford to lose three weeks' salary. Despite the chaos of Ralph's direction, everyone had believed him when he said their money would be there. It was Claudia who came up with the strategy.

"We finish the picture tomorrow," she said. "And then we steal it, or at least steal the last few reels. If Ralph is broke, he won't have had transfers made yet. So we hold the film until he comes up with the money."

They finished the final scenes by midafternoon and Ralph, in a gesture of bravado, arranged an impromptu wrap party at a Westchester restaurant. He bubbled around the room, thanking everyone for their work on the film and promising they would all be hired for his next project. They drank their wine and looked embarrassed.

Finally, Claudia spoke up.

"Ralph," she said, "we know you've been having a tough time with money. But everyone here is owed three weeks. Have you got our checks?"

"No," the director said, "not right now. But all the checks will be available from the production office on Friday. Anyone who doesn't want to make the trip downtown, just leave your address and we'll mail them out. Meanwhile, drink up and be happy. I've got to leave now but I've arranged for the bar to keep serving you until six PM."

After shaking hands and kissing them all, Ralph

left the restaurant. He was back in three minutes, red faced and shouting.

"You fucking ingrates! I'm calling the police. I'll have you all arrested unless the last two days' film is in my hand right now."

Bonnie Vine, the star, stepped forward.

"Cut out the threats, Ralph," she said. "We just decided to take out a little insurance. You come up with the money Friday, you get your film back. You don't—then you haven't got a picture. You can't reshoot the missing scenes because none of us will appear in them. We're sorry it had to come to this, but we've got to get paid."

"You'll regret this," Ralph said. "I'll sue you all. I'll see to it you never work again." Then he dashed out of the room.

The party broke up then. They would have left immediately, but the restaurant owner demanded payment: Ralph hadn't arranged for credit. They scraped up the money between them, left the bar and went their separate ways. It was the saddest wrap party Miriam had ever attended.

"So where's the film hidden, or do you want to keep it secret?" Miriam asked Claudia. They were driving back to Manhattan in Claudia's van.

"It's at your place, with your doorman," Claudia said. "We sent Colin, the grip, down with it before the party started. You're about the only one with a doorman."

"Oh, shit!" Miriam said. "What am I going to do with it?"

"Just keep it safe for a few days until we figure out our next move," Claudia said. "Maybe Ralph will come up with the money, or maybe we can find some fresh money ourselves. I don't know, though. Apart from the salaries, there's still all the postproduction work to be funded. This can't be the way they do it in Hollywood!"

Miriam found herself looking over her shoulder as she got out of the van and entered her apartment building. She felt like a thief. Carlos, the doorman, handed her three boxes of film and she scuttled into the elevator. She double-locked her front door and stood in the hallway, pondering what to do with her burden. Finally she stuffed the film canisters under the bed. Then she checked her answering machine.

There was a very cold message from Joe. In the unlikely event she wanted to speak with her husband, he said, he wouldn't be reachable for the next few days. He was going on a boat trip.

Just then she really wanted to talk with Joe. She wanted to tell him all her troubles and ask him if he wanted her to fly down and join him. At that moment the film business didn't seem at all attractive.

The second message was from Ralph Shannon: "I'm just back in the city and I'm with my lawyer. I'm holding you personally responsible for that film. If it's not in my hands first thing in the morning, I'm taking out a writ against you."

The third message, which must have come in only a few minutes before her arrival, was from Andy East, asking if she wanted to have dinner soon. She called him.

"God, it's good to hear your voice," she said. "I need a friend right now. I don't think I've ever been so low."

"Having trouble with the picture? Or Joe?" Andy asked.

"Both," she said. "You said dinner 'soon.' How about tonight?"

"Of course," Andy said. "You want to go to the Village, or somewhere uptown?"

"It'll have to be here, in the apartment," Miriam said. "I can't leave. I'll explain it all to you tonight. I know this sounds silly, Andy. But would you mind picking up a couple of steaks and some stuff for a salad? There's wine here, but I'm out of food."

He arrived at eight, with prime steaks, salad fixings, strawberries, cream, and a fresh Brie. She kissed him on the cheek and hurriedly locked the door behind him. He followed her into the big, bright kitchen and leaned against the refrigerator, looking at her quizzically.

"What is it?" he said. "They trying to evict you from this beautiful place?"

"Drinks first," she said, fixing them both a gin and tonic. "Now come into the living room and I'll tell you all about the Perils of Miriam."

Handing him a drink, she thought again how very good looking Andy could be—if he'd just *do* something with himself. His clothes always looked slept in. His shoes were expensive but scuffed. Oddly, his hair was always neatly clipped. His head seemed to be all Andy ever noticed about himself, and she wondered whether he had only a medicine cabinet mirror and never saw anything below his chest.

He listened carefully while she explained the fiasco the film had become, taking a calculator out at one point and feeding figures into it.

They had more drinks, a bottle of good Saint-Emilion with dinner, and cognac with coffee. By then she was relaxed and light-headed. The friendly confidence Andy gave her warmed her deeply. The strain began ebbing away.

"And what about Joe?" he asked, hesitant, as always, whenever he mentioned Joe. "You said there were some . . . problems."

"It's more than problems," Miriam said, determined not to cry this time. "I think it's all over. We just fell apart. Joe's changed. Maybe I've changed, I don't know. He started off just resenting what I'm trying to do, and now I think he hates me for it. He hates me for *some* thing."

"It can't be that bad," Andy said. "Just a rift?"

"No," she said, and detailed the bitterness between them. Andy's jaw set hard as he listened.

"You're not to blame," he said when she had finished. "Joe needs to grow up. But it sounds as if he's not going to. So—what do you want to do?"

"I don't know," Miriam said miserably. "Everything I do seems wrong." And then she did something that felt right. She moved into Andy's arms and let all his warmth and safety flow through her. He kissed her, and she kissed him back. His hand on her breast was gentle and she pressed him against her briefly before she stood and led him to the bedroom.

He worked her body gently, stroking and touching, easing away the pain and tension. Soon there was only simple desire. She thought, as she drifted in a golden haze, *this is the way it's supposed to be.* Love with a perfect friend. Love beyond guilt. Love in a simple way.

She stroked him and felt him getting stronger and stronger against her. Only the thin nylon of her panties was between them.

"Now, now," she cried, and Andy removed the fragile barrier and entered her. Long and deep and gentle, getting so far inside her, waiting for her, an incredible part of him knowing just what she needed. She climaxed many times, wrapping her legs around him, hoping to drain him. Her body kept coming, in so many engulfing waves, and he was content to let it happen to her. Sweat dampened his hair but there was no pressure on her to relinquish the pleasure washing over her. When he did climax it was like rain at the end of a long, sultry summer afternoon. It flooded her, reaching as high as her heart. For a few more wonderful moments, she felt fulfilled.

It was hard to breathe afterwards, as if filling herself with him had left no space in her. She lay there, his weight on her, and played her fingers up and down his spine, across his thin buttocks. He fell away from her and she moved gently on to him, softly kissing his nipples, nuzzling the tightly curled hairs on his belly, moving lower, taking him in her mouth, feeling him grow strong again.

This time he loved her without tenderness. He sensed her need to be taken and scourged. He thrust inside her fast and hard, and as he came he kissed her deep and wet on the lips and their tastes merged.

He was still inside her when Miriam fell asleep, a sleep deeper than any she had known.

Andy woke her gently, stroking her cheek. He had brought coffee and juice to the bedside and, understanding her daylight shyness, disappeared into the bathroom to shower. When he returned, dressed, Miriam was ready for him.

"Last night was wonderful, Andy," she said

shyly. "But we can't let it happen again. My life is already too . . . there's so much I have to sort out. I can't get involved now."

"Don't let's talk about it," Andy said. "I'm not going to push you and I understand what you're going through. But what I do want to discuss is Shannon's film. First, is it any good?"

She welcomed the change of subject eagerly.

"Any good? I've only seen the rushes," she said. "But with good editing and some dubbing, I think it could be okay. It's not as good as we set out to make, but it's not as bad as a lot of movies around."

"Okay," Andy said. "I've been running through the figures while you slept. You think another hundred thousand to pay off the salaries and do the postproduction. I've got some friends I think would be prepared to put up that much for, say, fifty percent of the action. Ralph Shannon won't like the deal, but I don't see that the man's got any choice. He and his backers will still have fifty percent of a film, which is better than a hundred percent of nothing."

"I don't want you getting involved." Miriam shook her head. "The film business is no place for sympathetic friends."

"I'm already involved," Andy said. "I'll talk to my people and then we'll make an approach to Shannon. I'll let you know what happens." He kissed her good-by, promised to phone that night, and let himself out of the apartment before she could gather her wits.

Andy put the deal together in three days. Ralph screamed and fought it all the way, but he was finally persuaded. There really was no other way he could have his film.

She was very relieved when the courier came to the apartment to collect the hostage film cans, and also relieved when Ralph, still sulking, told her he neither needed nor wanted her for postproduction. It left her free to decide what to do about Joe.

He was back from his boat trip and sounded quite pleased to hear her on the telephone. Yes, if she wanted to fly down for a few days, that would be fine.

The little house on the water was as pretty as she had left it, but inside were all the marks of a single person who couldn't cope. The kitchen had been taken over by dirty dishes, empty cans, and giant roaches; the bedroom was grubby and cluttered; the living room looked like the aftermath of one long party. Only Joe's study was neat, and she noted the growing pile of pages.

"You're getting some work done, then?" Miriam asked.

"Yeah," Joe said. "That's the one part of the arrangement that is succeeding."

He had met her that morning at Miami International and driven her down to Key West, saying very little on the trip. Anyway, the wind through the convertible had saved them from making conversation.

"Do you want me to hire someone to come in a couple of days a week and clean for you?" she asked. "You don't want anything interfering with your writing."

"I kind of hoped you might come home for good and take care of the house. And me," Joe said.

He looked wretched. He opened a beer and started pacing the room. "I'm sorry, Miriam," he said. "I guess I haven't tried very hard. But I can't do it. I can't live like this, married without a wife. I love you, but it can't be a part-time thing. I get so lonely that I go out and find some company. And then I get racked with guilt. I'm sorry, but either you come home or it's got to be a divorce." He was staring out to sea; he could not look at her.

"Oh, God, Joe," she said. "Please don't say that's the only choice. Some *time*, just give me some time," she implored.

"No more time," he said sadly. "You have to choose."

She stayed a week, fixing up the house again, making gentle sad love with Joe, walking by the sea. There was a great sense of loss hanging over both of them. They discussed the divorce only once, clinically, as if talking about some other couple. She would see their lawyer, they would sell the New York apartment and split the proceeds. With half of what was left of Joe's book money, she would get a total of about $200,000.

"I think you're both nuts," Mervyn Rutherford said. Miriam and Joe were sitting across from him in his law office. It was the first time Joe had been in Manhattan for six months.

"There's still time to forget the whole thing," Rutherford added. "The divorce won't be processed for another month." He looked at them and shook his head.

"Okay," he said, "but I feel guilty taking my fee. It's the most amicable case I've ever handled."

Miriam and Joe walked out into the sunshine of Madison Avenue.

"Please, Joe, take my hand, just for a minute," she said. She felt an overwhelming sense of obliteration, of everything ending at once. She started crying as Joe squeezed her hand and she saw he was crying too.

He pressed her hand again at the corner of Forty-eighth Street and left her there, heading east for Costello's Bar. Still crying, Miriam started walking downtown to her new, tiny bachelor apartment. She had to check the answering machine, to see if anyone had called offering her a movie.

She needed one, badly. Ralph Shannon's film

had just been released, was being sold to cable TV to get its money back, and wasn't going to do anything for her career.

Her career. It was all she had now. It would have to be enough.

PART TWO

Chapter Five

WINTER CAME EARLY THAT YEAR AND LASTED. MIRIAM retreated into the warm cave of her small apartment. She had books, the Betamax with a library of favorite films, and Villa Lobos on the stereo. She spent hours looking out at the sleet moving sideways past her window. She indulged her lethargy to the utmost. She didn't want to think about herself, where she was, where she had come from. She told herself she shouldn't leave the apartment or she might miss a call for a job, but as the weeks passed she cared less and less about not working.

At first, after the divorce, Miriam had been on an artificial high, born of shock. There was a fair amount of work and, between jobs, she enjoyed the city like a tourist. She did the museums, strolled in the park, shopped in the big stores, caught every new film and most of the Broadway shows. It was like the early years on the road with Joe, filling the days until he returned. Except that Joe was never coming back.

Andy East called regularly but she refused all invitations.

"You're crazy," Claudia said. "You've got to face your new life. You're single again. Date. Andy, for sure. He's just right for you."

"I can't," Miriam said. "It's hard to explain, but love is the last thing I want just now. If love were enough, I'd still be with Joe."

She stayed at home. She knew what was keeping her inside the apartment and she knew what kept her from seeing Andy. What she didn't understand, in the seconds she allowed herself to acknowledge the fact of it, was why she never thought about Joe. She didn't imagine his face. She didn't think about talking to him. It was as though, being the cause of her imprisonment, he must also not exist at all.

She questioned none of this.

Andy finally stopped calling. He had sounded hurt. He would be there if she needed him, he had said.

She and Joe wrote each other, however. They were difficult letters, because so much had happened and now there could be no more sharing, only a strained friendship. They reassured each other that it had all been for the best, what they had done was the sensible thing. Between the lines was a sense of loss, and of waste.

She shouldn't have been surprised when he wrote he was thinking of getting married. He'd mentioned the girl, Carol, several times. She was "good fun," "a real Florida girl." But the prospect of Joe's marriage forced her to face the fact: It was all over.

Miriam went out the night she got that letter from Joe. She didn't want to see anyone she knew. She took a cab uptown and strolled along Columbus Avenue near Lincoln Center, watching the early evening crowds heading for theaters and restaurants. She found herself near The Ginger Man and glanced in the big, fogged windows. There were two or three women dining alone; at least she wouldn't be treated with disdain for being on her own, banished to a table by the kitchen door.

She went in and sat at the bar and ordered a martini. The restaurant was comfortably crowded, the barmen young and cheerful. She relaxed and ordered another drink.

"Are you waiting for someone?" he asked. She hadn't noticed the man move to the stool next to her. "If not, can I buy you a drink?"

She knew the routine, had seen the mating game performed in so many bars. It would be easy to brush him off. No hassle. But she didn't want to brush him off.

"No," she said, "I'm on my own."

He seemed a nice man, fortyish, casual in blue blazer and gray slacks. A tanned face, good teeth, and graying black hair.

"My name's Clark," he said. "And I don't do this often, speak to women I don't know."

"Miriam," she said. "Neither do I."

They got along easily, talking about the weather and the Yankees, about shows they had seen and books they had read. He was in publishing. Textbooks, so she didn't have to worry about any connection with Joe. She said she was a teacher.

They moved to a table and ordered cherrystones and veal piccata and a dry Italian white.

"You're married?" Clark asked during the meal. He had noticed her wedding ring.

"Divorced," she said. "I suppose I should take it off. But it helps in New York, it saves you being . . ."

"Hassled by guys like me." He smiled gently. "I'm divorced, too," he said. "It's hard starting over, isn't it? You don't realize how cossetting even a lousy marriage can be."

She laughed at the old-fashioned word.

They went to his apartment in the West Fifties. Neither of them had to say anything; it was all understood.

PALACES

The apartment wasn't unlike her own: small, efficient, a place for starting over in a new, trimmed-down bachelor life. He fussed around, dimming the lights, opening the wine, putting a tape in the deck.

They kissed without real passion. She moved to the window and looked out onto the dark street as Clark pulled out the convertible bed. He came and stood behind her and ran his hands gently over her breasts. She stood there as he undressed her, unbuttoning her blouse and unzipping her skirt. When she was just in her panties she turned and helped him out of his clothes. They crossed to the bed.

He was patient and generous. He removed her panties and began to caress her body, first with his hand and then his mouth. She stopped him as his tongue flicked over her thighs. That was too intimate for her yet.

Miriam took him in her hand and stroked him gently but he remained soft.

"I'm sorry," he whispered. "It's been like this a lot lately. I want to. You are lovely and I want to give you pleasure. Just let me do all this to you."

She felt him slide down her body and did not stop him again. It was a mechanical pleasure she felt, a release of tensions but no real passion. He was almost firm now and mounted her and she guided him into her. The penetration was not deep and he came—very fast, too quickly for her.

"I'm sorry," he said. "You deserve better."

She got a cab downtown, stood under her shower for a while, put on a big fluffy robe and made herself a glass of hot milk. She lay on the bed and smoothed cream into her hands. She gazed at her ring finger for a while, then slipped the wedding band from it. It had cost sixty dollars, about all the money Joe had then. She put the ring in the jewelry box beside the bed, next to the photograph of her and Joe laughing in the snow outside the lodge in Aspen.

She tried again, letting a young man pick her up in the supermarket. Ted was tall, with muscular shoulders and long legs. He was handsome but not obnoxiously so. He had a cheerfulness about him that made her feel safe and drew her in from the moment they nodded hello. He picked her up at her place after dinner and they went to a quiet bar on Second Avenue in the eighties. Ted was easygoing, talking about his two years of premed, dropping out, working as an insurance salesman for a year and then coming to New York. Seattle wasn't all that bad, he explained, and he'd never had any special dream about New York.

"But I figured there might be something grand here for me, you know? Something I never thought about. I didn't have much to lose, and I was bored with everything I'd tried so far. I don't want to be a doctor and *nobody* wants to sell insurance, believe me. I guess, just because you don't have a goal in mind, that doesn't mean you can't make something happen for yourself, right?"

She was charmed by his lack of guile, the slow, careful way he used his large hands.

"I envy you a lot," he told her. "No hesitation about what you're after. Whew! I'd sure like to know what that feels like, Miriam."

She hibernated, scarcely leaving the apartment at all. A trip to the supermarket was agony; the effort of choosing between so many brands, pushing through the crowds of shoppers and facing surly check-out clerks too great. She grew pale and thin, eating little. She began to talk to herself as she wandered around the apartment. She thought about getting a cat. She was vague when people called, and she refused all invitations.

She was worrying about money, even though she knew she was better fixed than almost anyone else in her business. But she had no training, no job skills outside the tenuous film industry, and she began to have visions of her nest egg ravaged by inflation.

It was Claudia who snapped her out of it.

"You're carrying on like a child," Claudia said, pushing her way in one day. "A spoiled kid.

Moping around, refusing to see any of us. For Christ's sake, Miriam, grow up!"

Miriam shouted back at her, then began to cry. The tears flowed as Claudia hugged her and hugged her. When the crying was all over, Claudia made her dress and they went to lunch in Chinatown.

"We've got to use the time between jobs properly," Claudia said as they ate. "It's no use just waiting for the phone to ring. I've just gotten involved with the Female Film Workshop. It's people like us, still breaking in, but also women committed to making films from a female point of view."

Miriam went along to the workshop a couple of nights later. She was nervous at first; so many of the women seemed strident. She had never much identified with the sisterhood anyway, and some of these women were tough and butch, stereotyped lesbians. But as the evening passed she came to feel the mutual support.

Later a group of them dropped by Steve's Place for a drink.

"So what do you think of us, Miriam?" Jean Buxford asked. "A bunch of bull dykes?" Jean was an actress, slim, dark, and pretty.

"God, no," Miriam said. "I guess some of the group are . . . gay. At least a few look it. But for the first time in a long time I felt I belonged somewhere, here were people who could listen and understand what *I* was feeling."

"That's what it's about," Jean said. "Helping ourselves and each other, because until we do, no one else is going to. The gay element scares a lot of women off."

"It's just I'm not used to being around gay women," Miriam said. "A sheltered life, or something. They make me nervous."

"Do I make you nervous?" Jean asked, grinning.

"I . . . I didn't realize," Miriam said. She was confused and the others at the table laughed.

"Your first lesson," Jean said gently. "Things are not always as they appear."

Over the weeks she took a lot of strength from the workshop. Eight of them combined to make a short documentary about a Lower East Side daycare center. They shot it on secondhand videotape with borrowed equipment and had it accepted by PBS for an experimental film series. They used the $400 fee for fresh video stock and a small party in Miriam's apartment.

Jean stayed behind to help Miriam clear up, and later they settled down on the big stuffed couch for a nightcap.

"The group's been great for me, Jean," Miriam said. "Before I got involved, I was at rock bottom. I was just sitting in this apartment."

Jean lit a joint, inhaled deeply, and passed it on to her.

"The group helped you over a bad patch," she said. "You probably won't need it much longer. You'll be okay now."

The grass was strong and Miriam had never smoked much; it went straight to her brain. She started talking, telling Jean all that had happened to her in the past year, intimate details, and personal hurts she had never confided, not even to Claudia.

She was sleepy then, and grateful as Jean undressed her and put her to bed. She took Jean's hand and gestured for her to come to bed. It seemed the most natural thing in the world.

Jean did come into her bed and held her for a while. She stroked Miriam's bare shoulder and kissed her cheek. Then she spoke gently, the words coming through a soft cloud.

"You're beautiful and I would love to love you," Jean said. "But this isn't your scene. You've had a hard time with men, but it will work out for you. You've got to learn not to let them use you, that's all. If you ever need me, I'll be there. But we'll just be friends. That's all you need from me."

Jean left her then and Miriam drifted into a deep, dreamless sleep.

Phil Ashton called her a week later.

"I've got a picture starting at the end of the month. Do you want to be my AD?"

"You bet," she said. Then, cautiously, "I mean, I'll have to check my dates, but . . ."

"Six weeks' shoot, in Vermont," Ashton said. "Decent budget, good young cast. It's a love story, set in a ski resort. We were supposed to film in the Rockies but there's no damn snow this season so we're switching the production to Vermont. I want to use a New York crew, save some costs. That's why it's all such short notice. Can you ski?"

"Yes," Miriam said. She tried to keep calm. Ashton was one of a score of producers and directors she had sent resumes to. A top director, he had made a couple of features in New York before being picked up by Hollywood.

"Good," Ashton said. "There are a lot of ski scenes and I want an assistant who can move around on the slopes. I can't stand up on the damned things."

She decided to push her luck.

"It sounds like a tough job for the soundman," she said. "Slipping around with all that equipment. Have you signed anyone yet?"

"No," he said, "I was thinking of Bertoni. You have someone in mind?"

"I've got this friend I've worked with a lot," she said. "Top soundman and she skis like a dream.

Could have made the Olympics. Will you consider her?"

"Okay," Ashton said. "Bring her by the production office tomorrow. And get me an assistant cameraman, Miriam."

Claudia was wild.

"Except I can't ski," she wailed.

"Just don't tell Ashton that tomorrow," Miriam said. "Book yourself a package at Hunter Mountain later in the week. Four or five days up there, you'll pass."

Reading the script, she saw that Ashton meant to underscore the light story by moving the camera around steadily; no long shots, no brooding lighting, everything upbeat, the actors unguarded and cheerful. Without that mood, that temper, the picture wouldn't work. The shooting of it had to be bright. There wasn't enough to the story to take a more somber route.

For this project they needed an expertly sensitive assistant cameraman. It worried her that all she could bring to mind were names she didn't want. The right man would have to fall into her lap: She hadn't a clue where to go looking for him.

When a director friend suggested young Fletcher Harbor, she got his film clips and watched them in her apartment, excited and a little awed. His work was meticulous, glowing. The right man had in-

PALACES

deed fallen right into her lap. The cinematographer would be so pleased.

Fletcher Harbor—Fletch, he was called—sounded disappointingly young on the telephone, but going with the intuition that hadn't failed her yet, she hired him over the phone, crossing her fingers that the evidence in his clips was genuine.

It was the best thing she had ever worked on. The budget wasn't lavish by Hollywood standards but there was enough money to do it right. No more doubling up on jobs, no working until everyone fell over. Ashton's producer was observing union standards: ten-hour turnarounds, proper meals, decent working conditions.

The ski resort itself was run-down and its slopes were not challenging, which explained why the producer had been able to secure its exclusive use at the height of the season. But it suited the script, which was about a former ski instructor trying to make it on his own running a faded resort.

With crew and cast, they made up a party of fifty and had to double up in the rooms, a small inconvenience when they had the run of the comfortable old place with its snug bar, homey dining room, and roaring log fires everywhere.

"Pinch me," Claudia said on their first day. "We're getting paid for this?"

The atmosphere assured a happy set. Fred Royal, the producer, was old-fashioned: He didn't believe in conning anyone. He cared about the people on his pictures, right down to the lowliest grip, and was jealous of his integrity. And the director, Ashton, had no Hollywood hype about him. He worked steadily, without hysteria and without ego. He was a craftsman and he brought out in all of them the best of themselves. Within four days they were an integrated unit, all working toward the same end. Miriam knew it was going to be a film they would all be proud of.

Miriam and Claudia were roomies, of course, and they talked late into the night about the job and how much fun it was.

"I can't believe it," Miriam said. "I'm getting twelve hundred a week and there's nothing to spend it on. Just four features like this a year and I'll be keeping myself. Maybe this is the start of something big for us."

"I'd like to start something with Jeff Coleman," Claudia said. "He's beautiful. I was watching him on the set today and I was so enthralled I got a boom in the frame."

"Yes, I noticed," Miriam said dryly. "But you're right. He is beautiful."

There was a silence and then Miriam said, "He can't ski. Phil wants me to teach him what I can. I'll get him snowplowing, at least."

"You sly bitch," Claudia said, laughing. "All this and heaven, too. Getting paid to teach a Robert

Redford look-alike to ski. I guess you'll have an affair with him. Inevitable. As the star, he's got a bedroom to himself. You've got it made."

"No way," Miriam said. "I'm not getting into one of those on-set romances. I've got to keep my mind on my work. Anyway, you're more his type. All those California guys go for blondes."

"I sincerely hope you're right," Claudia said. "Put in a good word for me. When's your first lesson?"

"Tomorrow afternoon, if we get through the interior scenes on time."

They broke at noon and Miriam and Jeff took a packed lunch and rode the rope tow to the top of the mountain. It was a beautiful day, cold but sunny, and they had the slopes and trails all to themselves.

He was easy to teach, a natural athlete. He was executing a competent snowplow by the time they broke for lunch at two. They ate at a picnic table in a stand of trees, the banked snow protecting them from the breeze. Jeff produced a flask of rum.

"You're ready to ski the top trail," she told him. "A few more days and we could make you a downhill racer. How come you've never skied before?"

"I went through college on a football scholarship," he said. "And I was married. So skiing seemed too big a risk. Break a leg on the slopes and there would go my football scholarship. After that I got into acting and there was no time for any sport at all. Sandy and I had a couple of kids and I was working all kinds of jobs, waiting for the right part to come along. By the way, thanks for the lessons."

"All part of the job," she said.

"You do your job—I mean as AD—real well," Jeff said. "You're the first woman I've worked with. I wasn't sure how it would go, but it's great. You seem to have a calming effect on the set. It looks like it's going to be a real smooth production. God, some of the pictures I've worked on have been a bummer from day one. Isolated up here in Vermont for six weeks, we don't need any hassles."

She took another sip of the warming rum and began to wrap up their lunch.

"We can ski another hour before it gets really cold," she said. "Remember to take it easy and just let yourself fall over if you get out of control. Don't run into any trees. Phil will kill me if I bring you back disfigured."

In fact it was Miriam who crashed. She was sweeping down the trail ahead of Jeff, skiing between stands of fir trees, when she glanced back to see how he was doing. Her left ski caught a protruding root and she flipped over and landed heavily on her back. She lay there winded until Jeff reached her. He looked worried and fell over himself trying to help her up.

"Are you all right?" he said. "You fell awfully hard."

She struggled up. It hurt just below her shoulder blade but she figured it would be nothing worse than a bruise. She took it easy down the mountain to the lodge.

"I'm stiff and you must be hurting," Jeff said when they reached the bottom. "A sauna is what we need right now."

It sounded great. She went into the women's change room and stripped off her heavy ski clothing. She carefully tucked a towel around her and entered the dim little sauna room.

Jeff was stretched out on the top bench, quite naked and unself-conscious. He got up when Miriam entered and spread a towel on the bench for her.

"Half an hour of this and all the aches will be gone," he said. She was shy near his nakedness but could not resist looking at him. He was tall and lean, all muscle, an athlete. She kept her towel tightly around her and lay down on the bench. Sweat was running down her and the heat was making her drowsy.

"Turn over," Jeff said. "I want to see your back, where you fell."

She did and felt his hands part the towel. His fingers ran over her back, gently kneading her tense muscles. She relaxed a little.

"I give a pretty fair massage," he said. "As a

former jock I know how much good it can do." He was kneeling over her now, working expertly, his hands banishing the last of her pain. She looked sideways through half-closed eyes. His groin was very close to her face. And he had an erection.

"Does that feel better?" he asked softly.

She nodded.

"Does it hurt anywhere else?" he asked. "Just say. I'm enjoying this."

So was Miriam. The heat, the pressure of his hands, and the closeness of him were all doing things to her body.

She didn't want him to stop, but something was bothering her.

"Jeff," she said, "you mentioned your wife, Sandy, and the children. Are you still together?"

His hands were lightly stroking her bare bottom.

"Of course," he said cheerfully. "Sandy's going to come spend a few days on the set before we finish. Why? Did you think I was divorced?"

"Then," Miriam said, "I think we better stop this now, before it goes too far."

"It feels good, doesn't it?" he asked.

"It feels too good," she said. "I'm sorry, I just can't . . . make love to a married man."

His hands were still there. "Whatever you say. But I'd love to make love to you and we're going to be seeing a lot of each other over the next six weeks. What harm would we do anyone?"

She wasn't sure she knew, but she couldn't go against her code without having a better reason than feeling good. She turned over and sat up on one elbow. The towel fell away and Jeff smiled approvingly before she covered herself again.

"No," she said. "I know I'm naïve, but I can't help it. Please don't be mad at me."

"I'm not mad," Jeff said. "Just sorry. I think we would be good."

She didn't tell Claudia. She knew her friend would think her a square. She *felt* pretty square, too, when a couple of nights later, Claudia was not in her bed. Claudia returned to their room just before breakfast, looking exhausted and elated.

"Jeff Coleman is the greatest lay I ever had," she told Miriam. "He really cares about women. And he's so sweet and casual. No hang-ups. I lost count of the times I came. Honey, if you ever get the chance, make it with Jeff."

"I'm not his type," Miriam said.

Miriam skied with Jeff a couple more times, and he was just the same—friendly, open, available. Any time Miriam wanted to have an affair, it would be all right with him, was the message. Whenever she watched Jeff on the mountain, or before the camera, and when she thought about what Claudia had told her, or remembered his firm body in the sauna, she wondered at herself.

Miriam immersed herself in work. There was no

time for her to join the continual poker game in the bar, or the sessions of drinking and talking after the day's filming. There were always details, schedules to be prepared, egos to be soothed. She loved it all, the hundred and one things that had to be done to achieve just one good take. Like the clash between the cinematographer, Eric Benson, and the assistant cameraman, Fletch Harbor. Benson, an acclaimed Hollywood veteran, was the closest thing to a prima donna they had on this set. His work was brilliant but he had little time for the younger crew.

"Goddamned kids, playing at making pictures," Benson told Miriam after one not-too-successful day. "They take a film course or two, make a couple of grainy little films no one ever sees, and they think they're in the business. With people like me—they're so condescending. Like Hollywood is no longer *relevant* and I'm some relic."

Miriam was flattered that Benson didn't seem to be including her in his rancor. He must have thought her more experienced than she really was.

"Anyway," he continued, "I'm going to talk to Ashton about that fucking hippie he's given me for an assistant. He's hopeless. I want him off the picture. I'd be better off without an assistant than looking over my shoulder all the time to see what Fletch Harbor has screwed up this time."

"I'm sorry you're not getting along with him,

Eric," Miriam said. "What's the problem? Maybe I can help."

"Everything," Benson snapped. "His attitude, his work. I tell him to do something and he just stares at me. I want him off the picture."

Miriam was worried. She knew Benson could get his way if he insisted. But she liked Fletch and he was popular with the rest of the crew. If he was fired it would destroy the good atmosphere on the set. Fletch was only twenty, and he didn't have much experience. But he was brilliant behind a camera and had already shot two acclaimed documentaries.

She sought him out.

"What's the trouble, Fletch?" she asked when they were huddled over drinks in a quiet corner of the bar. "Why aren't you getting along with Benson?"

Fletch was a skinny blond kid who looked even younger than twenty. He was flushed and embarrassed and couldn't meet her eyes.

"He scares me," he finally said. "He's done so much, such great work, I'm scared I'm going to screw up. He tells me to do something, I freeze up. Everyone else is easy to get along with, but Mr. Benson has such a reputation and he's so demanding, I get scared." He looked down at his drink, despondent. "He's not going to have me thrown off the picture, is he, Miriam? I'd be ruined in the business before I ever got started. I just want to work hard for him, learn from him, but we can't get along. Either he acts like I'm not there or he yells at me."

"Let me see what I can do," Miriam said. She felt for poor, nervous Fletch.

It took two days to arrange, during which Benson became increasingly rude and hostile to his young assistant. But finally the film arrived from the New York rental agency and she explained the plan to Fletch. Then she cornered Benson after dinner.

"Eric," she said, "I think I know what the problem is with Fletch."

"I don't care," he said.

"Give him a chance," she said. "The problem is Fletch Harbor is in awe of you. He thinks you're the greatest cinematographer in the business and he just wants to please you. But when you speak to him he gets scared of messing up, so he does mess up. You're his hero and he doesn't know how to relax around the great man."

Benson didn't seem impressed.

"We can't be wet-nursing some film-struck kid."

"He's trying to learn all he can," Miriam said. "Just come with me and I'll show you something."

Benson followed her down the corridor to the room set aside for showing the dailies. She quietly opened the door. The projector was running, and down close to the small screen they could see the hunched figure of Fletch, intently studying the black-and-white film playing in front of him. She closed the door again.

"You recognized the picture, of course," she said. "*The Iron Man*. Fletch thinks it's your greatest work. He had a print sent up here and he studies it every night."

"Dumb bastard," Benson said gruffly. "He won't learn anything watching an old movie." He sighed. "You go talk to him when he's finished in there and tell him to come see me in the bar. I suppose they've got to start somewhere. *The Iron Man*, eh? It wasn't too bad."

"It got you an Oscar," Miriam said.

"All politics," Benson said. "But I wouldn't mind watching it again. I might go over it with the kid, show him a few of the tricks we used. Yeah, you tell him to come and have a drink with me when he's through."

After that, Fletch was taken in hand by the master and they worked as a team. Fletch tried to express his gratitude to Miriam but she brushed it off as part of the job. But for the rest of the picture, Fletch was always near her, offering to fetch and carry for her, admiring her work, treating her like a much-loved older sister.

They finished the picture on budget and four days ahead of schedule. They were all proud and happy with what they had done. It was a good film.

Fletch's camera work was technically fine, his vision mature. She still had trouble connecting the gawky young man with his brilliant artistry. Whenever he had free run, Fletch chose oblique shots, edges of scenes, corners of the action, nuances that spoke more clearly than stark shots. He worked slowly, deliberately, his blue eyes so intense they hypnotized her. Miriam sometimes had to shake herself out of a dreaming state that took hold of her when she watched Fletch working.

Fletch's low-key intensity brought to mind her father simply because the two were so different in their use of film. Her father had filmed his family in action to nail them down; recorded them so as to hold them in his pocket. Fletch took the opposite approach, his camera seeming to ask permission of its subjects. His work never intruded on the action it recorded but blended into situations, befriending people.

Only another artist would know Fletch's gentle persuasion for what it was.

The wrap party was staged in the ski barn next to the lodge. The set director and the wardrobe department had spent the day dressing the place up, the sound department had rigged a superb stereo system, and lighting had transformed the place into a pulsating disco. There was a vast table of hot

PALACES

dishes, and wine and spirits flowed freely. There was also a lot of grass, coke, and speed.

Miriam stuck with white wine as she moved around the happy throng. The celebration was underlaid with sadness, the knowledge that tomorrow their tight little family would break up. Outsiders could never understand the bonds forged on a film set. Miriam herself thought she would never adjust to the living together and dependence, all shattered when the final take was processed.

Claudia sidled up to her.

"You'll have the room to yourself tonight, kid," Claudia said. "I'm off for one last fling with Jeff. One night of love before the postpartum blues."

"Lucky you," Miriam said, feeling so alone then. She would have liked to finish the night talking with Claudia, figuring where their next job would be, sharing hopes and memories.

They were all pairing off. There was an imbalance of men to women, and those who didn't have a partner were settling down to heavy drinking or drugs or both. She didn't want to leave but the party wasn't her scene by then. She had a contact high from the revelry around her, the music and lights. She had started for the door when Fletch called softly.

"Are you going back to the lodge, Miriam?" he asked. "Can I walk you there?"

They walked across the snow to the lodge. It was a brilliant night with the moon shining on the snowy slopes above them and bouncing off the snow-packed roof of the lodge. Miriam shivered as she thought of her cold and lonely room up in the gables. Fletch pulled off his parka and draped it over her shoulders. In the lobby it was dark and quiet. They seemed to be the only people in the lodge, and behind them they could hear the sounds of the party.

"Do you feel like a nightcap?" Fletch asked. "I grabbed a bottle of champagne on the way out and I can get glasses from the bar."

"Okay," she said. "But it's so cold down here."

"We could go up to your room," he said shyly.

They went up the stairs together and into the little room, where she turned on the electric heater. Fletch uncorked the champagne, filled their glasses, then opened the window and placed the bottle in the snow on the ledge. She shivered again as the cold air entered the room and pulled Fletch's parka around her.

"It's been a wonderful experience," he said, warming his hands before the heater. "And I owe it all to you. I'll never be able to thank you enough for straightening things out with Mr. Benson."

She huddled down before the radiator with him. He was such a young boy, with his tousled blond hair and soft blue eyes and skinny build.

PALACES

"I didn't want anything bad to happen to you, Fletch," she said. "You've got a wonderful future with your camera. I know you're going to make it."

"I wish I had your confidence," he said. "You seem so assured. You know exactly what you want and how to get it. I guess nothing ever goes wrong for you."

"Lots of things have gone very wrong for me," Miriam said. "Lots of hurts and disappointments. But you pay the price and just hope you can keep on working."

"Someone told me about your marriage," he said. "I'm sorry. You must really love films to give all that up." He retrieved the bottle and poured her more champagne. Their hands touched as he handed her the glass. He took her hand in his then, and some of the wine spilled. She should have stopped it there but she simply didn't want to.

She let him kiss her and they sank back on the floor. Even through her bulky garments she could feel him hard against her. He was trying to touch her breast through the heavy sweater and she struggled to sit upright.

"I'm sorry," he said, crestfallen. "I didn't mean to try anything. I just thought—"

"Come to bed," she said.

He sat there on the floor gaping at her as she swiftly peeled off the layers of clothing. She stood before him naked for a moment, then slipped into bed. The sheets were icy and she shivered.

"Hurry up," she said. "It's cold in here."

He was flustered and undressed frantically, getting his feet tangled in his ski pants. He staggered and almost fell and Miriam was hard-pressed not to laugh. Then he was naked, skinny and shivering, shy, covering himself with his hand while trying not to.

She got him into bed and for a long time they lay there warming each other. At last the cold was gone and she felt passion in him. He was in a state of wonderment, tenuously touching her and gasping when she touched him. She had to guide him to her and when they were joined he came at once, his body jerking up and down. He was so light on her she held him comfortably, feeling all of him against her.

"I'm sorry," he said miserably. "I guess that didn't do anything for you. I feel like a fool."

"Failed your test with the 'older woman'?" she teased him. "Just relax and stay close to me like that. We'll get it right."

And they did. Fletch lost some of his awe and regained the virility of the young. They made love over and over and Miriam gladly lost herself in the sheer physical pleasure. In control, Fletch was a good lover. At first he was scared by the intensity of her orgasms and then he became proud of the emotions he aroused in her.

Sometime in the night they fell asleep, Fletch first, his downy cheek against her breast, their arms around each other.

The click of the door opening awakened Miriam and she looked over Fletch's head to see Claudia standing at the foot of the bed. Miriam put her finger to her lips as Claudia silently gathered some clothes and slipped out of the room to the bathroom down the hall.

Fletch was shy again when he woke an hour later.

"There's something I have to say," Miriam told him. "That was a wonderful night and you are very sweet. But it was just one of those things that happens. Nothing to make too much of. Just good friends."

He sat up in the bed, draping a blanket around his shoulders.

"Don't say that!" He sounded desperate. "It wasn't just a romp in the sack. At least it wasn't for me. I suppose you've had lots of experience and you think I'm just a kid. But, Miriam, I love you. I've loved you for weeks but I thought I'd never get a chance to show you."

"I don't think you're a kid, Fletch," she said gently. "But don't talk about love. We'll just be good friends. I haven't got time for love, even with someone as sweet as you."

He shook his head.

"We'll see," he said. "I'm going to make you love me. You can laugh at me, ridicule me if you like, but I'm going to make you love me."

She stroked his cheek and let him kiss her. But she stopped him when he moved against her.

"It's time you were dressed and on your way," she said. "We've all got to pack and head back to the city and look for our next job."

"Can I see you in town?" he pleaded. "And can we work together again? Dinner tonight? Please, I want to be with you."

"Not tonight," Miriam said. "I want to sleep for days, unwind. But if you want to, call me in a few days." She was letting him down as gently as she could. "Come on, now, it's time to get moving."

She watched as he pulled on his clothes, and lifted her cheek to him so he could kiss her good-by.

The blues didn't set in right away. There was the apartment to be cleaned and restocked, mail to be answered, bills to be paid. She slept a lot in the first few days and then began calling around, looking for tips and gossip that might lead to another job.

It was the letter from Joe that plunged her back into bleak depression. He was married, Joe wrote. To Carol. It had all happened in a hurry because, as

PALACES

he reported cheerfully, the baby was due in only seven months. He hoped she would find as much happiness as he had and that she would soon visit them in Key West.

The news shouldn't have upset her so much. He'd given her fair warning. But it was like the divorce all over again, and worse.

There was now another Mrs. Joe McDonald. She found herself thinking the silliest things. Should she revert to her maiden name? No, she would waste all her screen credits if she went back to being Miriam Cohen. How should she feel about this new girl, whom she had never met but who was now the wife of the person Miriam knew best in the whole world? And the coming child was what to her? After all her years with Joe, surely she and the baby had some relationship, didn't they?

In the end she wrote Joe and his wife a long, warm letter, praying they would always be happy and well and their baby strong and healthy and beautiful. She blotted the tears before they made the ink run.

It was two weeks before Fletch called. In that time she both hoped and feared he had gotten over his infatuation. The call dispelled that.

"I've waited as long as I could," he said. "I know you think I'm just a silly kid. Look, I've dated other girls and I've tried to get over you. But

I can't. Please give me a chance. Just let me see you now and then. I won't rush you."

And so they started dating. At first Miriam would only go with Fletch to places where she would not be seen by anyone who knew her. She was so conscious of the years between them. It was irrational, she knew, but it was how she felt.

It was Fletch who had the maturity to show her how silly she was being.

"Holy shit!" he said one night, when they were huddled in yet another out-of-the-way restaurant. "What are we sneaking around like this for? Why are you ashamed to be seen with me? Miriam, you're a young and beautiful woman. I'm filled with pride to be with you. Don't you see what you're doing to me, to both of us, by carrying on like this?"

"Okay," she said, finally, "you're right. We'll act normal."

It was ridiculous. He was young. He looked like a kid brother. Worse, he sometimes *felt* like a kid brother. He openly worshiped Miriam, which embarrassed her. He respected her work, loved talking with her, adored her body. It was ridiculous to allow herself any involvement with Fletch. Ridiculous, but she didn't say no.

She enjoyed him and was too weary, after Joe, to pretend otherwise. She enjoyed making love with him and she was always happy to see his shy face at her door, hear his voice on the phone. She told Claudia, told herself, that it would all be over soon, there was no future for her and Fletch, there couldn't be.

Claudia said nothing.

Chapter Six

SHE AND FLETCH BECAME AN ACCEPTED ITEM AMONG her friends. The boy seemed to understand her dilemma and spoke of his love for her only in their most passionate moments. The situation was, for Miriam, about as good as she could have hoped for. She had a friend and lover, someone from her own world, who didn't require anything of her. She knew it wouldn't last forever because, sooner or later, Fletch would either fall out of love with her or demand she declare her love for him.

She was out of town on a couple of jobs during that period and she was surprised by how much she missed Fletch. She wasn't in love, she told herself firmly. It was only that their arrangement was so comfortable.

She went to see her mother and sister in Wisconsin, flying to Madison and renting a car there. Driving, she made mental notes on what she would find in her sister's comfortable, undistinguished home. The outside would be fairly neat, the woodpile a little higher than necessary. Deborah always had a little more than she needed—but not much more. She was comfortable. Enough was what Deborah needed, and all she could tolerate.

Soon she was sitting in her sister's kitchen, eating or pretending to eat, a quickly put-together supper. "Why didn't you call me from the highway? I hate feeding you frozen stuff, Miriam. And you look like you could use a good meal. I suppose you think I'm . . . ordinary?"

Miriam shook her head, grinning. She loved Deborah. She loved the kitchen, which was never finished because Jake was always working on some other project and considered the kitchen last priority. She loved Jake's projects, his endless responsibilities to her sister's comfort and welfare, his insistence on Benny and Jenny having beautiful bedrooms and good clothes. "Benny *and* Jenny?" she had asked her sister only once, after the girl was born, and had gotten a funny look back. Benny and Jenny Berkheimer! Did they hate this ordinary place? Could a child of her sister's hate anything normal?

"Mama's always worrying about you," Deborah

said abruptly as they washed the dishes. "I don't think—"

"Would you like the movies? Dad's home movies?" Miriam asked quickly. "It's not fair that I've got them all."

Deborah shrugged. "What for? I'd never look at them. And, anyhow, you're a moviemaker yourself. It makes sense for you to have them. Keep them, Mir."

Mir. But she had never been able to call her sister Deb or even Debbie. She wanted to say, "I never look at them either. And I probably never will." But she knew there was nothing there her sister would understand.

After going to her sister's, Miriam spent an obligatory long afternoon with her mother in the ranch house outside Madison. Her mother looked not a minute older than fifty-five; she was a little gray, a little stout. She still dressed very nicely, pantsuits and scarves and a little jewelry. She still cooked for herself and took a long walk every noon. And she still had nothing to say.

Miriam asked questions about the house, about her niece and nephew, about the neighbors who were still there and the neighbors who had moved away. It was always that way, Miriam rattling on compulsively, desperate to keep her mother talking. She couldn't let the conversation flag, for if it did, her mother might come to realize that she and her daughter had nothing to say to each other. Miriam had realized that as a child and she never knew why she always tried so hard to keep her mother from finding out how different they were. She knew only that if she talked enough, telling her mother far more about her life than her parent could absorb, she would succeed in keeping her mother ignorant, keep her from being hurt.

It's not Mother's fault—I'm a duck in a family of hens, Miriam thought, and was relieved that her mother asked only perfunctory questions about Joe. She shouldn't have been surprised: Her mother never pressed, never probed. During that sunny afternoon in the kitchen, watching her mother's total concentration as she measured the ingredients for bran muffins, Miriam thought, *why, Mother's like Joe*. He never probed, either. But where Joe was self-absorbed, her mother simply had little imagination. *What's the difference?* Miriam told herself. *It's the same aloneness for me.*

On the plane back to New York the feeling of aloneness was intense. The sun was setting as the plane began its approach to Manhattan and she looked down on the Hudson, a river of gold. Beneath the illusion, the water was ugly, filthy, but the surface glittered. It was just like the city that spilled its debris into it; glitter over ugliness. But this city was her home and she understood: She was learning to live on the surface.

Fletch met her at the airport. She was ridiculously pleased to see him. They kissed among the crowd at the baggage area and Miriam didn't care if they attracted attention.

"I missed you horribly," Fletch said. She just grinned at him.

Fletch retrieved her bag, and she moved toward the waiting cabs but Fletch led her to a big, black limousine at the curb. The driver took her bag and ushered them into the deep rear seat. A bottle of champagne was nestling in a silver bucket of ice. Fletch busied himself opening the bottle, looking away from her.

"You shouldn't have done this, Fletch," she said. "You can't afford it." She spoke more sharply than she meant to.

"I'm sorry," he said, his head down. "I wanted to welcome you. I suppose it was silly."

She reached for his hand and brought it to her lips.

"No, no," she said. "I've just got the blues, I guess. It was a sweet, lovely idea. Thank you." She kissed him, their mouths hungry. "Will you stay with me tonight?" she asked.

The limo glided into Manhattan and down the East River Drive. Miriam caught a glimpse of the apartment building where she and Joe had lived.

She drained her glass. They took the rest of the champagne up to her apartment and drank it after they had made love.

They stayed together. They went out in the evenings, neither of them having work the next morning. They ate in cozy restaurants—nothing like Elaine's—and saw films or walked long walks, winding up back at her apartment. His was cramped and, as they both said, crummy. They spent a good deal of time in her bed, long, slow nights of making love and falling asleep together. She was happy.

It was the last thing she'd expected, after Joe, to love someone. She promised herself that she didn't love Fletch, would never love again. And to love a man whose work was the same as hers! Miriam wondered which was greater, her delight or her surprise. She kept herself calm by reminding herself that, no, she didn't really love him. But even she didn't believe that after a while.

Fletch had a job in New Jersey that week. At least one of them was working. Miriam, when she wasn't worrying about where her next film was coming from, spent the time pondering what to do about Fletch. She knew she loved him and she had almost forgotten the difference in their ages. But she was so afraid of being again possessed by someone else. She had paid so dearly for her independence; she wouldn't do anything to jeopardize it.

PALACES

She spent the day in the Museum of Modern Art, then hurried home to the answering machine, ever hopeful. It was the usual mix: Claudia saying her boom job had been canceled; a solicitation to take the *New York Times*; three hang-ups; and Solly Behn asking her to call.

She guessed Solly wanted her for another Foot Haven commercial, which would at least pay this month's rent. But he had left his home number.

"Hey, I've missed you," Solly said. "It's been too long. There's something I want to talk to you about. What are you doing right now?"

"Nothing, Solly," she said, glad to hear his voice. "I was about to thaw something for supper."

"Then jump in a cab and come up to my place," Solly said. "Have supper with Mrs. Behn and me. We old fogies eat early, but we eat well. Just come as you are, right now."

Solly's doorman wasn't impressed by Miriam's old jeans and sweatshirt but he buzzed up to the penthouse, then showed her to the elevator.

Solly was waiting for her and gave her a huge hug. He led her through the grand apartment to the kitchen, where he introduced his wife. Mrs. Behn could have been his sister, jolly and round and welcoming.

"I'm so glad you could come," she told Miriam. "Solly has told me so much about you. He says you're very talented—and very brave. Living alone in this city, a pretty little thing like you. And not eating right, I'm sure. I'll fix that. It's cook's night off, so you're having pot roast. You two go off and have a drink and I'll call you when it's ready."

They sat by the big windows looking out over Central Park. It was a magnificent apartment of vast rooms and high ceilings, high enough above Fifth Avenue to escape the traffic noise. She sipped the dry martini Solly had made for them and watched the lights come on across the park.

"It's beautiful this time of year," Solly said. "All green and growing, before the summer heat. I think spring's the only time New York seems like I remember it. Gentle, beautiful. People saying good-day to each other. Time to stroll the streets. It's a pity summer has to come." He moved around the room, turning on lamps. "Speaking of which," he said, "what are you doing this summer? Are you free?"

"I haven't got a booking yet," Miriam said. "There are supposed to be all kinds of features shooting here but so far no one's clamoring for me. Are you planning some new commercials?"

"No, I've got something else in mind," Solly said. "I'll tell you about it over dinner."

The three of them ate in the big kitchen rather than the formal dining room.

"We like it better in here," Mrs. Behn confided.

"It's silly, the two of us clattering around this big old apartment. The children are long gone and far away but Solly won't consider moving out. So here we are, sixteen rooms and we use three of them."

"If I do move," Solly said, "it won't be to another apartment. I'll make the big shift, all the way to California. Grow oranges, learn to play tennis, laze in the sun. That's where you'll end up, little Miriam: a big-time Hollywood director."

"I'd settle for being a small-time director, anywhere." Miriam smiled at him. "I've only worked ten days in the past two months. It's getting me down."

"Well," Solly said, sitting back in his chair, "I might have something to interest you." He lit a cigar. "You know, I've made a lot of money from Foot Haven. A few years back I set up a trust to form a ballet company in Chicago for youngsters who might never otherwise get the chance to dance. I think it's succeeded. Anyway, this summer the company plans to do its first professional season. What I want to do is get a record of it all— from rehearsals right through to opening night. On film."

Miriam wasn't too excited at the prospect of making a home movie for Solly. It wasn't quite the career boost she had in mind.

He sensed her disappointment.

"I'd want it to be a very professional documentary," he said hastily. "Something worth entering in festivals. I'm prepared to spend half a million dollars on it. Could we make something respectable for that kind of money?"

"Half a million? You'd walk it in," Miriam said. "Half a million will get you a top director, union crew, the works. If you're going to spend that kind of money, you'll get the best. Would you like me to shop around among the directors I know?"

"No need," Solly said. "I know who I want to direct. You."

Miriam was about to refuse. She was scared. A budget that large resting on her shoulders?

"I've watched you working on my commercials," Solly continued, encouraging. "You know what you're doing, you don't panic, and you work well with everyone. So maybe you're young and you haven't had that much experience. But the ballet company is young, too, so you'll all get along. Will you do it?"

She looked across at him and smiled.

"Yes, Solly," she said. "I'll do it and I won't let you down. I'll give you a film you'll be proud to have your name on."

"Great," he said. "And don't worry about the money. Spend what you like. I've been very lucky in my business. I guess I'm worth two hundred million. So what's half a million here or there, for a good cause. Anyway, it's a tax deduction. We'll

PALACES

open a bottle of wine now, celebrate, and then you'd better get home and start rounding up the people you want to work for you. I'd like to get this started within six weeks."

Miriam knew whom she wanted for the project. She had worked with all the best of the young filmmakers and this was her chance to let them display their talents. Claudia was her first choice for sound and they lunched together to talk about some of the other crew.

"Dan Bridge for lighting," Miriam said. "He's good and he's easy to work with. Denny Stone for key grip. Marie for makeup . . ."

"You're ducking the important one," Claudia said, teasing. "Who do you get for camera? Who's the brightest young documentary cameraman we know?"

"I know," Miriam said. "It should be Fletch. But I've got a problem there."

"What problem?" Claudia asked. "If the director and the camera are bedded down together every night, they'll be able to get all their angles worked out and save us time."

"That's the point," Miriam said. "I *am* the director and there're going to be times when we clash over something and I'm going to have to make the decision. I can't favor Fletch. Or you, for that matter."

"I think you're worrying about nothing," Claudia said. "But, as you say, it's yours. Handle it in your own way."

Miriam waited until Fletch had been back in town a couple of days before she spoke to him about the Chicago job.

"Do you know anything about ballet?" she asked.

"Nothing," he said. "Or opera. I haven't had time yet to learn about the arts." He grinned. "You want to start improving my mind?"

"I'll explain later," she said. "Tonight I'm taking you to Lincoln Center."

He was restless throughout the ballet and she had to dig him in the ribs and hiss at him to pay attention. After the performance they sat at an outdoor café and drank espresso.

"Sorry," he said. "It didn't do a thing for me. I'd rather watch a bad movie anytime."

She looked at him across the table and thought again how very young he was, a kid in so many ways. Not exactly intolerant of new experiences, just indifferent.

"I'm not trying to give you an instant course in arts appreciation, Fletch," she said briskly. "I want to know how you think you'd go about filming a ballet."

Then he was interested.

"Because," she said, "I'm going to direct a documentary about a ballet company this summer, in

Chicago. And if you're going to be the cameraman, you'd damn well better know what you're doing."

His thin face lit up and he reached across the table for her hand.

"You're directing! Hey, that's wonderful. And we get to work together. Listen, I'll go to dance class if it'll help the picture. Oh, boy, a job together!"

She told him about Solly, and he whistled when he heard the figures.

"That's great money," he said. "We can do something classy with that. My last thing we made for seventy-five grand."

"The money, and the fact that Solly's a friend who's put so much faith in me, are why I've got to be extra cautious on this project," Miriam said. "Fletch, even if you and I weren't together, you'd be my first choice for this job. But because we are together, I actually thought about hiring someone else."

He was bewildered.

"You know I can do it," he protested.

"Yes, I know you can," she said. "But don't you see the position I'm in? I'm going to be giving you orders."

"What are you getting at, Miriam?" he demanded. The smile was gone.

"If you're going to shoot this picture for me,"

she said, "you and I suspend our . . . relationship . . . for the duration."

"That's bullshit," Fletch said.

"You think I'm a square old lady if you like," she snapped. "But I'm deadly serious about what I do and I'm not letting any personal relationship come between me and the best picture I can make."

He paled. "It's just . . . you know I love you. It hurts when you suggest I'm too immature to take direction from you. I thought we trusted each other."

He looked so wounded. But she was determined to stick to the course she had charted.

"There are enough tensions in making a film without letting personal lives intrude," she said firmly. "So that's the situation. If you're shooting this one for me, the affair goes on hold."

He stared down at his cup, then looked sharply up at her.

"I don't want the job," he said. "No job's worth losing you. I guess I've known for a while now you were . . . uncomfortable about us. This sounds like your way out of it. Right? Let me down gently. Be just friends on the picture and hope the kid will be over his infatuation by the time the picture's finished. I may be young, but I can see through what you're doing."

"No, Fletch, I swear that's not true," she said. "I think I do love you. But it's all been so unexpected.

PALACES

You've got to give me time to work out what's best for both of us."

In the end, of course, he won her over.

"Don't leave me, Miriam," he whispered as they were falling asleep. "I'm so afraid you're going to leave me. You and I are what matters."

She soothed him with soft words and felt him drift into sleep. She didn't think about what would happen to them after the picture. That would have to wait. She didn't know what she wanted later. She did know she had a job to do and already, even as the boy slept in her arms, she was planning the film.

Solly had told his ballet company she was coming but they were slow to make her welcome. Miriam spent most of her time with the dancers, absorbing their routine, trying to become one of them. She and her crew would have to be a part of the company if they were to capture their energy and dedication.

The company had a quaint old refurbished theater on the South Side. Its director, Leonie Taylor, was a handsome young black woman. She and Miriam quickly became friends. She made sure Miriam was included in all meetings and in the relaxing moments when rehearsals were over.

"Some of the dancers are hostile when whites come around," Leonie explained. "Sure, they're pleased to have Mr. Behn's money, but they don't like to feel beholden to anyone. Once they see you're just doing your job, like they're doing theirs, you'll fit in."

She fit in so well, in fact, that within a week she seemed one of the company. The dancers held nothing back. That was how she learned of the bitter dispute over the importation of a guest star for the summer season.

About a third of the company felt that using Marylyn Bell, one of Chicago's most accomplished dancers, as guest star in their company was demeaning to them.

"It's not that she's white," argued Cable Dunn, leader of the *corps de ballet*. "But this is supposed to be the Inner-City Troup showing what *it* has achieved." Many felt the same way.

The fight raged for days and Leonie presided over it, calmly and with good humor, never imposing her authority. Finally, though, she cut the debate off.

"Miss Bell is going to dance with us," she told the company. "We need her to make the season a success. We can all learn from her. We're damn lucky she's agreed to do it."

That meeting went late, too, and broke up only when more than half the company declared themselves in favor of the guest artist.

"I guess I'm not sensitive enough," Miriam told Leonie while they were drinking coffee in the rehearsal room, enjoying the calm after the tumult. "At first I couldn't see their objection to bringing in someone they all admit is a star performer. Now I think I understand, and I don't know which side I support. It's a good starting point for the documentary. I'll have to recreate the situation, restage the meeting."

Leonie groaned.

"Just don't start the fight all over again, honey," she said. She stood up and stretched. "I'm going to grab a drink down the road. You want to come?"

"No," Miriam said. "I'm beat. I'll catch a cab outside and go back to the hotel."

Outside the theater, it was hot and still. She waved good-by to Leonie, waited a few minutes for a cab, then began strolling up the well-lighted block. Soon she took a wrong turn and found herself on a darker street. She strode on, confident despite the empty street. When she passed two figures lounging against a car she saw they were only kids, white teen-agers. One of them whistled at her as she walked by and she kept her face straight ahead, impassive.

She had gone another half block when they struck. The taller of the two boys grabbed her around the waist and the other rammed her with his shoulder. They forced her into an alley, her scream cut off by a hard hand over her mouth.

They were in the alley now, lit just a little by a

single street lamp nearby. The taller youth produced a knife and she started moving back in terror as its wicked blade snapped out. He held it to her throat and brought his mouth to her ear.

"Shut up," he hissed. "I'd just as soon cut you, so don't make me."

The other boy was grabbing for her shoulder bag.

"Take it, take anything you want," Miriam gasped. "Just don't hurt me."

"That's the way. Beg," the tall one rasped. "I like the sound." Anyway, what's a white chick doing down here at night? Getting some nigger cock?" He moved the point of his knife to her breast. "White boys not good enough?" He turned to his companion. "Robbie, let's show this chick what she's missing, fucking niggers instead of fucking her own."

The smaller boy nodded, his eyes glazed. He looked like a small, rabid beast.

The big one moved against her and thrust his hand up her dress. She pulled away but was tripped by the other boy and fell down onto the garbage cans. A steel lid clattered to the pavement.

The big one fell on her, the knife still in his hand.

"That was stupid," he snarled. "There's nowhere to run to. No one down here is going to help a white chick. Now, you're going to do exactly what I tell you or I'm going to cut your nipples off."

PALACES

She shuddered as he flipped up her dress and put the knife against her bare thigh. She felt the blade slice through the elastic of her panties, and she lay rigid with fear as the boy rocked back on his knees and unzipped himself. In a second he moved on top of her. She heard a shriek of pain and thought it had come from herself.

But it was her attacker who was screaming, lifted clear off her body by a massive foot connecting with the side of his head.

She didn't dare move while the drama played around her. The alley seemed filled entirely by the newcomer, a huge black man towering over the three of them. The tall boy had landed several feet away but was still clutching the knife. He staggered to his feet and faced his attacker.

The big man grinned down at the knife, took one step forward and, with startling speed, grabbed the youth's arm. He spun him around once and there was the sickening snap of bone. The boy was thrown across the alley, face forward into the brick wall.

The other boy was crouching behind Miriam as if she could shield him from this terrible force. The black man reached over her and put one big hand around the boy's throat, lifting him. He slapped the boy twice—long, lazy, looping blows that sent the boy's head snapping back. Then he tossed him across the alley, into the wall beside his fallen companion.

Miriam pushed her dress down and slowly lifted herself.

"No point calling the police," her rescuer said. "We'd be waiting here all night. They hurt you?" His voice was soft.

"No," she said. "No. You came just in time." She wanted to explain. "I'm working over at the ballet theater and they grabbed me when I started walking home."

"It's no place to be walking on your own," he said. "White punks, black punks, no difference." He ambled over to inspect the youths. He kicked each of them in the ribs, casually, and they lay still. "Punk kids," he muttered. "Give the neighborhood a bad name."

He walked her out of the alley and back along the street to the theater. They waited until a cab rolled toward them. He halted it by stepping into the road, his vast size blocking it. He opened the cab door and helped Miriam inside.

"You take care now," he said as he closed the door.

"I can't thank you enough," she babbled. "Can I see you and. . . ?"

"No trouble," he said. He slammed the door, gave her a little wave, and ambled back down the street.

PALACES

The crew arrived in Chicago ten days later and Miriam took strength from their presence, their bustling around. They all trusted her to do her job and she had no doubts about her ability. She was brisk and efficient and surprised herself by the ease with which she coped.

"You're a marvel," Claudia told her. "For a while there I didn't think you'd make it. I don't mean the work—I knew you could do that. I mean being on your own. You were always so much a 'couple person.' "

"I guess I was," Miriam said. "But I found out you can't have both, marriage and your own life."

They were sitting on a wide balcony, looking out over Lake Michigan. Solly had installed them in his house, complete with servants, and they were all enjoying the unaccustomed luxury.

"Miriam," Claudia said, "I think you're strong and brave and very talented. But you don't have to go overboard, from being a dutiful wife to not trusting men at all. If you're careful, you can be independent and in love."

"It's myself I don't trust," Miriam said. "I've come this far and I'm damned if I'm going to risk losing it all, or again losing someone I love. So I'm trying not to be in love."

"I should have such problems," Claudia said.

"Married guys and gays, that's all I ever see. Thank God for work."

"Thank God for Solly," Miriam said. "I've got a good feeling about this job. Everything's falling into place."

Except that the trouble over Marylyn Bell was still there, and mounting. The company was now evenly split on the issue, with the "no guest star" faction gaining supporters every day. It made good documentary film, the angry clashes between the two sides and the bewildered Marylyn Bell just wanting to do whatever was right.

Then it spilled into the streets. Local black militants adopted the cause and began picketing the theater, accusing Solly and Leonie Taylor of selling out, of betraying the city's black artists. They demanded the company join them on the picket line.

Miriam filmed the crisis. It was confrontation at its most powerful, and even if it wasn't what Solly had expected, it gave new depth to the documentary.

Solly flew in when most of the company had joined the picket lines. He was bewildered and angry. He tried to speak to the protestors but was shouted down.

At the height of the day's uproar, Miriam imagined Joe's voice ridiculing her:

These people are fighting with everything they've got, Miriam, and you're standing around, getting in their way, just so you can take pictures. Pictures of things, Miriam, that's all you're about anymore.

Pictures of things.

Her father had always been holding a Brownie, and carted the black Bell & Howell everywhere they went. Her mother, exasperated, told him he never *saw* anything because he was so busy recording it all. He grinned, snapping off two shots of his wife's impatient face as they rode the ski lift over the Gatlinburg mountains. She was lecturing him and he was, as usual, laughing, delighted.

Pictures of things, she told herself. Of all we saw and everything we did. Any excuse for a home movie—a first day at school or cousins visiting, standing stiff and self-conscious while Uncle Jack filmed them. Dance dresses, tried on to show Dadsi, and she and Deborah would twirl in red or blue while he held the camera on them, grinning.

When Dadsi died Mother sent the seven crates of film canisters to Miriam. Nothing had been said, but she and Deborah evidently decided they belonged to Miriam because she was a filmmaker herself now. And Miriam had not even opened the crates, had never wanted to look at those home movies.

"'I feel sick to my stomach,'' Solly told Miriam when they returned to the house that evening. ''I wanted to give them the best, a chance to be seen performing. It wasn't my idea to bring in a guest star, but I was happy to pick up the tab for her. Anything to help the ballet. Can't they see that?"

"It's rough on Marylyn," Miriam said, "but I think you're going to have to give in and drop her, if you want to have a show at all this summer."

"I'm willing to capitulate," Solly said. "Anything for the troup. But Leonie won't hear of it. It was her decision to bring in Miss Bell and she's sticking to it. So I have to support her." Solly looked tired and old. "Well, Miriam, *don't* I have to go along with whatever Leonie wants?" He made an impatient gesture. "This is a *dance* company. It's got nothing to do with black and white. Don't the dancers themselves see that?" He shook his head. "I don't understand, I really don't."

Tempers rose with the heat and the controversy began to attract media attention. This gave protection to Miriam and her crew because the demonstrators assumed they were just one more television news team. They played up to them, to all the cameras.

Later, Miriam tried to figure out just how their cover had been blown. Somehow, the crowd learned who was behind Miriam and Fletch and Claudia, and in a second, the demonstrators turned on the crew, calling out to them in the vilest terms, screaming and hollering and, finally, moving in on them.

They were jostled; their power cables were slashed; trash was hurled at them. At one point Miriam looked into the fighting crowd and recognized the huge bulk of her rescuer from the night in the alley. Their eyes met. He shrugged, resigned, then turned away.

"We should be getting combat pay," Claudia said after the second day of harassment. "I'm getting scared. Something bad is going to happen."

"Me too." Miriam said. "But we can't just pack up. Some of the footage is great. The time poor Solly broke down and cried . . . the rage and frustration when Leonie was talking. We came here to make a nice little documentary about ballet, but what we've got is a piece of film about what happens when people can't get along."

"How long can Solly stand it?" Claudia asked. "Surely he's going to just say to hell with it and forget the whole thing."

"He still hopes for a break-through, that the show will go on," she said. "I guess I sound silly, but I encourage him in his hopes. And I want us to see this thing through, no matter how it ends."

The next day they set up in the little park across from the theater. Leonie Taylor was making a final plea to the protesters, begging them to let the ballet go ahead. It was the hottest day so far and everyone was impatient and jumpy. Dust rose as the crowd, about a hundred strong, milled around the rock Leonie was standing on. Miriam and Fletch were mounted on a flatbed truck parked in the center of the crowd, Fletch's camera doing slow pans of speaker and audience, moving back and forth.

"I don't like the feel of this," Fletch said to Miriam. "They're in a dangerous mood."

"Nothing's going to happen," she reassured him. "A lot of noise, that's all." His hands were shaking as he focused his big camera, and she reached out and touched one. It was a gesture of love and he looked back at her with love and gratitude.

"Christ! Look at that!" the assistant cameraman shouted. Jed Groom was behind them, mounted on the cab of the truck, surveying the crowd.

They looked out to the edge of the park where he pointed. A group of tough-looking whites was swinging into the park, forty or fifty of them. Some carried picket signs, but others had baseball bats. They did not look like ballet fans. But their signs demanded Marylyn Bell be allowed to dance.

The protesters turned away from Leonie toward the white invaders, the rumble of fury growing stronger. Very soon, the confrontation both sides desired was under way.

It was a short and brutal battle. The whites flayed out with baseball bats and the blacks responded with rocks, bottles, and fists. The fight was all around the film truck and Fletch, pale and still, kept his camera running. Then a hand reached up and clutched at the camera support. It rocked and would have collapsed into the mob if Fletch hadn't stepped on the grasping fingers.

Another hand grabbed his leg and Fletch was dragged from the truck, screaming, down into the crowd. Miriam screamed as she saw him, so tall and fair and slight, flaying out at the mob. One moment he was above them, and then he was thrown to the ground. A scream of heart-felt pain, and the mob parted, everyone backing away in horror.

Fletch was on his knees, clutching his stomach, blood spurting from the terrible knife wound. Silence fell over the park. The opposing sides watched in awe as Fletch slowly toppled onto his side, lying much too still in the blood and dust. Then the combatants fled the park, all of them, black and white, leaving Miriam and her crew and the ballet company all standing stock-still.

The scene would stay frozen forever in Miriam's mind. The only movement came from Jed Groom, beside her on the truck. He had stepped behind the camera when Fletch was dragged from the truck. Jed was still filming. Later, all the networks would try to buy the film and the police would take stills from it in a vain attempt to identify the one with the knife.

She flung herself down from the truck and stumbled across the bare earth to Fletch, kneeling beside him. She picked up Fletch's body and cradled it fiercely, holding him as hard as she dared. No one came near them. She talked to him, first in her mind and then aloud in a harsh voice. She told him she loved him, forcing her mind to the specifics of why so that she could tell him every bit of it. She talked to him about their work, and then she went back to talking about love. That Fletch wasn't there anymore didn't touch her mind. She talked, making herself say everything she thought he should hear.

Finally, she lowered him very slowly to the ground. Two ambulance men approached, and took him. She followed close behind, riding with him to the hospital.

The rest of that day and night, Miriam spoke to no one. She stayed mute while Solly protected her from intrusions, arranging for the crew to fly back to New York and for Fletch's body to go with them. It was not until they were through the airport and she was alone with Solly in his limousine that the numbness began wearing off.

"It was my fault," she said. "We shouldn't have been there, in the park. We knew it was getting ugly." The Manhattan skyline had a steel-gray cruel look about it. "He did as I told him, even when he was scared and wanted to leave."

PALACES

Solly took her hand. He was drained and old and did not know how to ease her grief.

"No one's to blame," he said heavily. "It's one of those awful random things that can happen anytime, anywhere. You mustn't—"

"I must!" she shouted. "You don't understand! He was in love with me. That's why he was there. He didn't want to be there. He was scared. He was there for me. And I gave him almost nothing in return."

"I do understand, Miriam," he said gently. "We all knew about Fletch and you. But he was also a filmmaker, doing what he wanted to do. He was where he wanted to be, not just because you wanted him there."

Could she believe that?

She kept hearing his voice. "Don't leave me, Miriam. I'm so afraid you're going to leave me." How many times had he said that, especially right before they came to Chicago? In the end, he had been the one to go.

I'm so afraid you're going to leave me.

Miriam stayed in her apartment, seeing no one. She stayed numb for weeks, for which she was grateful. Numb was best. She took one chance at feeling when she opened a couple of her father's crates of home movies. Reading the labels, she took the one marked "Summer Vacation, Michigan Lakes, 1968" and threaded the film into her projector. It was the first she'd seen of her father's movies since they were made, and she expected a jolt of some kind. She got none. She watched the jerky scenes for twenty minutes before they stopped keeping Fletch at bay. Then she turned off the projector and left the apartment, walking for an hour or so. Returning, she put the film back into its canister and the canister into its crate. All seven crates were stored away again. There was nothing in those movies for Miriam.

After a while, she came to see that she was the only one who could make Fletch's death something less than pointless. She had the means. Ending her period of mourning, she moved into a downtown film studio and there, with an editor and all the film they had shot in Chicago, she began putting together her testimonial to Fletch.

The idea she had had in Chicago, before the disaster, became a compulsion. She worked twenty hours a day to satisfy it. When she was finished, she called Solly.

"I want you to get all the crew together," she told him. "Come down to the screening room with them. There's something we've got to decide."

They came two days later, slipping into the makeshift theater one by one, nobody looking at anybody else. Miriam waited until they were settled, then walked to the front of the room and spoke.

"I've taken all the work we did and put it together. I hope it's a tribute to Fletch. I hope it will make people think. But, after you have seen it, if any of you thinks it exploitive, I'll ask Solly to burn the film."

The lights went down and the film rolled. There was no sound track yet but they needed none. They were silent as the film showed the tensions building, feelings reaching fever pitch. Then the camera pitched and shook for a few seconds before focusing on Fletch in the midst of the angry mob. There was a sharp intake of breath in the screening room as the camera stayed on Fletch, alone now, clutching his stomach, surprise and pain and grief on his face. Slowly, the camera pulled back from his body, now lying alone in the empty arena.

The screen went black but Miriam did not move to the lights. She sat listening to the first sobbing. People on either side of her took her hands and slowly they all linked hands, sitting in the dark, bound by their loss.

"It's finished, Solly," Miriam said, a month later. "The narration, sound track, some linkage in the early parts. Do you want to see it?"

"No," he said, "I couldn't bear it again. Maybe when it's in the movie houses, one day, I'll. . . . I don't know how you've survived, running it over and over."

"Working on it was what I wanted," she said. "It made me determined. I guess I've grown a tough shell."

"Not tough, not you," Solly said. "You've just learned that life must go on." They were sitting in Solly's office and he shuffled some papers on his desk. "What do you think about distribution?" he asked. "I've got half a dozen companies who want to handle it. They all want to release it fast, because of the news value. It's sick."

"No, they're right to rush it out," Miriam said. "We all knew there was an element of sensationalism. It can't be helped. As long as the film is honest, it doesn't much matter."

Confrontation was treated like a major feature film, with simultaneous release in twelve cities. It was a harsh, sobering documentary, and it struck its audiences full force. The critics were unanimous in praising its depth and honesty.

Miriam refused all requests to go out on the lecture circuit to show the film and discuss it. Meantime, there was plenty of work to choose from. She turned down two documentaries and accepted a medium-budget feature, a rip-off of *Urban Cowboy*. She took it because it meant another director's credit for her and because it was being shot away from New York.

She got back to New York in February, a month after the release of the Vermont feature she had worked on a year before. She had already seen the good reviews of the film and noted the satisfactory grosses reported in *Variety*.

She watched the film alone, at an afternoon session on Thirty-fourth Street. They had given Philip Ashton a credit right after the main titles and followed it with her own name, almost as big as the director's. She smiled wryly and hoped Ashton wouldn't mind the producer's cashing in on her slight fame.

She could not keep track of the film itself because she kept watching the Vermont locations, remembering what it had been like to be there, just a year ago, with Fletch. The theater was half empty and no one noticed her weeping. The rest of the audience shuffled out as the final credits rolled but Miriam stayed. She almost missed the assistant cameraman's credit, it went by so fast. Poor Fletch: The producer hadn't realized he had another name worth a prominent credit.

It was dusk, and cold, when she left the theater, walking through the crowds to Park Avenue. She was hungry for human contact with someone from outside her circle of professional friends. Without thought she turned down Park Avenue to the Hotel Bancroft.

"Andrew East, please," she said to the desk clerk.

"I'm sorry, m'am," he said, "but Mr. East isn't

in residence. He'll be either at the Boston or Philadelphia hotels. I could check for you."

"No," she said, "it doesn't matter. I was just passing by."

She went out into the dark and walked straight home.

"Don't argue," Solly said. "It's all booked and paid for. First-class United—we could meet someone important on the flight—and rooms at the Beverly Hills."

"I don't want to go to the Oscars, Solly," she said again. "We're not going to win anything. *Confrontation* only got a nomination because it was in the headlines. There are far better documentaries. The nomination was enough."

"Sure, so we won't win," he said. "But I want to be there, just in case, to show some respect for the Academy. And it will be good for you to meet all the top people in the industry. Maybe you'll be offered a property and maybe I'll finance it. At seventy-two, what's there to learn about the shoe business? I might like to become a big shot producer."

In the end, he wore her down.

There was a limousine to meet their flight and suites waiting for them at the Beverly Hills. She looked around the rich old lobby. The last time she had been there was with Joe, on his book tour, when she had joked about one day bringing him there for the Oscars. She squeezed Solly's hand as they started for the elevators and he smiled at her. She decided not to be so grumpy.

There was champagne and flowers in her suite, and telegrams from her mother, Claudia, Phil Ashton. And one from Joe, wishing her luck and saying he and his family would be watching her on TV, rooting for her.

The hotel buzzed with Oscar fever. Miriam and Solly spent the morning of the awards beside the pool, caught up in the excitement. The public address system crackled all the time, paging the stars and the deal-makers. So many of the faces around the pool were familiar, images she had watched on a thousand screens.

"I feel like an imposter," she murmured to Solly as they lay in the bright sunshine. They had one of the choice cabanas at their disposal, reserved, Solly informed her, strictly for nominees.

"Just enjoy it," he said. He was loving playing the tycoon and she noted he had switched from the vile little cheap cigars he usually smoked to big, expensive ones. "We've both earned some time in the limelight." He waved to a waiter. "Have a drink, lie back, and look like you're enjoying yourself. We could swing a big deal."

There was no big deal for them that morning, but

Miriam was surprised at how many people knew who she was and stopped by to wish her well.

"See," said Solly, "you're famous."

After lunch she went up to dress for the big night.

Before putting on her gown, she did her nails and her hair—still lit with blonde lights and still about shoulder length—very carefully. She gazed down at her hands, amused. She was as dressed up as she'd ever been; ready for the crowd at Chandler Pavilion and looking the way an Oscar nominee ought to look. But she didn't feel any different. And as far as the holy awards were concerned . . . she was there only for Fletch, for their film, not for herself.

Solly, his plump body squeezed into a dinner jacket, escorted her through the jammed lobby to the hotel portico. It was bedlam there, limousine drivers all looking for their occupants.

"No funerals in LA County on Oscar Day," Solly said. "The undertakers have hired all their limousines out."

It was bumper to bumper all the way to the Dorothy Chandler Pavilion, perhaps a thousand limos jammed in with the regular commuters. No one seemed perturbed at being out there in the bright sun in evening dress, crawling toward a ceremony staged at a ridiculously early hour so that

PALACES

East Coast viewers could watch it during prime time.

As they inched up to the entrance Miriam let her window down and the hysterical sounds of the Oscar-watchers came pouring in. There were thousands of them perched on makeshift stands, pushing at police barricades, surging this way and that, trying to get close to a star. They screamed on cue for the television cameras and subsided to a low roar when the TV lights left them.

She and Solly were hustled out of their car and into the theater, hurried by the frantic usher who took them to good seats on the main floor. They sat for half an hour until the ceremony began. Latecomers were still pushing in, and people already seated showed boredom as the winners of technical awards were announced. It annoyed her more than a little: This audience should have known it was the craftsmen, as much as the actors and directors, who made the industry work.

It was only when the ceremony began being televised live that the audience paid it full attention.

Miriam's category was one of the first of the televised awards and she began to shake as the nominations were announced. Solly held her clammy hand and squeezed it when their names and *Confrontation* were called. She heard respectable applause for the documentary but thought the other films had more audience support. It didn't matter.

Just getting this far was more than she had ever dreamed of.

And then they announced the winner. "*Confrontation.*" The applause was loud all around her. Solly was pulling her out of her seat and pushing her into the aisle. She frantically shook her head. Solly, the producer, should accept the statue. But he pushed her again and she found herself tripping down the aisle to the sound of applause, down all the rows of staring faces, up the steps and onto the vast stage. The lights blinded her and the presenter had to steady her as she stepped to the rostrum.

Of course she had not prepared a speech, but words came, her voice clear, no tears yet.

"All of us who worked on *Confrontation* hope it will bring some understanding to this country," she said. "This Oscar is dedicated to Fletcher Harbor."

She ran from the stage, tears pouring down her cheeks as they moved on to the next award.

The rest of the night was a blur. She stayed in her seat, hugging her gold statue and trying to pay attention to the major awards. It was only a small heavy gilt statue, up close. She'd heard of stars who used them for doorstops. It wouldn't change anything. It certainly wasn't going to bring happiness, or security. She still didn't know where her next job was coming from.

They went on to the Oscar party and drank

champagne and accepted congratulations. She danced with Solly and several handsome young men and at one o'clock they reclaimed their limo and cruised back to the hotel.

There was no sleeping late. The first phone call, from Claudia, filming in Boston, came in at seven AM, followed by a flock of telegrams and flowers and more calls. Breakfasting downstairs with Solly the calls kept coming, and the waitress, smiling, decided it was easier to leave the phone plugged in beside their table.

She was on her third cup of coffee when he stopped by their table.

"Congratulations," he said. "You deserved the award. I loved your picture." He was tall, about forty-five, nice looking, tan. "I'm Howard Veitch, of Palace Productions," he added. "We've got a project right now you might be interested in. Why don't you give me a call at the studio when all the fuss has died down."

He gave her his card and left the restaurant, smiling and nodding around the room.

Solly whistled.

"President of Palace Productions," he said. "And such a young man for the job. I read about him once in a while. The studio brought him in when they were in trouble, a couple of years ago. He's got them back in the black. One of those 'baby moguls' the trades are so excited about. It looks like you're going Hollywood, little Miriam."

"I wouldn't get too excited," she said. "I can't see the big studios getting into documentaries, and that's my reputation. No money in that. They're only interested in projects that cost zillions."

"See him anyway," Solly urged. "It can't hurt."

PART THREE

Chapter Seven

HOWARD VEITCH'S OFFICE SUITE WAS THE PENTHOUSE of the Palace Building and Miriam had to run through three sets of receptionists, each older and less pretty than the one before, to reach his presence. The last barrier was a formidable woman in her fifties who studied Miriam with evident distaste.

"Miss McDonald? I don't have you on Mr. Veitch's calendar. What's it about?"

"Mr. Veitch asked me to come to see him," Miriam said. "Yesterday. I called him last evening, here, and he said to come by now. I guess everyone else had gone for the day and he forgot to tell you about it."

The woman sniffed.

"I wish he wouldn't do things like that. It upsets the routine."

"I'm sorry," Miriam said meekly. "But he did ask me."

The woman sighed and rose, looking martyred.

"I'll see what it's about," she said. "You sit there and wait."

She reappeared a moment later, no happier.

"Yes, he did make the appointment," she said. "But it happens to be in the middle of his workout. He's in the gym. Follow me."

They passed through Veitch's office, a vast room of leather and chrome and masses of plants. Through the greenery were magnificent views over Century City to the hills. Off the office was a full-size gymnasium where Howard Veitch, trim in a Gucci warm-up suit, was working out under the eyes of a slim, leotarded young woman. He broke off when the secretary brought Miriam in.

"Hi," he said, picking up a towel and wiping his brow, "I'm just about through here. This is Jersey," he said, indicating the young woman. "You put yourself in her hands and you'll keep in shape. You got room for anyone else in your class, Jersey?"

He turned back to Miriam. "Jersey's got the hottest gym in Beverly Hills," he continued. "She comes over here to me every day, as a favor. She's got a waiting list for her classes. But she'll take you on as another favor to me. Won't you, Jersey?"

The girl nodded and began gathering her things. Miriam thought it all very Hollywood: She didn't

PALACES

have a job yet, but already she was involved in an exercise class.

Veitch turned to his secretary.

"Mrs. Johnson," he said. "Take Miss McDonald into the office and get her a drink or whatever. I'll be in, in a minute, when I've showered and changed."

The secretary fixed Miriam a mineral water from the lavish bar in Veitch's office and left her there alone. Miriam carefully toured the room, her heels sinking deep into the burgundy carpet. Wherever there wasn't glass were pictures; Howard Veitch with the stars, with sportsmen, with politicians. And framed industry awards to Veitch and to Palace. At least there wasn't an Oscar, which put her one up.

"Hi," he said, coming in from the gym, dressed.

Howard Veitch was handsome in the way fourteen-year-old girls think of handsome. He was extremely well turned out; too smooth, really, as though a high-priced interior decorator had designed him. He had dark brown hair, done just so; cold brown eyes; a perfect body which attracted her not at all; and the obligatory tasseled brown loafers to go with the brown pants and cream silk shirt. There was nothing wrong with his appearance or the way he carried himself, but nothing enticing, either. His manner alone made her long for dear old bald, weather-beaten Solly.

"Sorry to keep you, but I won't miss my daily

workout. It's the only way to keep on top of the job. Be fit. It's the wave of the future, you know, personal fitness. Maybe you'd like to make a documentary about *that?*"

"That could be interesting," she said politely, secretly appalled. "But you mentioned a project the studio already had which you thought might suit me."

"Oh, yes," he said, a little annoyed because she had changed the subject without permission. "There was a picture I thought you might like to have a look at." He buzzed the console on his desk and the stern-faced Mrs. Johnson appeared. "Gracie," he said, "get me the *Second Chance* folder."

"She's a tough old bitch," he said as the secretary left. "I inherited her when I took over the studio, and now I couldn't do without her. The broads with the big knockers in the front office are just there for show. It's old Gracie who knows where everything is."

When he had the folder he sat down at his desk and leafed through it.

"This," he said, "is something else I inherited. No one quite knew what to do with it, but I had an idea for it recently and I think you might fit the project. It's not a difficult feature, and it would suit a woman starting out as a director."

She flushed at the put-down but let it pass.

PALACES

"I think I'd be willing to take the chance with you," he said. "I believe in—I am committed to—getting more bright young people into the industry. Particularly women. You know, there are people who think women are only capable of being script assistants. Not me. I want to give them a chance for the very top. So why shouldn't I start with you?"

He stood up, dropped the folder in her lap, and began pacing the office.

"You ever been to Rio?" he asked. "That's where the picture's set."

Rio!

"No," she said. "But wait a minute. You just signed me up for a Beverly Hills exercise class and now you're talking about making a picture in Rio."

He waved a hand.

"We won't be shooting until January, February. I want to use Carnivale time. They all go nuts."

"It sounds great," Miriam said. "I guess I'm used to films that start tomorrow. But if we can work out an agreement, I'll make sure I keep a couple of months free."

"Shit, no," he said. "That's not how it works. If we do a deal, I'll take you on now. There're five or six months' preproduction work involved, anyway. And it will do you good, hanging out here at Palace, learning the ropes. I'll help you all I can. We'll pay you seventy-five thousand to direct and spread it over the year, beginning now. And we'll give you, say, four points."

"Gross or net?" she asked.

"Net, of course," he said. "Hell, the budget's only four million on this one. It'll be in net profit a week after release. You'll make out."

Miriam smiled to herself. Even with her limited knowledge of Hollywood deals, she knew she would never see a cent from her four points of the net profit. But what did she care? The chance to direct a feature for a major studio, to fly down to Rio, to work with big names here in Hollywood. And seventy-five thousand dollars.

"When you read that," he said, indicating the folder, "you'll see there are a few areas still to be straightened out. Nothing major, but I'd welcome any ideas. Certainly there's enough to keep you occupied the nine months before we go on location."

"We?" she asked. "You're going to Rio, too, Mr. Veitch?"

"Call me Howard," he said. "You bet I'm going, I never miss Carnivale in Rio. I'll be there as executive producer, holding your hand all the way. I'm going to have to stick you with young Peter Kraft as producer, but you shouldn't have too much trouble with him."

"Why should I have *any* trouble with him?" she asked.

"Kraft is a spoiled, wasted little son of a bitch on his last legs in Hollywood," Veitch said, "but some of the old guard here think we still owe him something because his father was Murray Kraft, who directed the old Palace's biggest hits. His mother was Mary Avon, America's sweetheart. Christ, it was so easy to make pictures in those days. Anyway, while I do have absolute control over this studio, I still humor the board. And they feel we owe young Kraft a last chance. He's a burned-out case—booze, pills, coke, heroin. But, like I say, I'm willing to humor them and put him on one more picture. Don't worry about it. He'll be producer in name only. I'll steer you through the project."

"So when do we decide whether we've got a deal?" Miriam asked. "I'm flying back to New York tonight."

"What the hell, we've got a deal," Veitch said. "I'm willing to take a chance on you. You return to New York, do whatever you've got to do, and be back here in two weeks. We'll draw up a contract, I'll fix you some office space, and you can start coming to grips with the project."

She told Solly all about the meeting while they were flying home.

"It sounds too good to be true," he said flatly.

"It is," she said. "I read the stuff he gave me about the picture. Years ago the studio bought the rights to a novel—a so-so novel. It's set in Boston and the main character is a man. The studio's had half a dozen treatments done and it's now set in Rio, if you please, instead of Boston, and the man is now a woman. There's no real script, just a series of outlines, all by different writers. Each outline is more confused than the one before it. And none of what's there has much to do with the novel, which is probably just as well."

"So do you want to do it?" Solly asked.

"Of course," she said. "You think they would have given it to me if it was a nice, strong story with no problems? I don't think anyone with real experience would touch this. But I'm sure as hell going to give it my best shot."

"You'll make it work, Miriam," Solly said. "You can make anything work."

Claudia drove down from her Boston job for Miriam's celebration party. Miriam had asked about forty people to her apartment: the film crowd she had worked with, the girls from Steve's Place, Solly and his wife.

"You'll miss this apartment," Claudia said. They were in the little kitchen, cutting vegetables and cheeses.

"I know," Miriam said. "I just realized, getting ready for the move to LA, this is the only place I've ever had that was all mine. I went straight from my parents' house to Joe. That's why I'm only going to sublet it. There'll be something to come back to."

"You won't be back, though," Claudia said. "A year on the Coast and you'll be a convert."

"Leaving New York is so hard. I never made a lot of money and my name wasn't up in lights but, hell, I survived here. It's a tough city, but once you feel you belong, it gives you so much back. I don't know if I want to be a plastic Los Angeles person," Miriam said.

"It's film that matters," Claudia said, "and LA's still where they make most films. You're never going to get a deal like Veitch's in Manhattan. And anyway, you won't be stuck in LA all the time. A couple of months in Rio is some kind of compensation."

"If it happens," Miriam said. "There's an awful lot to be done before we get that picture into production. I want you for it, of course, but, listen, don't turn down any great jobs in the meantime."

"I'll take the risk," Claudia said cheerfully. "Two months in Brazil beats two months of northern winter anytime. I'll practice my Portuguese while I'm waiting for the signal."

"What's the Boston job like?" Miriam asked.

"So-so. They've just about run out of money and we're working mad hours, but there's some good footage in the can. And I'm having the wildest affair with the director. It might even be serious. How's your love life?"

"Nonexistent," Miriam said. She frowned. "I've given all that up. I can't be bothered. I don't want involvements and I don't feel right about one-night stands. No, I'm just going to stick to my work."

"You can't live like that," Claudia said. "Honey, you've got to give yourself another chance. Don't turn your back on the world."

The party was crowded and happy. They all wished her well and she knew how much she would miss them. Some of the people in that room were her real family now, and she was leaving them. And leaving the city she had dreamed in and lived in. But, as they all said, she could always come back. They knew how precarious it would be in LA, how different from the New York film scene where they all tried to help one another.

She waved the last of them off well after midnight. She was tired but she didn't want to go to bed. It was her last night in the apartment that had protected her through the worst times of her life. She wandered around, straightening things, touching objects, remembering. A new life was starting tomorrow—even before she had finished with the old one.

She had to wait half an hour to see Howard Veitch and even when she did get in, he was distracted.

"I'm just rushing off to Rome," he said. "I'd forgotten you were coming this week." He was shoving things into a briefcase. "The contract will have to wait until I get back."

"Okay," she said. "I need some time to get myself settled, anyway. I'm still at the hotel." Thank God she had enough money to get by on. She would have hated asking Howard for an advance when her contract wasn't even drawn up.

"One thing, though," she said. "You mentioned an office. I do need somewhere to work."

"Gracie will find you a space," he said. "Just ask her for anything you need. You better make contact with Peter Kraft, too. Might as well find out now what it is you're going to have to cope with."

"I think we're going to have to get a writer working on this project as soon as possible," Miriam said. "None of the outlines so far—"

"Do what you like," Howard said, gripping her elbow and steering her to the door. "You're the director. I'm late for a plane."

It wasn't the kind of welcome she would have designed for herself, but Miriam was not too unhappy over Veitch's abrupt departure. His absence gave her time to settle in.

Gracie Johnson turned out to be a big help. She took Miriam down to the third floor, to a tiny office, just bigger than Howard's desk.

"It's not much, is it?" Mrs. Johnson said. "When

I started with Palace, we still had the old studio complex, back lot, the works. All the directors had suites of rooms. Now we work in a regular office tower and all the filmmaking goes on someplace else."

She made sure the phone was working and gave Miriam a parking lot pass.

"Where do you think you'll live?" she asked.

"I don't know," Miriam said. "I don't really want to get involved with running an apartment. But I can't afford to stay at the Beverly Hills for long."

"There's a good residence hotel only a mile or so from here," Mrs. Johnson said. She wrote down the name and directions. "Tell them you're with Palace. A lot of our young people stay there."

"Thanks," Miriam said. "One other thing. I'd like to get in touch with Peter Kraft soon. Does he come into the office?"

Mrs. Johnson laughed.

"Peter Kraft? I doubt he knows where the office is. That poor young man. Such a tragedy. His parents were industry royalty. He seems to have done everything he can to denigrate their name."

"But you know him?" Miriam asked. "What's he like?"

"If it weren't for his . . . problems, he'd be a very pleasant young man," she said. "Maybe even talented. It's certainly in his blood. But there's no way to find out, not the way he carries on."

"Am I going to have much trouble working with him?"

"Quite a lot, I'd say," she said dryly.

"And Howard? Mr. Veitch?"

"He's not easy, either."

The hotel was all right; three levels of studio apartments built around a small swimming pool. It was the hassle-free environment Miriam was looking for and she moved in the next day. In the afternoon she visited a used car lot in Century City and bought an old Mustang convertible.

And then she was ready to meet Peter Kraft, her producer. She called him at ten o'clock the next morning. The phone rang and rang and she was about to hang up when he finally picked it up and shouted, "Shit! Whatever it is, I don't want it." He hung up.

She dialed again.

"Mr. Kraft," she said, "this is Miriam McDonald and I'm directing your next picture."

She heard a groan.

"What time is it?" he demanded.

"Just after ten," she said. "Sorry, but I thought all you Hollywood people were up at dawn."

"Not this one," he said. "Hold on." He was back after a long silence. "Sorry," he said, "I had to get some coffee. Now, what picture are we talking about?"

"Howard Veitch has made me director of the Rio

picture," she said, wondering why she was having to explain all this to her producer. "He thought we should get together and start things rolling."

"Howard said that?" He didn't sound very interested. "That little number's been hanging around for years. It's a dog. So Howard wants to load it off on me. That figures. Who are you, anyway?"

Miriam had had enough.

"I think we better get together, today, and work that out," she said. "Where do you want to meet? I'm at Palace now."

"Christ," he said, "I had a bad night. How about next week."

"Today," she said.

"Jesus, you're all business, aren't you? Okay, lunch then. Ma Maison. Put it on the studio. You book us for two o'clock and I'll find you at your table."

He didn't arrive until two-forty-five, by which time the waiters had given up trying to persuade Miriam to order. When he finally ambled to the table and dropped into the seat across from her, she allowed her anger to show.

"You may think this project is a joke, Mr. Kraft," she snapped. "But I take it seriously. I'd at least expect you to be on time."

He raised a hand wearily.

"Don't expect anything of me," he said. "Howard must have told you I'm a has-been, never-was, all washed up at the age of twenty-seven. Anything Howard's assigned me to isn't going anywhere." He beckoned a waiter and ordered a tequila and tonic. She nodded for another mineral water and asked for the menu.

She studied him while he nervously waited for his drink. He was painfully thin, tall but hunched over, a stubble of blond beard on his chin, an unkempt mass of hair falling down the back of his cotton shirt. His eyes were a tired gray, and red rimmed. He was young, certainly, but he had the beaten aura of a much older man, a failed man.

He gulped down the drink and ordered another.

"Okay," he said, "so you're going to take this seriously. I suppose I have to go through the motions. You better tell me who you are. You already know who I am."

She picked at her salad and briskly ran through her career, putting only a slight gloss on it. He didn't seem to be listening, but when she had finished he suddenly smiled and for the first time she felt there might be some hope for Peter Kraft. The smile was sweet and boyish, and he suddenly seemed like another person.

"I see why you're so anxious," he said. "It's all happened to you in an awful hurry." He sighed ruefully. "I guess I better fill you in on this great picture we're making. It's been on and off forever, as you know. If it's on again, it's for one reason only. They moved it to Rio because there's a fortune in captive American money there. It's an exercise in laundering US dollars for wealthy Brazilians who otherwise can't get their money out. The picture will have a real budget of, say, three or four million. It'll go on the books, though, as costing twelve or fourteen million. Everyone will be happy and no one will give a damn what kind of picture gets made. The cost of making a piece of junk is meaningless if it allows them to move an extra ten million out of the country."

"But why does it need to be a piece of junk?" she asked. "Why can't we make a good film regardless of what their purpose is?"

"You mean, 'Let's put on a show in the barn'?" He laughed. "Because it doesn't work that way. Howard's the new breed of studio head. He's more interested in the deal than the product. He doesn't *want* to get a releasable film out of this setup."

"So why don't we just surprise Howard and do our best?" she suggested. "I'm here to direct a movie, not run a foreign exchange scam."

He smiled at her again. "Why not?" he said. "I've got nothing better to do. It won't work, but we can try. And I'd love to send that big bastard into shock." He laughed. "Old Howard, he wouldn't know a good picture if it ran up to him and bit him on the ass. You want to try and salvage something from this exercise, I'll help you all I can."

"That's all I want," Miriam said. "You'd be helping yourself, too," she added. "Surely, with your name, your background, you aren't ready to leave films already?"

"My name," he said. "I'll tell you all about that sometime. I managed to turn it into a handicap."

"So here's your chance to make a fresh start," Miriam said. "Neither of us has anything to lose. I think we might just surprise them all."

He studied her across the table, looking sober and responsible.

"Look, I'll level with you," he said. "I will try and help but you can't rely on me. I've got too many bad habits and I've had 'em all too long. I'll probably let you down. Understand that."

"No," she said firmly. "No one's going to let anyone down."

Over the next couple of days, Peter helped. He called her with ideas and names. Spaced out he might be, but Peter Kraft was a child of Hollywood and knew the people who made the industry work. He even visited her one afternoon in her Palace office.

"First time I've been in the building for three years," he said. "If Howard had his way, they'd have taken my pass away, but there are still a few guys on the board who remember my parents and feel they owe me. That's why Howard has to keep throwing me bones like this one."

"It's going to be more than a bone," Miriam said. "We're going to make it a very good picture."

"You wouldn't guess it from the size of this office," he said. There was scarcely room for the two of them. "In my dad's day you judged how important the picture was going to be by the size of the office they assigned."

"I don't care about that," Miriam said. "But I do care about the way they used to make pictures. And your parents. Are they both dead?"

"Dad was killed in a car crash when I was twelve," Peter said. "Mom had given up the screen, and she had nothing left when he died. She started drinking. She's still alive, living in a discreet rest home up in Carmel. I see her . . . now and then."

"It must have been rough, growing up alone," Miriam said.

"No worse than the other screen brats," he said. "All their folks had split, or were about to. None of us had any security. Even before Dad died and Mom cracked up I was boarded out with cousins here in Hollywood while my parents worked around Europe."

She watched him talking. Burned out, yes, but still, near the surface, there was a sensitivity there. She was going to need him on this picture, but Miriam also wanted him to succeed for his own sake.

"Do you blame them for your own . . . life?" she asked gently.

"The drugs and the booze and the goofing off?" he said. "No, it's all my own damn fault. It's been a while since I had my act together. Just can't seem to be bothered. There's still a little bit of money left, and my folks' name still gets me by the gate at Palace. When that's gone I guess I'll move East, try something new where no one ever heard of the Krafts."

"You won't have to move if we make this one go," Miriam said. "But it's not going anywhere until we get some kind of script together. Have you any ideas?"

"Yeah," he said. "David and Paula Tomkins would be the best I could get. They're young and they're hot but their latest project's just been canceled. I know them well—hell, I went to school with Paula—and I figure I could get them to at least have a look. They turn down more than they accept but they might go for this. The way the property is now, it's about the biggest challenge they're ever going to face."

"Sounds good," she said. "I've seen some of the Tomkinses' work and I like it. When can you talk to them?"

"They're coming by my house Friday," he said. "There's a bit of a party going on. The Hollywood Outcasts." He laughed. "A lot of people the industry has forgotten. Apart from the Tomkinses, that is. Maybe you'd like to come along. It'll end up a cast of hundreds so there's a chance of your running into someone interesting. And you'll like David and Paula. I guess they're about the straightest of my friends."

It had been a grand old house, in the best part of Brentwood. Now the grounds and the façade looked tatty, neglected, and the drive was overgrown. Miriam imagined she could feel the disapproval of the rich, neat, respectable neighbors as she squeezed the Mustang into a space between a battered pickup truck and a green Mercedes convertible.

The door was open and sound came blasting out. There were certainly hundreds inside. At the door she had to step over a couple entwined on the floor, both naked to the waist. She debated turning around and heading back home, but half a dozen new arrivals came crowding in behind her and she was pushed through the throng.

The blasting of music was deafening but Miriam seemed the only one bothered. The others all looked stoned. A few were dancing in the big main room but most were draped around the walls, keeping time with the beat and blinking to the strobe lights. She was glad she had eaten: The catering appeared to consist of pizzas and jug wine and that was all. A little of the Old Hollywood style would not have gone amiss tonight, she thought.

PALACES

She came to a smaller, well-lit room, probably the study. There was a cluster of hypodermic syringes in a bowl on the table. She left the room.

She found a bar toward the back of the house, where older guests were congregating. She felt more at home there, in the air of alcoholic bonhomie instead of the fazed-out, vacuous atmosphere drug users produced.

"You're Miriam, right?" said the man in the white suit. He was a little fat fellow, probably in his sixties but trying not to let it show. He wore a yellow polka-dotted bow tie, and had a cane in one hand and a drink in the other. In this crowd he looked hopelessly elegant.

"I'm Ted Monte," he announced, as if she should know that without being told. "Young Peter's been talking to me about working on his picture but I said I must meet you first. I never take an assignment unless I know I have a rapport with the director."

Then she remembered. Peter had mentioned Monte for set designer. Monte, Peter said, was an alcoholic, an old queen, and a vicious gossip. He didn't get much work now because he despised the new Hollywood and let everyone know it. But he was good at his job and worked cheap. It was only a matter of whether she could get along with him.

"I know," she said, smiling at him. "I'm one of your greatest fans. The sets in *White Bank*—the whole look of that picture—were what won it all those awards."

"Yes," he said, nodding, "that was one time they let me have my creative head. I'm very good with those exotic settings. And your picture's in Brazil." He rapped on the bar with his cane. "Let me get you a drink. Better have a Scotch. Every other liquor our young host has provided is el cheapo."

She sipped her drink and leaned against the bar as Monte introduced her to his companion, a tiny, wrinkled little walnut of a man.

"This is George," he said. "He used to be a jockey until the demon drink unhorsed him. George was just telling me the sad story of a mutual friend who passed on this week. Another lush—like us."

"Yes," said George. "Poor old Vinnie. He'd been in the bar from noon until nine, when he started to go home. But he fell into the cellar instead of out the front steps. They never revived him. You should have come to the ceremony, Ted. It was touching."

"Did they bury him or cremate him?" Monte asked.

"Cremate," George said.

"Christ," said Monte, "they'll never put him out."

Miriam took her drink and went out into the garden. There, on the patio beside the pool, she found Peter and half a dozen people with him, sprawled in deck chairs. The center of attention was a bowl of cocaine on a table near Peter.

"Welcome," Peter said, waving to a chair beside him. "Come sit down with us and have a toot. This is the oasis of sanity in this house. I'm not going back inside until they've all gone."

She sat in a deck chair but declined the coke.

"I just met Ted Monte," she said. "He seems to drink a lot."

" 'Course he does," Peter said cheerfully. "Most of the people you'll be working with have one problem or another. But they're all good. Like Willy." He leaned forward in his chair and called to a group in the pool. "Willy Lee! Come out and meet your director."

She watched as the Oriental man levered himself up out of the pool. He had the torso of a weight lifter, massive arms and chest and shoulders. As more of him emerged over the rim of the pool she saw he was naked. And massive there, too. But as he stood up Miriam saw that his legs were short, spindly and horribly misshapen. The bottom half of Willy Lee was that of a dwarf, the top a linebacker. As they waited he draped a sarong around his waist and limped over to the table.

"Miriam McDonald, Willy Lee," Peter said. "Willy is going to be our cinematographer. The Brazilians won't know what to make of him. The only mutant Chinese cameraman they ever saw, I bet."

The Chinese nodded to her and reached for the coke bowl.

"Willy used to work for my dad," Peter said. "But then there was the scandal. It was only a little bit of opium, and the girl looked an awful lot older than fifteen, but Willy suddenly got unemployable. He only gets to shoot X-raters these days, but he's real good."

Willy Lee sucked in his coke and looked across at her.

"I am good," he said. The voice was flat. "I need the chance to prove it again. Don't worry about this shit," he said, gesturing with the coke spoon. "It's just something to make up for not being in the industry."

"Yeah," said Peter, "I guess we seem like a bunch of druggies to you, Miriam. But, the moment they shout 'action,' we all snap out of it." He laughed and Lee laughed with him.

Miriam shivered. What kind of a crew was Peter putting together for her? She wanted to work with nice straightforward professionals. Were these *all* weirdos?

"Don't worry," a soft voice said at her shoulder. "Peter knows talent. When this crowd gets to work, they'll really roll."

She turned to face a man of about her age, curly haired, smiling. To her relief, he was totally normal looking.

PALACES

"Hi," he said, "I'm David Tomkins. This is my wife, Paula, and it looks like we're going to be doing your script. We saw *Confrontation* before we decided to take the assignment."

Paula Tomkins came in out of the shadows. She was younger, slim and small, with long dark hair framing a tiny oval face.

"We have a few mutual friends," Paula Tomkins said. "David's a New Yorker and we spend a lot of time there. That's where we get sane. Phil Ashton's one of your fans."

"You will do the picture, then?" Miriam said, delighted. "I'd have been too embarrassed to offer it to you. I mean, all your credits and such classy stuff. This project is a real mess."

"Yes," David said, "it has the stamp of Howard Veitch on it. They bought a book they shouldn't have, then parceled it out to a bunch of hacks they owed favors to. We'll have to junk everything that's been done so far, but we might as well keep it set in Rio. Then we'll all get a nice trip out of Howard."

They chatted, Miriam pleased to talk business as the party degenerated around them. When the Tomkinses finally said good-night she was ready to go, too.

She went to look for Peter, but the crowd from inside had spilled out into the garden and patio, bringing their music with them. She was about the only one still wearing clothes, and she picked her way through the couplings, dodging the hands grasping at her, veering away from offers of drinks and drugs. She felt so out of place, and she was very sad: This scene was what talented, bright people called having a good time. The waste!

And then she saw him, leaning against a tree, surveying the revelers with bemusement, as much out of his depth as she was.

"Andy!" she cried.

He turned. The look of delight on his face made her ashamed of all the times she hadn't answered his calls.

"Hello, Miriam," he said. "I saw you earlier but you looked busy." He took her hand gently, and she was surprised when he made no move to kiss her. After all, they were old friends.

"Busy is right," she said. "I'm only here because of business. I'm sorry, but this is not my scene."

"Nor mine," he said. "I came with a starlet, last seen in a back bedroom shoving things up her nose. I've just been standing here on the sidelines, watching the natives."

"I looked for you in New York, a while back," she said. "I called at the hotel but they said you were working out of town." She wanted him to know she had tried to see him. It seemed important that he not think she had used him and forgotten him.

"Yes," he said, "I've been on the run. We opened a couple of new hotels, same lines as the

Bancroft, small and European. That's why I'm out here. Opened a place in Bel Air a couple of months ago."

"Are you going to be staying here for a while?"

"Sure, at least until the hotel's established," he said. "Are you out here on a picture?"

"Yes," she said, "and it's going to take months and months. That's why I'm so pleased to see your friendly face."

"That's me," he said, not smiling. "The friendly face. But I thought you'd have lots of friends out here now. The Oscar should have made you a big deal in Hollywood."

"Andy," she said, looking at him carefully, "I'm sorry about what happened, all the calls I didn't take and the invitations I turned down. I didn't mean to hurt you. I just had to be on my own through . . . a very bad time."

"And now?" he asked. "Are you still on your own?"

She sighed. "I'm setting up a film. I work long hours and I do my best. It's what I wanted, the chance to work."

"It's what we all want," he said. He was trying to keep the bitterness from his voice. "But working at what you love doesn't have to exclude everything else."

"For me it does," Miriam said. "At least, it seems to." She tried to soften it. "But you know how fond of you I am. Us Madison kids have got to stick together, out here on the wicked West Coast."

He glanced around. A girl with enormous breasts, clutching a jug of wine, came staggering toward them, singing to herself. She was naked except for a pair of bright red sneakers.

"I'd like to get out of here," he said. "How did you come?"

"I drove myself," Miriam said.

"Debbie, or Ginny or whatever her name was, drove me," Andy said. "Would you give me a ride back to the hotel?"

They didn't say much on the short drive back to his hotel.

The hotel was an old, mellow building, four floors set in large grounds. The pool and two tennis courts were still lit up among the trees.

"It's lovely," she said as they walked through the small lobby. "Just the kind of place they need in Bel Air. You should get all the serious people here."

He laughed as he ushered her into the elevator.

"Yeah," he said, "I have visions of writers working undisturbed, then coming downstairs to the bar to talk business with serious filmmakers. So far, all the trade I'm getting is the spill-over from dentists' conventions. And they all complain it's too quiet, no $200-a-night hookers hanging out in the lobby."

He opened the door to his suite on the top floor. It was comfortable, not luxurious, but it had a settled look to it. Unlike her hotel apartment, Andy's place was a home.

"A glass of champagne?" he asked, moving to the refrigerator. She nodded and he opened a bottle of Dom Perignon, picked up two glasses and sat across from her in the living room. "Would you like supper?" he asked. "Our room service is one of the best features of the place."

"No, thanks," Miriam said. "I can't make too late a night of it. All the studio people start so early out here. Not like the night life we're used to in New York."

They both sipped their champagne to cover the awkward silence descending on them. There was a sexual tension in the room: Miriam could feel it and she flushed. She knew she wanted Andy to make a pass at her. She felt a physical need for him, but he was wary of her and she didn't know why.

He reached over to refill her glass and their hands brushed. She looked at him squarely, challenging him to make a move. Instead he gave a slight shrug, settling back into his chair, watching her.

"I'd like us to keep in touch, Andy," she said. "It's . . . so hard to find people to talk to out here."

"Sure," he said. "Now you know where I am, call any time. We'll have lunch."

She finished her drink quickly then and Andy escorted her down to her car. He kissed her lightly on the cheek and leaned over to her as he shut the door.

"I do want to see you, Miriam," he said. "Your way—just friends. But I'm not going to make a fool of myself again, so it's up to you. When, where, and how often we get together, and on what basis. It's all up to you."

"You mean platonic?" she said, smiling. She didn't want to drive home to her empty bed.

"Whatever suits you," he said. "Just so long as I don't feel I'm being used to relieve a career woman's tensions."

Just then she knew that was exactly what she wanted him for. She made her longing subside and smiled as brightly as she could.

"I deserve that, Andy," she said. "I wasn't using you—or I didn't mean to. It's just that at this stage of my life I can't get into complications."

"Love doesn't need to be complicated," he said, stepping away from the car. "You'll find that out, someday. You better get home to bed now, Miriam."

He stood staring after her as the car moved down the gravel driveway.

Chapter Eight

WHEN SHE ARRIVED IN HIS OFFICE, SHE FOUND HOWard fuming. He slammed the Rio project file down on his desk and started pacing the room.

"Jesus!" he said, "I knew you were a novice in this business but I didn't expect you to be gulled into signing a bunch of misfits and deadbeats for the picture. I've only been away a couple of weeks. Why in hell didn't you wait for me to return before you arranged all this? You've stuck yourself—and Palace—with a crew guaranteed to produce a disaster!"

"Mind if I sit down, Howard?" Miriam said calmly. He just glowered at her so she placed herself in one of his big leather chairs.

"First," she said, "I am the director and I don't have the final say in crew or casting. You know that. It's Peter's job. But I do go along with the people he's hired. They're oddballs, but there's a lot of talent among them. I can work with them."

"Tell me that when you're in production," Howard said. "I can see nothing but trouble, from Kraft on down." He brightened. "At least a first-class fiasco should get Kraft out of my hair once and for all. He brings in a four-million-dollar bomb, those sentimental old farts on the board will feel they've discharged their obligation to his goddamned parents."

"I wanted to ask you about the budget, Howard," Miriam said. "I got the preliminary figures from accounting and it looks like one hell of a lot more than four million dollars has already been allocated. There's all kinds of figures that don't make sense and several people on the payroll who don't seem to exist."

"Don't you worry about the figures," Howard said hastily. "That's my department. I do have to load some costs onto your picture. It's just an accountancy thing, some overheads we need to charge off."

"I sometimes get the feeling the whole project's just an exercise in fancy bookwork," she said.

"You want to make the picture or don't you?" he snapped. "You can pull out right now if you like. There's a hundred *experienced* directors out there who'd jump at it."

"Of course I want to make the picture, Howard," she said. "I've just got to be sure the studio wants it made. I don't want my name on some dog of a film no one's ever going to see."

"You make it and I'll see it gets the best treatment," he said. "But I think you've given yourself a handicap right at the start with some of these people. That fucking pansy Ted Monte! Vicious son-of-a-bitch. When I left the network for this post, he spread a story I'd been fired because they found out my mental age was the same as the average viewer's. Christ, I'm the man who got the network back to number one. Who do you think came up with 'Celebrity Pets'? And 'That's Outasight'? Or 'Surf Bums'? All top shows, all with the stamp of Howard Veitch on them. Old-timers like Monte think television's just junk. But I'm proud of what I did for the network."

Miriam hid her smile.

"You don't need to take any notice of Ted Monte," she said. "He's just envious of your success. But he is a good set director and we got him cheap."

"Just keep him out of my way," Howard said. "Anyway, at least you've got a top script team. Those Tomkinses have a great track record. I never saw anything they wrote, but I saw the grosses. Have they started work yet?"

"Just," she said. "It's going to be a hell of a job

pulling together the original book and all the treatments that have been done over the years. It's really starting all over again."

Howard was bored with the subject by then, and had exhausted his temper.

"I don't care what they do with the book," he said. "Just so we keep the title *Second Chance*. The studio paid a lot of money for that title." He picked up the phone, dismissing her. "Anytime you want to tap my brain, just come on up," he said brightly. "That's what I'm here for."

She nodded politely and left.

"Howard Veitch is such an asshole you almost feel sorry for him," Paula Tomkins said. "The only reason they appointed him to head Palace was that the money guys in New York liked his television background. He's got a television mind. Everything Howard knows about film he learned from in-flight movies."

Miriam was dining with the Tomkinses in their Benedict Canyon home. They were tossing around ideas for the script. She had quickly gotten to like and trust the Tomkinses and she enjoyed their easy relationship with each other. It was a pleasant, relaxed evening.

They took their coffee onto the deck. It was a gentle, warm night and the stars hung low in the dark sky. David Tomkins lit a joint and they passed it around the table. Miriam was mellow, content, and confident.

"Okay," David said. "What we've got is a story about two kids who fall in love, fall out of love, meet again in Rio at Carnivale, and score their second chance. Not much there but if we put enough gloss on it it might work."

"What if she's a singer or a dancer or something?" Miriam said. "Her career drives them apart. He resents it, wants to be the breadwinner. Then, in Rio, he sees it can work, you *can* have two successful partners in a marriage."

"But who'd believe his earlier resentment?" Paula asked. "Surely, these days, everyone wants his or her partner to realize their full potential."

"Not so," Miriam said, shaking her head adamantly. "You and David are among the lucky ones. I know lots of people who still feel threatened if their wives go out for a career."

"Are you speaking from personal experience?" David asked gently.

Miriam nodded.

"And is it worth the sacrifice?" he asked.

"I'm still finding out," Miriam said. "So far, I think so."

The picture began to take over Miriam's life. Peter Kraft was proving more helpful than she had had reason to hope for, but there were still dozens of details only she could straighten out.

"I think David and Paula's latest draft is good enough to go with," Peter said one evening when he met her for drinks at Chasen's. "Which means we better start thinking about casting."

"That's your department, thank goodness," Miriam said. "I wouldn't know where to start. I've never cast a movie."

"It's really quite simple," he said. "The people you want either aren't available or ask too much. So you work through agents until you arrive at the most acceptable compromise. Anyway, we've got no choice about the male lead. Dear old Howard already sent me a note telling me who we're going to hire."

"I thought this was supposed to be *our* film," she protested. "It looks like it's becoming a vehicle for Howard to pay off his accumulated debts. So who's he stuck us with for the lead?"

"Tom Richards," Peter said. "Palace got him cheap before he got big in his TV series. They have to use him soon, before the option runs out. Actually, it's not too bad for us. Richards isn't much of an actor but his series is rating big, which means we've got a chance of getting some of the kids in our audience. He's young, good-looking and a pain in the ass, but you'll cope with that."

"Okay," Miriam said, "at least we get to pick the female star."

"Not exactly," Peter said, grinning. "Tom Richards has a clause in his contract giving him script and co-star approval. So there's not much point in talking about the female lead until we've discussed it with Richards."

"Damn Howard," she said. "Everywhere you turn you come up against one of his sneaky little deals."

"And the studio loves him for it," Peter said.

They met Tom Richards in his trailer on the set of his series, "Phoenix." He was about twenty-five, coolly handsome and aware of it. He didn't bother getting from the couch when Peter and Miriam came in.

"Hi," he said, "Howard told me to expect you. I might as well make this clear from the start: I don't want to do whatever the movie is. Veitch screwed me for a ridiculous figure. I'm a star and I'm worth ten times what he contracted me for. But my agent says it's a binding contract and I've got to play or pay." He stood up, went to the bar and got himself another cold beer. He didn't offer them anything. She watched him moving around the trailer. He was tall and lean and his face was expressive, even when settled in a pout. She didn't like him, but what mattered was that Tom Richards had that look that spelled *star*. It would be up to her as director to bring it to the screen.

"You, Kraft, I know all about," Richards said, settling himself again. "Another of Howard's liabilities. But at least you're only the producer. I won't need to take any shit from you."

Miriam felt Peter bristle and she put her hand on his arm.

"But as for you, Miz . . ."

"McDonald, Miriam McDonald," she said.

"Right. As for you, Ms McDonald, I don't know." He took a long pull on his beer. "I don't like the idea of working under a woman. I like to be on top."

Miriam allowed her anger full expression.

"You can cut that sexist crap right now, Mr. Richards," she said. "I'm the director and if it's you I have to direct, so be it. I'll tell you now you weren't my choice. But I'm willing to make the best of it. I suggest you do the same."

"We'll see," Richards said. "From the way you sound, this picture is going to end up one of those sisterhood sob stories. I don't go for all that feminist bullshit and I don't intend having my career jerked around for The Cause."

"Just because I stand up for my rights, I'm a whiner?" Miriam shouted. "Go see *Confrontation*. I directed that. Then tell me gender has anything to do with my work."

"Take it easy," Richards said. "I'll give you a chance. I've got no choice." He turned to Peter. "Howard gave my agent the dates and locations. I can fit 'em in, but only just. If you go one day over it's going to cost a fortune in penalties. You brought me the script?" He tossed the bulky folder onto a table in the corner. "I'll look at it. Now, about the female lead, you know I've got approval?"

"Yes," Peter said. "But I figured you'd be too busy, with the series and all, to worry about that. I'm sure we can find—"

"Uh-uh," Richards said. "There's no need for you to find. I've got just the girl. Lisa Cobden. She did a guest spot on my series and she's fabulous. Before that she was on Broadway, and she's done a couple of featured spots in pictures out here."

"I'll be pleased to meet with her, Tom," Peter said. "Who's her agent?"

"I guess I am," he said, smiling broadly. "I've been watching over her out here. You want to meet, you better come by my house tonight. She's living with me."

When they got out of his trailer, Miriam groaned.

"It's not bad enough we get stuck with an insufferable TV actor like Tom Richards," she said. "Now we're going to get landed with his girl, too. And if she can stand living with a prick like him, what kind of person can she be?"

"Yeah." Peter shrugged. "Life wasn't meant to be easy. But he's got us over a barrel. At least he's hot on television and he should sell us a few tickets."

Fortunately, they saw the other side of Tom Richards that night. They arrived after dinner and Richards welcomed them with chilled wine and a gentle smile. When they were seated with their drinks he produced Lisa Cobden, leading her into the room, holding her hand, obviously seeking approval.

"This is Lisa," he said. "Isn't she beautiful?"

She was. Tiny, slender, with big brown eyes and a pert face fringed by sweeping honey-colored hair, Lisa looked about seventeen. And pure.

"Hi," she said shyly. Her voice was gentle but the actor's training was there. "Tom shouldn't have dragged you all the way out here," she said, smiling at him. "I'd have been very happy to come to you. I really want this part and if I get it I'll work very hard for you."

"You've got the part, darling," Richards said.

"No, Tom," she said. "I'll have to test for it, and I'm sure Mr. Kraft and Ms. McDonald have lots of other people they'll want to consider. I don't want the part just because you've got a clause in your contract."

Peter and Miriam waited for Richards to throw a fit. But the star, clearly besotted, accepted the condition.

"You'll get it on your own merits, and or looks," Tom said. "Won't she, Peter? Miriam?"

"I'd say she's got it already," Peter said. "It's only a matter of working out terms. Miriam?"

"I think you're perfect, Lisa," Miriam said. She

looked at Richards and allowed herself a small smile. "You know what you're talking about, Mr. Richards."

"For God's sake, call me Tom." He grinned back at Miriam. "You bet I can pick a winner."

They stayed a while, talking about the film. Miriam and Lisa also talked about New York, how different it was from LA and how much they missed it. Miriam's first impression of the girl was reinforced: Lisa had a radiance to her that was even more captivating than her physical beauty.

Driving back in Miriam's car, she and Peter were jubilant.

"I was so prepared for disaster," Miriam said. "You'd figure Tom Richards' girl would have an ego this big—or else be a dishrag. But she's delightful. And he behaves himself when she's around. It's going to make working with him so much easier."

"Yes, a different man," Peter said. "You'll notice, though, there were no apologies for all the shit he put us through this afternoon. Cross your fingers nothing happens to their romance before or during the picture."

"You want me to drop you at your house?" Miriam asked.

"No," he said, "it's too early for me. I guess I'll stop by the Jungle for a while, check out the action.

You want to come with me? It's not even midnight yet."

"Okay," she said.

The Jungle Bar was packed and noisy but Peter got them a table by the wall and ordered beers. Two of his friends, rock musicians busy forming a new band, joined them for several more beers and Miriam found herself drawn to the older of the musicians. Chet was a wry, funny guy, gently putting himself and the industry down.

"Look at me, thirty years old and still wedded to rock n' roll," he said. "My folks keep asking when I'm going to get a job. But I always dream the next band we form is going to be *the* one. Cover of *Rolling Stone*. Hit after hit." He laughed. "I've been in so many bands now, I can't remember all their names."

"But you like what you're doing," Miriam said. "That's the important thing."

"Oh, sure," he said. "I just love being up there with my axe, turning on a crowd. But the gap between me and the audience is getting wider and wider. I'm an old man in music terms."

There was a well-worn look about him, not just the faded jeans or the hint of gray in his ponytailed hair. His long thin body was slumped, as if in resignation, and his pale blue eyes were tired.

"Hey, you're in Peter's picture?" Chet said. "Sounds like it's going to be a blast. Rio!" He looked across at Peter, deep in conversation with a girl who couldn't have been more than fifteen. "Peter really knows how to have a good time, but it's nice to see him working again. There was a time when I thought we were going to lose that boy."

"Actually I'm not *in* the picture," Miriam said. "I'm the director."

"Better still," Chet said. "I don't think I ever met a lady director. You must be smart."

"Not smart, just persistent," she said. "If I were *smart* I'd be in some other business."

"I just had an idea," Chet said. "You're making a picture, you're going to need music. The new group, we don't just play rock. Hell, we can write bossa nova if that's what you need." He called to Peter across the table. "What do you say, man? Old Chet does the soundtrack for you?"

He turned back to Miriam. "We'll go back to our pad in a while and play some stuff for you. I think I'll invent a new form. Rock samba."

They did eventually move the party to Chet's place. The old house Chet, Dave, and some of the musicians were renting was in North Hollywood. It was seedy and run-down, just a place to flop. The only things kept well were their instruments and their sound equipment.

And they could play. Miriam lay on a broken couch, drank warm white wine from a peanut butter jar, and let the music wash over her. Chet began playing alone on his electric guitar and two or three others drifted in to join him. They jammed for an hour, sad gentle South American rhythms, with overlays of cool jazz and the raw strength of rock underneath. When they finished, Chet ambled over to sit beside Miriam.

"Well?" he asked softly. "Is that the sound you're looking for?"

The music had taken her away from the dingy room, and it took her minutes to gather her thoughts.

"It's beautiful," she finally said. "I think we might get something going."

He didn't reply. He had fallen asleep. She felt a piercing tenderness for him, poor tired desperate musician. And she was frustrated. She had been prepared to take their new friendship a lot further. She smiled ruefully at the sleeping Chet and moved away carefully so as not to wake him.

Miriam found Peter in the next room, staring into space, smoking. The young girl was sleeping in his lap, her skirt draped over her naked body. It had grown cool in the early morning.

"You want a ride home?" she whispered.

"No, I'll stay," Peter said. "See you tomorrow."

She had lunch with Howard Veitch, who was supposed to have read the latest draft of the script. He didn't seem all that interested and she guessed he hadn't had time to read the Tomkinses' work.

PALACES

"It sounds fine," he said. "You're doing very well with this. Just keep it up. No one expects the movie-of-the-year from this project."

Was he ever going to give her a little enthusiasm?

Peter called her late in the day.

"I was too strung out to work," he said. "I'll make up for it tomorrow."

She told him about her lunch with Howard.

"Yeah, that's par," he said. "Howard doesn't want to know until the film's in the can. Then, if it's good, he'll take the credit. If it's a dog he'll say it was all our fault. You can't win. Anyway, what did you think of Chet's music? We'll need some tracks from somewhere and we can get him real cheap."

"I want to hear more," she said. "But, so far, I'm impressed."

"Good," Peter said. "I just left Chet's place and he said if I was talking to you, how about you join us again tonight. He's got a friend playing at the Troubador, then we can go back and listen to some more of his stuff."

"I'd like that," she said. "Only not so late tonight. We've got a lot of work to do."

It was fun at the Troubador and Chet was awfully nice to be with she decided. He was so laid back, dreamy. It added to his charm.

He draped his arm around her shoulders on the drive back to his place and she wished they were by themselves. Listening to his music could wait. Miriam would rather be alone with Chet. He was so soft and vulnerable. She shivered when she thought of snuggling up to him. They would be so good for each other.

It wasn't to be, not that night, anyway. Chet played again, as well as he had the night before. There was wine and grass, and silent people moved through the rooms. When he had finished playing Chet drifted off somewhere to the back of the house and Miriam, after waiting half an hour, realized he wasn't coming back. She drove home alone.

Peter appeared in her office at eleven the next morning, uncharacteristically early.

"Sorry it was so quiet last night," he said. "But you did say you wanted to finish early. I think we should give Chet the chance to put something down. He's got his problems but he's a good musician and it's not like we're going to be taking him on location or anything."

"What problems?" she asked, as casually as she could. "He seems pretty normal. Nothing a few nights' sleep wouldn't fix."

"Smack," Peter said. He saw her look of puzzlement. "Chet's a heroin addict, deep into it. It's all he lives for, smack and music. He doesn't eat, or sleep, or fuck." It must have shown on her face be

PALACES

cause Peter suddenly reddened, looking at her closely.

"Oh, hell," he said. "I hadn't thought of that. I guess he's an attractive guy if you don't know about his habit. Sorry, Miriam."

"That's okay," she said levelly. "It was only a passing fancy. If you think he's safe to use on the film, then use him."

They discussed other business connected with the film. It was time for Peter to be going to Rio to obtain the rights and permissions they would need, to see to accommodation for the cast and crew of sixty, to arrange catering and extras and all the rest.

It was Peter's job and she would have to trust him, but she wished she were going along. There was little preproduction work left for her, and right then she wanted to be busy.

The late summer weather turned savage, the sky a sullen gray from brush fires. Dust and ash swept down on the city, pushed along by the hot, fierce wind. Anyone who could got away from the city and she felt an envious anger that Howard and the rest of the moguls were away in the gentle New York fall, catching the Broadway shows, doing deals in comfortable restaurants, while she was in this insane place. Miriam was tense and tired all the time. The dust and the heat were always there, on her skin, in her hair, inside her. She felt parched, drained, useless.

When she could stand it no longer, she called Andy East.

"Hi," she said, "I'm glad you're still here. Everyone else seems to have fled. I can see why."

He sounded pleased to hear her voice.

"I know what you're going through," he said. "Nothing you've been told prepares you for the Santa Ana. Just be grateful it doesn't last too long."

"It's already been too long," she said. "Hell, Andy, can we get together soon?"

"Of course," he said. "I've missed you. I'd have called but I figured you were awfully busy."

"Not anymore," she said. "It's all ready to go, but for the next few months I've got to sit here and mark time. Everyone else on the project has skipped town but I've got to stay here in case anything comes up."

"What you need is a quick vacation," he said. "Can you take a couple of days away from Palace Productions? Just a couple."

"There's no one here to miss me," Miriam said.

"All right, then," said Andy. "why don't we fly down to Mexico? There's a place I have to look at, a new resort they're planning on the coast. I may put a hotel there. It's still fairly primitive but there's accommodation of sorts and the beach is a gem."

PALACES

He came for her the next morning, driving a white Mercedes 450 convertible. He looked embarrassed when she admired the sparkling car.

"I've got to drive something," he said. "And the staff have been sneering at my old VW."

There was a private Lear jet waiting for them at the airport and, when she saw the way the crew greeted Andy, she knew it wasn't a rented jet.

They were out over the ocean, drinking a chilled Chardonney, when she started giggling. He tried to look stern, but then he, too, broke up.

"I know what you're thinking," he said. "We're not doing badly for a couple of kids from Wisconsin."

"But Andy," Miriam said, "I can't believe all this." She waved her hand around the plush aircraft. He again looked embarrassed, and boyish. He was still as rumpled and gawky as he'd always been. Only the externals had changed. But how they had changed!

"I'm not too comfortable with all this," he confided. "But my advisors say it's good for the image. And it's all a tax deduction." He was shy again. "The plane actually makes sense. I have to travel a lot, to the other hotels."

"How many hotels have you got?" she asked. Andy was a tycoon, but the fact was just sinking in.

"Ten in the US," he said shyly. "And another

three or four to open over the next year. Mexico, maybe, and one in Bermuda."

"But the last time we talked, you said you just had 'this little operation.' "

"It grew quickly," he said. "Seems the idea was right. It's almost as big as I want to get now. Too many more hotels and I wouldn't be able to keep personal control of them."

She found it hard to adjust to the new image of Andy. He hadn't changed to fit a new image. He was still just Andy.

"We'll be landing in a minute," he said, looking out the window. Below was a lush green coastline splashed by white waves.

The plane made a wide low sweep and set down on a dirt airstrip ringed with palm trees. There was activity around a small tin shed at the strip's edge and a big old black Cadillac moved slowly across the strip to their plane.

"The welcoming committee," he said as if apologizing. "They're very keen to get this development going. But I promise there won't be any business on this trip. We're here to relax."

The car took them to the tin shed where a group of local authorities waited with cool drinks and anxious smiles.

"They've got you mixed up with El Exigente," she whispered.

"Stop it," he whispered back. "This is serious. Don't start me laughing."

But as the authorities fussed around him, it *was* like the coffee commercial. She had never seen Andy so in charge, so businesslike, the center of everyone's attention.

At last he satisfied the officials that they had done enough for him. The car and driver were put at his disposal and they set off along a rough track to the coast. As they topped a rise she saw the village and the ocean glimmering before them.

"It's beautiful," she gasped. And it was. The vivid blue of the ocean, the white-crested waves rolling in to a golden-sand beach, the rich deep green of the jungle.

"I know," he said. "If we do develop here we've got to keep the place the way it is. If I had my way, I'd just build a house for myself and leave everything else untouched. But the people here are desperate for tourists, and if it has to be done, well, at least we're not as rapacious as some developers."

They were taken to the village inn, which was a collection of thatched mud cottages built around a central restaurant and bar. The whole staff, twenty people, were on the front verandah to welcome Andy. Two boys in stiff white jackets carried Miriam's one case between them.

Her room was basic but delightful. There were tropical flowers everywhere and the scent was rich and sensual. The big wooden bed was covered with a mosquito net. The wide windows were unglassed and a gentle onshore breeze stirred the white net curtains.

As she finished unpacking her few things Andy knocked.

"Is it okay?" he asked. "It's not the Ritz, but—"

"It's lovely," Miriam said. Impulsively, she kissed him. "I can't thank you enough. It's like escaping to another world. Just what I needed."

"If you want a swim," he said, "get changed now and I'll meet you in the bar. Then we just walk across the beach and into the water."

She put on a green print bikini and draped a yellow sarong, supplied by the inn, around her hips. She found Andy in the bar, talking with the jolly fat bartender. Andy was in brief white shorts, his body deeply tanned.

They strolled across the perfect half-moon bay and into the water, the gentle surf pulling at them. Miriam felt all the grittiness and tension of Los Angeles wash from her. They swam a little way and rolled on their backs, the sun hot on them, the water cool.

When they swam in again there were deck chairs, umbrellas, and a smiling waiter. Miriam put on her dark glasses and watched Andy as he ordered drinks. There was a new air about him now, the air of a man who had achieved a great deal and was satisfied with himself.

"I thought we'd have a light lunch here on the beach," Andy said. "Then I want to walk around a little, look at some sites. You're welcome to come with me but I thought you might like to lie down in your room. It gets awfully hot down here in midafternoon."

They lunched on fresh raw fish marinated in lime juice, thinly sliced smoked ham, and chilled tropical fruit. A bottle of Bollinger rested in a silver bucket.

"I didn't think a little quaint place would run to such luxuries," she said, watching the bubbles rise in her champagne glass.

"I sent the plane down yesterday with a few necessities," Andy said. "They're not really geared for tourists here yet." He said it without affectation, as if sending a jet-load of champagne and food was nothing special.

She could feel the sun beginning to burn her and she was grateful to Andy for suggesting she nap. He saw her to her door and she went in, lowered the grass shades on the windows, and stripped. She washed the salt water from her body in the small bathroom and slipped between crisp sheets, noting without surprise Andy's hotel crest on the linen.

She lay there waiting for sleep, all of her relaxed

in the pleasant warmth of the room. She could see the glare around the edges of the shades but in the room it was dark and peaceful.

As she drifted toward sleep, her mind wandered over all the times Andy had called and she hadn't had time to talk with him, the dinner invitations she'd been too busy for. Was he still angry with her? Or was she just ashamed of herself?

She slept. The brightness around the windows was gone when she heard the tap at her door. She sat up in bed and pulled the sheet up to her chin.

"Come in," she called softly, and Andy came through the door. He had been out in the full sun wearing only shorts, and his body glistened.

"I thought I should wake you," he said, his voice husky. "You don't want to sleep too long and miss the sunset." He stood there, uneasy, wondering whether to go or stay, and Miriam knew what she wanted him to do.

"Come here, Andy," she said very softly. She let the sheet fall, exposing her breasts. He moved across the room to her bedside and she could feel her nipples harden as he stared at her, mesmerized.

She cast the sheet aside.

Andy stripped off his shorts. He was big and hard and white against the rest of his tanned body. He lay down beside her and studied her for long moments before taking her in his arms. She reached up and touched his face, tracing his mouth with her fingers. They kissed, and he was hard against her, groin to groin, chest to chest.

She came even before he entered her; just the closeness was enough. She heard herself crying out and felt his hand gently covering her mouth. Then he was inside her, reaching deeper and deeper, and her passion flooded over them. His sweat, sun scented, mingled with hers and their bodies moved frantically to climax again and again.

After they had dozed and then awakened, she said, "Thank you." She looked into his eyes and saw sorrow. But why? Even this closeness wasn't enough for him. "Oh, Andy." She sighed. "What can I do?"

"You won't let yourself love me and I can't help loving you," he said. "So use me all you like—and don't expect me to give up loving you. I'll just stop saying it."

They made love again that night. After a romantic dinner and a stroll on the beach, they lay down under a palm tree. The sand scratched the back of her thighs and twice they were almost discovered by people walking the beach. It didn't matter. All that mattered was the fierce sense of herself, of her womanliness and Andy's release inside her. She sensed she was taking from him more than she was giving, but there was no point in dwelling on that.

They flew back to LA late the next day, Miriam squeezing his hand and thanking him for all he had done. He grinned and shrugged and acted as if it had all been nothing. He was determined to play it cool. He wouldn't push her, and she was grateful.

After their Mexican vacation, she saw Andy only a couple of times before she left for South America. They spent a day and night on board the first yacht Miriam had ever seen up close. Abraham Walker, their host, made no secret of his admiration for Andy, Andy's business acumen, his fresh outlook, his intelligence.

Walker had made his millions by dumb luck, inventing pantyhose at his wife's urging. He knew he wasn't a match for Andy's ingenuity and he was generous enough to admire the younger man without envy. He chattered to Miriam all afternoon, Andy-this and Andy-that until she was thoroughly annoyed. Why did there seem to be a conspiracy to throw her at Andy? Watching Walker's wisps of white hair blowing in the strong ocean breeze, she wanted to tell him she'd groped with Andy in the backseat of a car when she was fifteen. Then she was ashamed: Andy *was* terrific, and she seemed to be turning into a real bitch. What was wrong with her?

Chapter Nine

FOR THE EIGHT-HOUR FLIGHT DOWN TO RIO, THEY HAD the rear section of the jumbo jet all to themselves. Miriam had no chance of concentrating on her Portuguese phrase book because of the festive mood. There was drinking and laughter, and she was pleased to see crew and cast mixing right from the beginning. Ted Monte, seated beside her, had consumed six martinis by the time she stopped counting. Even Ted's acid tongue had found nothing to criticize yet.

"A nice mixture," Ted said, nodding and waving his hand around, meaning their party. "Enough bright young people and a few of us veterans," he said. "And such an exciting place to work. Rio at Carnivale! You don't know how it will grab you, my dear. Everyone goes stark, raving mad. You have this tight Catholic society released from their bonds for a couple of weeks. *Anything* goes. The rest of the year the majority of the people live in poverty and priest-enforced discipline, so for Carnivale they try to cram all their lusts and dreams into a frenzy of dancing, drinking, and fucking."

"You've been to Carnivale before, Ted?" she asked.

"Once, years ago," he said. "I was living with a very famous star, Hollywood's most popular romantic lead in those days. Of course, we had to keep our affair very quiet. He brought me to Rio for Carnivale and, for the only time in our affair, we were able to go around together openly. Everyone was too frantic having a good time to bother about who was up who. Dear Rodney," he said. "We went to the big masked ball together—him in drag—and danced all night. Wouldn't the *National Enquirer* have loved that!"

Lisa Cobden, who was sitting with Tom Richards in the next row, leaned over the seat to talk with Miriam. All through the long journey she was fresh and bright. Lisa Cobden glowed.

"I can't wait to get started." She smiled at Miriam. "The final draft is wonderful. I already feel I am that girl, that it's her flying in this plane. I want to be so good in this."

"You will be, Lisa," Miriam said, smiling back.

PALACES

"If you and Tom can bring your own feelings to the film, there won't be a dry eye in the house."

"Don't worry about Tom," she said, dropping her voice. "He wants me to be a big success and he'll do anything to make this work. Why, he's not even drinking. He's fallen asleep with the script."

"Tired, not bored, I hope," Ted said.

Soon everyone was crowding to the windows on the right side of the big jet. Below them were the lights of Rio, ringing the dark, vast bay. Rio sprawled over the hills, an unplanned city, untamed and exotic.

Peter and his retinue of assistants were waiting for the party when they got through Customs. He looked nervous among the hordes of khaki-uniformed police who swarmed everywhere in the airport.

"At least you're on time," he said as he kissed Miriam on the cheek. "Jesus, this country at this time of year. Nothing happens when it's supposed to." He shouted at the handlers he had brought along and they began organizing the baggage and the cast and crew into the two buses and six limousines he had waiting at the curb.

"You look strung out," Miriam said, praying it wasn't drugs and high living.

"Wait until you've tried to organize a picture here," he said. "Everyone's crazy. They don't come to work because they're off practicing their sambas. The atmosphere is great but it's hell to work in."

"Any real problems?" she asked when they were in their car.

"I guess not," he said. "Nothing we can't fix, anyway. Accommodation has been the biggest headache. The town's been booked for a year. I managed to find an old hotel in the unfashionable part of town. On payment of several bribes the owner agreed to kick out his regulars and make it available to us. At only ten times the normal rate. It's run-down, but it'll do. As for our stars, I got two suites at the Copacabana. Bribery again. I guess you'd prefer to bunk down in one of them."

"No," Miriam said. "I want to be with the others. You can have the suite."

"I've been using it as a production office," he said. "But it's too hard working out of there. I keep gazing out at the beach. I guess we'll keep the suite, though, despite the cost. Dear Howard's liable to show up demanding the best room in town."

Miriam let down the limo window and the warm, scented night air flowed in. They were passing a village and she heard the rhythm of the samba. She caught a glimpse of people swaying under the lights, richly costumed.

"Still two weeks to go to Carnivale," Peter said. "But they've been practicing all year, the samba schools, that is. They're building up to a peak now. After a while you don't hear it anymore, like New York City traffic noise."

"God, I hope we can capture the atmosphere," Miriam said. "I'm happy with the script, the cast and all that side of it. But what's going to make this film special is getting the feeling of being here."

"You'll probably capture it," Peter said. "You can't avoid it. It gets to everyone."

She glanced across at him, seeing his face in the passing flash of street lights.

"You're caught up in it?" she asked. "I mean, have you been . . . all right?"

"Have I been fucking around with drugs and sex and rock 'n' roll?" he said. "Look, Miriam, you don't have to worry about me. I've as much invested in this as you. The difference is that Howard *wants* to see me fail. With you, he just doesn't care one way or the other. The only coke I'm doing on this job is purely for medicinal reasons, just enough to keep me going. Don't worry. You couldn't ask for a more serious producer than I am right now. I won't let you down."

The hotel was small, old, and far off the tourist track. Miriam was pleased. They were living in the streets of the real Rio, far from the glittering beachfront high rises. True, almost no one on the staff spoke English but the moviemakers coped with the help of phrase books, sign language, and much good humor on both sides.

They filmed street scenes the first few days, easy stuff, long distance of Tom and Lisa strolling through the crowds, setting up shots of the traffic on the boulevards, street vendors, quaint shops.

"We need some police to control the crowds," Willy complained. "Every time I move my camera there's a bunch of kids in the way. And the noise! I don't know what Claudia's going to do when we need sound."

"Peter tried for police help," Miriam said. "They quoted him a hundred dollars a day per man. We can't afford it. Anyway, the crowds will get bored with us when Carnivale starts."

"I'm not worried about the extraneous noise," Claudia said. "I can tone it down later in the studio. And we'll be using wireless mikes for the outdoor stuff, anyway. What does bother me is all the equipment. Some of the kids hanging around look like they'd steal the shirt off your back. Can you spare me an extra grip to protect all my stuff while I'm working?"

"See Peter," Miriam said. "Personnel is his problem, thank God."

She and Claudia ate out of the hotel that night, at a traditional Brazilian barbecue restaurant. They attracted a lot of attention, two young women without escorts, but easily fended off the men.

PALACES

"You can't beat New York training," Claudia said as she waved off another crestfallen Latin. "Though I'm not sure I won't succumb to all those dark eyes and flashing teeth before the picture is over. What about you? Are you still the iron maiden?"

"No time for anything else," Miriam said. She didn't mind when Claudia teased her; she knew her friend really cared. "I just put my personal life on hold when I'm doing a picture."

"And between pictures?" Claudia asked, looking at her hard. "You haven't told me what you've been doing all those months out on the Coast. Have you been bedding some idol of the silver screen? Or a big-shot producer? What about the yet-to-be-seen Howard? Everyone assumes you bedded him to get this job."

"No one who knows Howard Veitch assumes that," Miriam said quickly. "Howard's too busy making deals and too worried someone may be moving up on him. Actually, Hollywood's kind of sad. All those rich and beautiful people scared they're going to lose what they've got. It's not the kind of place for real relationships."

"You haven't gone celibate?" Claudia pressed her. "It's not natural."

"Well, not exactly," Miriam said. "Andy East and I spent some time together in the past few months."

"I like Andy. And I think he's cute," said Claudia.

"But he's . . . serious," Miriam said, embarrassed. "About me. I've had to discourage him."

Claudia shook her head in disgust.

"You don't like having casual affairs and you shy away from a guy who gets serious. You've got problems, kid."

"I'm happy," Miriam said. "I'm making pictures, which is what I like to do."

They were filming in a cabaret, Lisa playing a singer. The place was packed with extras but there was no need to coach them. The girl was good and their applause was genuine.

"Christ," Peter said, "she's so talented. She's going to steal the picture from Tom. I wonder which will win out—his ego or his love."

"He's okay," Miriam said. "He's a pussycat as long as she's around. He won't mind if she steals it from him. He's already a star."

They got the scene in only three takes and broke for the day. The extras were still clustered around Lisa by the time the grips had packed everything away.

"You want to come have a drink with me?" Peter asked. "I've got this journalist I'd like you to talk to. He's the *New York Times* bureau chief here and he's preparing a long piece on the resurgence of the Brazilian film industry. It could be a help for us, because it won't be coming out for a few months, maybe even close to our release date. I don't know how you feel about reporters on the set, but if you haven't any objections I'd like you to let him hang around for a few days."

Mac Hunter was waiting for them at a table in the beachfront bar of the Copacabana. Peter didn't need to make any introductions. Mac unwound his long frame from the table and greeted her with a kiss.

"Miriam!" he said. "What in hell are you doing here?"

"Actually, I'm the director of this movie," she said. "That's what I do now. Make pictures."

"Hey, that's wonderful," he said. "You always were interested in film, I remember. And where's Joe? Is he here with you?"

"Joe and I split up quite a while ago, Mac," Miriam said. "He's married again, living in the Keys and writing."

"Hell, I'm sorry," he said. "I didn't know. I don't hear much gossip down here. I knew about Joe's book, of course, but I figured you two would be living a life of luxury in the Big Apple."

"We're both very happy," she said. "With our own lives."

"I'm impressed with you already," Mac said. "Big-budget feature film, exotic location. Woman director. I'm glad I picked this project for the story. Peter told you what I'm doing?"

"Yes. It could be a big help to us," she said. "We'll give you any assistance we can. Wait till you meet Lisa Cobden. She's worth a story by herself. She's going to be a big star."

"I think I saw her on Broadway a few years ago," Mac said. "Cute little girl with a big voice?"

"That's Lisa," Miriam said.

"I'll see if I can get something in Arts and Leisure," he said. "The main story won't appear in the magazine for months. There are three or four more movies being shot down here later in the year, so I'll cover them, too."

"The later the better," Peter said. "If we can get some ink in the *Times* when the picture's in release it'll help."

"I'll stall as long as I can," Mac said. "That's one of the things I like about the *Times*. They have infinite patience if it's not a news story."

"How do you like being posted down here?" Miriam asked. "It's got to be one of the most romantic places a bureau chief could go."

"This time of year, yes," Mac said. "All the jet set are here for Carnivale, the city relaxes its rules, everyone gets crazy.

"But it's a long way from the newsroom. You have to fight for space on the foreign pages and you worry they're going to forget about you down here," he said. "Still, there are compensations. The women are a knockout."

The three of them looked out over the beach and Miriam and Peter nodded agreement. The beach, as always, was crammed with sun worshipers, predominantly women. They were uniformly thin, tanned deep brown, and nearly naked.

"It's a funny country," Mac said. "Going topless is forbidden by law but those swimsuits they wear, the *tanga*, have to be the briefest in the world."

"Yes," Miriam said. "I've ventured onto the beach in my old bikini and felt positively overdressed. And overweight. They're all so thin."

"Being thin and brown," Mac said, "is the badge of being rich in a nation where ninety percent of the people are shockingly poor. Rio is a city of extremes. There are stunningly rich Beautiful People who operate outside all Brazilian moral codes. It's more frantic than Manhattan. And the rest of the people are poor, overworked, and under the thumb of the State. That's why Carnivale is such an excess. The authorities know if the poor can't feel as rich and free as their ruling class for a little while, something would erupt. Bread and circuses."

As if on cue, a group of painfully thin children came running in from the beach to their table, begging money. The waiter shooed them away.

"There are thousands of those kids," Mac said. "Orphans, runaways, living outdoors. But don't be fooled by their big brown eyes. They are the best sneak-thieves in the world. They've got to be. It's how they live. Take your eye off your possessions for just an instant and they're gone."

The sun went down behind them and the beach began to empty. Soon there were only a dozen men moving through the twilight, scouring the sand with metal detectors. With the twilight the samba rhythms started up again, all around them, as if all Rio was one gigantic band. It was the night of the final dress rehearsal for the Carnivale parades, and in every suburb and village the competing groups were putting final touches to the elaborate costumes they would march in, and making sure they were step-perfect in their parade routines.

"What are you doing for dinner?" Mac asked. "I know a little place up in the hills where the tourists don't go."

"I'd love to," Miriam said. "I didn't expect to be free tonight so I've nothing planned."

"Yeah, but don't forget we've got a dawn call in the morning," Peter said. "We're shooting the young lovers on the beach."

"Mac," she said, "my producer's warning me to make it an early night. Is that all right with you?"

"Sure," he said. "You won't join us, Peter?"

"No," Peter said. "I've got to call in at the film

processing place and make sure they're doing the dailies. And I have to call LA to see what's happened to this week's cash transfer."

She enjoyed the evening. She and Mac talked of old friends in New York and she found herself explaining about her and Joe. Mac was a good listener and she appreciated the chance to talk it all out.

"Do you think you did the right thing?" he asked her when she had been silent for some minutes.

"Looking back, I guess I had no choice," she said. "Neither did Joe, I suppose. We wanted different things. Perhaps if I'd been involved in films from the very beginning of our marriage it would have worked, but I found a vocation at the time Joe was ready to drop out."

"How do you cope, being on your own after years of marriage?"

"It's hard sometimes," Miriam said. "You were so used to having someone there, to talk to, to love. You did things together and you seemed stronger than two individuals. Sometimes I feel so vulnerable. The freedom is great, and not worrying about anybody—but then, there's no one worrying about me, either."

"What about sex?" Mac asked casually. "Did you find it hard, stepping back into the singles scene?"

"Yes," she said. She laughed. "You have a casual affair and then expect someone to admonish you for it. It takes ages to realize you're only responsible to yourself and at first it's a very scary revelation. I can cope with it now but it took a long while."

"Will you come home with me tonight?" he asked. Then he poured more wine and waited for her reply. They were sitting at an outdoor table under the stars. It was a romantic night. Mac was an agreeable companion and an old friend, and it would be easy to say yes.

"Not tonight, Mac," she said. "I've got a dawn shoot. I'll have to be up at four AM."

"I'll run you back to your hotel, then," he said. "But let's have dinner again soon, when you don't have an early call. Maybe you'd like to come with me to the Governor's Ball. It's the big social event of Carnivale and I think you'd enjoy it."

"That would be great," Miriam said. "I'll have a look at the production schedule tomorrow. The ball's next Friday, right?"

They drove down the mountain in the dark, their headlights picking up bands of revelers getting an early start on Carnivale. Across the valley the huge statue of Christ glowed white against the mountainside.

At her hotel Miriam kissed Mac on the cheek and thanked him for the evening.

"Sorry to have to cut it short," she said. "I had a marvelous time. I'm very glad to see you."

"I'll drop by the set in the next couple of days," Mac said. He fumbled in his wallet. "Here's my card, where you can reach me anytime. I suppose you've had a few hassles already. Some of the lower-level cops have to subsidize their salaries with bribes. If there's any serious trouble, I might be able to help."

There was a heavy mist on the beach at Ipanema but Miriam was assured it would burn off with the first rays of sun. They set up quietly in the pre-dawn, shivering in the chill. She felt sorry for Lisa and Tom, who were doing the scene nearly naked.

"My goose bumps are bigger than my nipples," Lisa laughed as the crew bustled around her. "That's going to look great in close-up."

"I'll warm you up," Tom said, cuddling her to him. He looked around. "Christ, Miriam, do we have to have all these people on the set? The crew seems to be getting bigger by the minute."

"Stop bitching, Tom," Lisa said. "No one gets up before dawn if they don't have to. Not even to gaze at my boobs."

At last the sun began to push up out of the ocean and the mist dispersed. Miriam called softly for quiet and Willy rolled the camera. Claudia was crouched in the sand off to one side, straining to keep the fifteen foot-boom in position, its microphone just over Lisa and Tom but out of the frame.

They did four takes and Miriam was almost satisfied. Lisa, clad only in flesh-colored panties, and Tom, bare to the waist, had warmed up with the arrival of the sun and they were enjoying their scene, oblivious to the people around them.

"Oh, shit!" Willy called, and Miriam glanced up and then looked around. They were no longer alone on the beach. Huddled down in the sand, all around them, were little knots of revelers who had been sleeping the night off, and numerous young boys, the homeless children she had seen the day before.

"I think we better pack it in," Willy said. "We've got what we wanted."

"No," Miriam said. "Just one more take for safety."

They went on filming and the onlookers slowly tightened around them. At first it was just a low murmur, but then the noise built. The boys pressing down on them were uttering high, birdlike sounds. All their eyes were fixed on Lisa.

It happened suddenly. A tall youth dashed forward and stood in front of Lisa and Tom. He unbuttoned his tattered pants, exposed himself and began to masturbate. Another youth broke from the crowd and lunged at Lisa, grabbing her breast and squeezing it hard.

Tom Richards roared in fury and tackled the youth, punching him viciously to the ground. The cries became angry and fearful. Miriam heard Claudia scream as a man snatched at her boom pole and tried to wrest it from her. Two of the gaffers ran to her assistance and another fight broke out. And then all the beach around them erupted. Willy, Miriam, and Peter concentrated on protecting their camera. In a minute they heard klaxons blaring and two big black cars came bouncing onto the beach. The mob broke instantly, fleeing in all directions as the cars disgorged a number of dark-suited men, pistols in hands.

"Thank Christ," Peter said. "The cavalry's arrived."

They waited for the police to come to them. Lisa was sobbing, Tom's arm around her bare shoulders, an ugly scratch reddening across her breast.

The police looked as menacing as the mob. They surveyed the situation, pistols still exposed. Two of them advanced on Lisa. They grabbed her roughly by the wrists and, when Tom tried to push them off, gestured him away with their guns.

Peter rushed up.

"What's happening?" he demanded. "I thought you were here to protect us. We've got permission to film."

"You have caused a riot," the leader said in heavily accented English. "The girl, she bares her breasts in public. She is arrested for disturbing the peace."

One of the grips got close enough to hand Lisa her robe and the arresting officers allowed her to pull it around her. Then they hustled her up the beach to their cars.

"Arrest me, too, you Fascist pig!" Tom yelled, chasing after them. "I want to go with Lisa."

The policeman shoved Tom backwards, then turned and joined his fellows. With klaxons blaring again, the cars lurched off the beach.

Miriam and Peter drove to police headquarters, a vast, tomblike concrete building. No one seemed to want to help them. It was twenty minutes before they could even locate an English-speaking officer. He explained they'd have to wait until at least ten AM, until arrest reports came in.

"Bullshit!" Peter said. "This is an American citizen, a *star*. We want action, right now."

"From what you have told me, the young lady has broken the law," the officer said. "Now the law will have to take its course. I suggest you go and get coffee and come back here after ten. Ask for me and I will try then to find where your star is being held."

Glad they had left the raging Tom behind, they went to a café across the square from the threatening police building. The other patrons seemed to be waiting, too, casting anxious glances at the building. Occasionally someone would jump up and run out to greet someone coming through the doors of the police building, blinking in the bright daylight.

They returned at ten o'clock and located the officer.

"I am sorry," he said. "Our paper work is not as efficient as it should be. There are no reports of your lady. I even called the district office to which she would have been taken but there is no information there."

Miriam could feel Peter about to explode. She put her hand on his arm.

"What should we do?" she asked the officer. "This is a very young girl we're talking about. She will be terrified. And it's holding up a major Hollywood motion picture. I don't want to have to bring the American consul into this, but. . . ."

"The American consul could do no more than I have done for you," the officer said sharply. "And making threats will not help you. You do not seem to understand that your activities have caused us a great deal of trouble. *We* are the injured party. You brought a riot on yourselves by your scandalous conduct on one of the beaches of which we are so justifiably proud. I suggest you return to your hotel and wait for word from the young lady. If you wish, I can provide you with a list of attorneys. You will need one."

She got Peter out of the building as fast as she could.

"This is fucking ridiculous." He finally let go as they stood in the street. "That poor kid is locked up somewhere for nothing. We've got to make a big fuss. I'll call Howard, get some action."

"For Christ's sake, don't do that!" Miriam hissed. "The last person we need throwing his weight around is Howard Veitch. He'll offend the whole city and get us all locked up. We're just going to have to be patient."

Back at their hotel there was a stack of messages from Tom at the Copacabana. Miriam called him.

"Where is she?" he screamed. "I've been calling every police station and no one admits knowing anything. She could have been raped and murdered by now. We don't even know they were police who took her away."

"I'm sure she's all right, Tom," Miriam said reasonably. "We just have to wait until we get word."

"To hell with waiting," Tom said. "I already called Palace in LA, to try and get Howard off his ass. I knew you and that fucking airhead producer wouldn't get anywhere, so I called the head office. You know what they told me? They told me Howard Veitch was here in Rio, supervising production! What the hell is going on? Where's Veitch and who's running this picture? I tell you now, the next call I make is going to be the Screen Actors Guild. You can't allow your actors to be treated like this. I'll get SAG to go to the President. Reagan'll care. Reagan knows how to handle tinpot dictators."

"Tom," she said, trying to soothe him, "I know how terrible you must be feeling. We all want Lisa back safe. But I don't think involving the White House will help us at all. I'm sure she's going to turn up any minute."

"Shit," he snarled. "I should have gone with my instincts and refused to do this picture. What could you expect, letting a woman run things."

It had been such a harrowing day. Would she have to see Howard, too? Was he really in Rio? If so, he would lecture her about the trouble she had caused the studio. She did not need Howard Veitch just then.

"Tom, I know you're upset," she said. "But be fair. No one could have anticipated what was going to happen this morning. It was just bad luck, but we'll sort it all out."

"*I* may sort it out," he said. "I'm certainly not going to rely on you. The way I heard, you got your cameraman killed on your last picture. Well, you're not going to 'sort out' Lisa." He slammed down the phone.

Miriam was too worried about Lisa to be upset by Tom's abuse. And as the hours passed she began to despair. It was afternoon when she remembered Mac Hunter and called him at the *Times* office.

"The police minister's secretary is a friend of mine," he said. "But you've got to understand this is a wild time in Rio. Everyone's crazy, the cells are filled with drunks, and a half-naked American girl could get treated like any other reveler. Stay where you are and I'll get back to you."

Two hours passed. She and Peter snapped at each other in between taking more abusive phone calls from Tom Richards.

Mac called her at three-thirty.

"You can pick her up at headquarters in about half an hour," he said. "She's had a very close shave." He started laughing. "She acted her way out of it. The guys who grabbed her were not your friendly neighborhood policemen. They took her to their barracks and were all prepared to have a little fun. They figured a girl who takes her top off for a dirty movie was easy pickings. Anyway, she convinced them she was a big star from New York, a personal friend of the US ambassador and his guest in Brazil. Then she sang them the whole score of *Evita!* Sure, it's the wrong country, but it impressed the hell out of them. They dressed her up in a police uniform and took her on a tour of the other precincts. She sang for every district cop in Rio, a one-woman USO show. She's worked her way all the way up the ladder to the deputy police chief's office and she's ready to leave, now. The only thing she's suffering from are strained vocal cords."

Miriam called Tom with the news. He was mightily relieved but didn't offer an apology for his outbursts against her and Peter. The three of them drove to headquarters to find Lisa waiting at the entrance, surrounded by admiring police brass.

"Hi," Lisa called, still signing autographs. "Sorry about losing a day's shooting. But it was out of my control." Tom kissed her and put an arm protectively around her shoulders, pulling her away. He glowered and Miriam feared a battle.

She got the picture back on schedule within three days and called Mac to tell him she would love to go to the Governor's Ball with him. It wasn't gratitude. She really wanted to see him.

He picked her up at 9 PM. Tall, blondly handsome in a perfectly cut dinner jacket, Mac was a dashing escort. She was glad she had packed the soft beige silk Zandra Rhodes evening dress. They would make a handsome couple, even beside all the wealthy, glittering Brazilians and exotic visitors.

"You look lovely," Mac said when he'd settled her in the car. "No one would believe you'd been working on a hot film set all day." He negotiated through the traffic and out onto the road to the yacht club. "What's your call for tomorrow?" he asked casually.

"A nice late one. Noon," she said.

"Good," he said, and they both understood that the night was taken care of.

The yacht club, jutting out over the bay, was ablaze with lights. Fleets of limousines were jammed up to the entrance. Mac flashed his press card and got them into a roped-off parking area.

"My God, how formal it is here," Miriam whispered as they passed between the marine honor guard into the club.

"Give it a couple of hours and they'll all be raving," Mac said. "No one, even the highest society, is immune to Carnivale fever."

Mac knew everyone and he introduced Miriam to the governor, the US ambassador, and the bright lights among the rich young Brazilians. She danced with a series of tall, dark handsome young men, drank French champagne from the finest crystal and watched with amusement as the pace of the party stepped up and the formality crumbled away. There was a floor show in which incredibly lithe men and girls danced what Mac assured her was a traditional Brazilian folk ballet but looked like an explicit mating ritual. The dancers were all but naked and their sexuality pervaded the ballroom. She watched the guests watching the dancers and smiled to herself at the irony: innocent Lisa Cobden arrested for baring her breasts on the beach while the *crème* of government and society applauded simulated sex at a formal ball.

Mac took her into supper at midnight and she marveled at the splendor of the feast—tiny red lobsters, mountains of oysters, huge pink salmon, sides of rare beef. Again there was the contrast between all this and the grating poverty of the mass of people outside. They took their plates out onto the terrace overlooking the dark bay, sitting at one of the little white wrought-iron tables preset with champagne and caviar.

"It's a brilliant evening, Mac," she said. "Thank you for bringing me. Just the break I needed in the middle of filming."

"There's a lot of the night to go yet," he said.

They were returning to the ballroom when she saw the familiar figure at a corner table. He was sitting with a tall blonde who was bursting out of her strapless red gown. Miriam steered Mac to the table, signaling to him with a look but not explaining. There wasn't time for that.

"Howard!" she called as they approached the table. "Fancy meeting you here. Tom Richards called the studio the other day . . . we had a little crisis . . . and they said you were in Rio, but we thought they were wrong because we hadn't seen you."

He didn't rise when he saw her and he appeared to be drunk.

"I've been here a week," he said sullenly. "But I've been very busy working on developments. I'm sure you're coping fine without me. I might come visit you next week. Where's your production office?"

She told him. He didn't seem at all ashamed not to know where their office was. She introduced Mac. That brought Howard to his feet, finally.

"The *New York Times*!" he said. "Great! Sit down with us and have a drink. This is Cindy Horan, my executive assistant. I'm showing her what life is like on location."

He signaled a waiter and ordered himself a Scotch. The others were happy with champagne.

"I'm glad you've got time to liase with the media, Miriam," Howard said. "Any publicity helps, of course, but you can't beat the *New York Times*." He turned to Mac. "You will be doing something about our picture, right?"

"Probably," Mac said. "Maybe as part of a look at the whole film scene in Rio. But Miriam's an old and dear friend from New York, so tonight isn't business."

"I bet it isn't," Howard said. He gave his executive assistant a squeeze. "It's a time for playing, not working."

When they had left Howard's table, Mac said,

"He seems like an asshole. How could he be here a week and not see you?"

"He's not the world's most admirable human being," Miriam admitted. "And his commitment to film is . . . a little vague. But he has a reputation in Hollywood—or, more important, in Wall Street—as a great deal-maker. For example, this picture wouldn't have been made if not for the deal Howard put together." She stopped. After all, Mac was a journalist. "Anyway, I'm happy Howard isn't nosing around the set. We've got enough problems without him."

They danced some more and when, at two AM, Mac asked if she'd like to go home, Miriam was ready. The streets still pulsed with life and Mac drove slowly, dodging couples who staggered into their path. The top of his car was down and the night air was soft, warm and flower scented. She thought of the dark, sexy dancers at the ball and felt desire rising in her. She let her hand brush Mac's thigh and he glanced across at her and smiled.

His apartment was the penthouse of an old Portuguese-designed building. A sleepy doorman rode them up in the creaking elevator and, wistfully, wished them good-night.

The apartment was softly lit, filled with flowers and plants. Around three sides was a wide balcony with views across the city and the water. The incessant beat of the samba floated up to them and there were lights everywhere, as there would be all night.

"Do you want a drink?" Mac asked softly. They were on the terrace and his arm was lightly draped around her bare shoulders.

"No," she said. "There's nothing more I want."

He turned her around and kissed her and she pressed against his body. They stayed that way for a while, savoring each other.

He walked her back through the living room and into his bedroom. The room was painted deep blue. The lights were low and she could see out over the city through the open windows.

Mac shrugged off his dinner jacket and pulled his black tie apart. He came to her and kissed her again, then carefully unhooked the back of her fragile gown. It dropped to the floor as Miriam stood, letting him tend to her. He pushed aside her bra and lowered his head to her breast. She remained still as he sank to his knees, running his lips down the front of her. She gave a little cry as he brushed aside the thin silk panties and buried his face there.

They scrambled out of the rest of their clothes and tumbled naked onto the cool sheets. She could see all of him, the strong slim body, the firm buttocks, the pulsing manhood. His hands and his mouth had made her more than ready and she moved his body onto hers, crying out again when he entered her. She arched her hips to draw him farther in. She looked down, watching in awe the place where their bodies were fused. He was so big: It should have hurt her. But it was as if he was sharing his manhood with her, as if he was part of himself and part of her, a magic joining them.

It was a long lovemaking and she came many times, the impulses starting deep inside and flowing in waves all through her body. She wanted it never to stop and he understood and kept time with her. And when at last he could hold back no longer she climaxed yet again, a crashing finale perfectly orchestrated between the two of them.

They lay back, spent. Lights from cars on the road below swept across the bedroom ceiling. The scent of night-blooming flowers mingled with their own musky fragrance. The air was soft and warm.

His arm was around her tightly and he kissed her earlobe.

"Old friend. Dear friend," he whispered, and she could feel him grin.

They sat on the terrace, Miriam wrapped in his robe, and drank coffee laced with brandy as the sun came up and the first of thousands of brilliantly colored kites soared into the cool dawn air. The kites flew from every hilltop around them, garish against the deep green jungle and the light blue morning sky.

"A new day after a wonderful night," she said. "I feel so good, so free, as if I know myself for the first time." She looked at Mac, sprawled naked on a lounge. "I think what I want is physical love with someone I like."

He laughed easily.

"It's what we all want," he said. "But most times the other feeling—emotional love—blows everything apart. I have fought very hard not to be in love. If you were going to be around much longer, I'm not sure I could keep up the battle. But I mustn't be in love. I'm too selfish for that. There are too many things I couldn't give up for love. But you're not selfish—and I think you do need to be in love, no matter what you say."

"No," Miriam said sharply. "I think I'm like you. Career, independence, the belief that I can make it on my own—they've all become more important to me than the empty place love could fill."

Mac studied her face. "It's a lonely road we've chosen."

An hour later he drove her back down the hill to her hotel. No one looked at her oddly for being in her ballgown; there were many other couples still dressed in evening finery. She kissed Mac lightly and he promised to call.

But there wasn't the opportunity for another night with Mac. The production moved on to twelve-hour days, making the most of the vast expense of location. They had to finish on schedule, or the company would be up for all kinds of penalty payments. Tom Richards was due back in Hollywood to resume his TV series. The crew survived on amphetamines. Everyone was tense and snappish, but the work got done.

Howard paid them one visit. When he saw the frenzied pace of work he nodded approval, remarked that he would just be in everyone's way if he stayed, and retreated to the Ipanema penthouse he'd rented with his blond assistant.

Mac stopped by the set a couple of times but he was all business, the reporter at work. He asked savvy questions and got frank answers; they all trusted him after his help with Lisa and the police.

Finally they had it all in the can, a day under schedule. Miriam and Peter shared a bottle of champagne in the production office.

"You've been wonderful," Miriam told him. "I had no right to expect so much help from you."

He smiled a twisted grin.

"You mean, when Howard first foisted me on you?" Peter said. "I wasn't very promising material, but you weren't put off and you gave me a chance. So I gave it my best." He drank. "Actually, I wasn't so sure about working with you, either. A woman, and her first feature. I'm glad now I didn't let it scare me off."

"You think we'll work together again?" she asked. "I mean, after this one?"

"I don't know," he said. "If you stay with Palace, it's Howard who's going to decide who you work with. And Howard doesn't like me. I believe I mentioned that."

"He will when he sees the rough cut of this picture," Miriam said. "You'll be a hero. And while you've got your producer's hat on, how are we doing on budget? Is there enough to throw a really good wrap party tomorrow night?"

"On *my* budget we're in good shape," Peter said. "What I don't know is how many extras Howard has loaded on. We always knew this picture was a tax scam for the wealthy Brazilians. Shit, what's the difference? They're going to rip us off. Spend what you like on the party. The cast and crew deserve it."

She hired a beautiful restaurant across the valley from Sugarloaf. Carnivale was over, and everything was available.

"Why don't you invite Mac?" Claudia said the afternoon of the party. "I mean, your last night in Rio."

"I'd rather keep it family," Miriam said. "You know wrap parties are awful for outsiders, all of us sobbing on each other's shoulders."

"Well, I'm bringing a guest, even if you're not," Claudia said. "A nice local boy, rich as sin. He wants me to stay on a couple of weeks down here, meet his family."

Miriam was taken aback. When had Claudia found the time?

"Don't look like that," Claudia said. "We can't all be like you, wedded to films." She took Miriam's hand. "Honey, you've got to loosen up. Sure, we've been one big family on this job, and we will be on the next. But you need something of your own between jobs. Can't you call Mac and invite him?"

Miriam wouldn't. The party was her responsibility, and she could not be encumbered by her own interests on this last night.

It was a typical wrap: They all drank too much, there were drugs around, and everyone cried at least once and promised to keep in touch. Back in the hotel, after the party, Miriam felt a great loss. This had been her project. She had brought them all together and she had been responsible for making it work. She lay in the lumpy bed listening to the night sounds of the foreign city and wished for Mac beside her.

Miriam stopped off for a couple of nights in Manhattan before returning to Los Angeles. She had a delightful dinner with Solly and Thelma, in their apartment.

"So what now?" Solly asked as they sat in the study waiting for Mrs. Behn to call them into the kitchen. "After shooting a feature in Rio, I don't think you'll go back to making commercials for me."

"I don't know, Solly," she said. "I've got to do the postproduction, and then I guess it's up to the studio. If they like what we've done, they might offer me another picture. If they don't—well, I'll be very grateful if you need a director for your commercials."

"I don't think you'll ever have to do that," he said gently. "You're on your way now. But I wouldn't be too distressed if you didn't get another picture from Palace. I know some people on Wall Street and they talk to me about your industry. It's not like old times. Some of the studios have been taken over by the money guys and they're more interested in money than pictures. You, you don't belong with deal-makers. You are a picture person."

She smiled at him with love.

"It's all I want to be, a filmmaker," she said. "But these days it's harder and harder to separate money from films."

"There's always independent production," Solly said. "I've got some money. Your friend, Andrew East, has money. And good sense, too. We could maybe put up a little for the kind of picture you want to make."

"How do you know Andy?" she asked warily.

PALACES

"I put up some of the money for a new hotel in Chicago," Solly said. "He is a very impressive young man. And he loves you—like we all do." He was worried. Had he gone too far?

She was angry, but she knew there was no real cause.

"I don't need Andy's help," she said sharply. "I can make it on my own." She hadn't meant it to be so blunt but there was no backing away. "I don't want to be dependent on anybody, Solly."

"I'm sorry," he said meekly. "There was a time when we were all of assistance to each other. I am only saying we might repeat that someday. Please don't think I'm interfering."

Anger became remorse. She got up and ran across the room to him, tears in her eyes.

"I'm the one who's sorry, Solly," she said, hugging him. "I owe you so much. And Andy—oh, the only thing he ever did wrong was to love me more than I can stand to be loved. Please forgive me for sounding so ungrateful. I'm really not."

He hugged her tightly.

"I understand," he said. "And you'll make it on your own. Just remember, though, there are some of us who care for you very much and we will always help. Helping someone doesn't always mean you want to own them."

After Miriam left, Solly and his wife sat in the kitchen and talked about her.

"She has to make it," Solly explained carefully. "Miriam's not like you and me. She's never going to have kids and she's not right for our kind of life. Me," he shrugged, "I liked business well enough to make out for myself. You have to like business or you fail. But that's all there really is to it. With film, you have to be a fanatic."

"Miriam's not a fanatic, Solly. She's a marshmallow." His wife smiled at him, ready for the rebuttal. He wagged a finger at her.

"She isn't any different from any other obsessed person, Thelma. She looks mild because she doesn't care about making an impression. I can't explain it exactly. But Miriam's made of fire and steel and only because of that will she make it. And she's got to make it. Film is her marriage—even if she gets married again film will always come first. It did with Joe. I don't think she knows that, but it's true. Film is her child. It's also the father she wasn't really comfortable with, the mother she has nothing in common with, the sister ditto."

His wife sighed. "And if she fails, Solly?"

Solly shook his head very slowly.

"If she fails, I will never stop worrying about her."

She flew on to LA and moved back into her apartment hotel, quickly beginning the lonely work of cutting the film. Peter Kraft had stopped off in Aspen and Howard Veitch was in New York; she and her cans of film seemed to have been totally forgotten. Already Rio seemed a dream.

But as she did the rough cut Miriam grew excited again. Somehow, for all her inexperience, the film was all there. It moved with color and exotica. Lisa was brilliant and Tom played off her expertly. Miriam knew enough about movies to feel that this one was going to do very well among the people who cared. It was not going to be a blockbuster, but it was a good, solid piece of work.

She finished the assemblage in four weeks, with still no word from Howard. Her year with the studio was almost up and she had no idea what would happen next.

Miriam hated herself for doing it. She seemed to have taken from him in so many ways and given nothing in return, but he was the one person she trusted, and, she admitted it, loved. And she had to talk to someone. She called Andy the day after she had handed over the film to the studio.

"Look," she said, "you'd be within your rights if you told me to go to hell. But, Andy, I'd like to try a new beginning with you . . . if you care about it. I need a friend and I guess you're the best one I ever had. You don't ask for love, I won't expect sex. You want to try?"

He laughed. It sounded, on the phone, a little

hysterical and she wondered if she should just hang up before she made an even bigger fool of herself.

"Honey, that's the silliest proposition I've ever heard. Only a little hayseed from the Midwest could offer anything so naïve. And only another hayseed could accept."

But after that he didn't laugh. They kept the bargain and became loving friends. Miriam began taking a real interest in Andy's business. She began to feel she was contributing something to their friendship. There was still sometimes a tension there, times when he looked at her with such devotion, such longing. Times she would have given anything for his body warm beside her. But for the most part it seemed an ideal arrangement. At least, it seemed so to Miriam.

Solly called her from New York. He made jokes, talked again about moving out there and growing oranges, then came to the point.

"What have you done with the Rio film?" he asked. "I have a friend who owns a lot of Palace stock. He tells me everyone in films is short of product this summer. The studios all cut back on production. I mentioned your picture and he said he would ask around. So, where is it?"

"I think I know where it is, Solly," she said. "Prob'ly sitting in Howard's office. But as for what anyone plans to do with it, don't ask me. I haven't heard from Howard in weeks."

"But it's ready to go and you're happy with it?" Solly insisted.

"Ready as it ever will be," she said. "And, yes, I'm happy with it. It's going to make a big star out of Lisa and it could make some money for the studio."

"Okay," Solly said, "sit tight. I think you'll get some action very soon."

His friend must have owned quite a block of Palace stock. Two days later Howard called. He managed to ignore entirely the fact that two months had passed since their last conversation.

"The board would like to look at *Second Chance*, Miriam," he said. "I assured them it was ready. You wouldn't let me down, would you? It *is* ready?"

"Howard, the film's all ready," she said. "I left it for you six weeks ago."

They arranged to show it in Palace's screening room the following week. Just the board, their wives, and a few people influential in the industry, Howard explained.

"I'm nervous," Miriam told Andy the night before. "I haven't shown it to anyone, not even you. I know the board won't like it. It's a good picture, but it's a small one."

"Can I come to the screening?" Andy asked. "Give you an unbiased opinion?"

"I'd love it if you would," Miriam said. "I already feel I'm being thrown to the wolves. It would help to have one person there I can trust."

The screening was at eleven AM and Miriam was there early. Her heart sank as the members of the board and their cronies drifted in, all looking like they had been dragged away from much more important things. They did not look desperate to see this picture. They smoked cigars and talked to each other about money. She was glad Andy was there beside her and she smiled thanks when he squeezed her hand.

The untitled film began to roll and she winced at the rough cut. Surely the board would understand there was lots of cosmetic work still to be done. Some of the dialogue was out of sync and Chet's music track hadn't been inserted yet. She huddled in her seat, blinking through clouds of cigar smoke, wishing the ordeal over. She was glad the film finished abruptly, without credits. Then, stunned, she heard applause all around her. These businessmen who had paid for her movie were actually clapping for it. She pressed Andy's arm, wanting to jump up and shout and sing and dance.

Then Howard was in front of the audience standing in front of the blank screen.

"Thank you," he said. "I think this film marks

PALACES

new era for Palace. We labored long and hard on this picture. We endured the most difficult location shooting, and the hideous expense that entails. But, gentlemen, I think you'll agree it was worth it. We have a picture Palace will be proud to release."

They crowded around Howard, congratulating him. They talked release dates, campaigns, the number of film prints to be made, and profits.

"Only fourteen million in full?" she overheard one of the men saying to Howard. "I didn't know you could still do a class picture on location for that kind of money. The other studio heads are going to hate you for this, Howard."

"It's just a matter of supervision and tight control, J.B.," Howard simpered. "I wouldn't let this picture start until I was satisfied with the shooting script, the cast, the crew." He looked up and saw she was listening, but he was unabashed. He beckoned her over. "J.B.," he said. "I want you to meet my director, Miriam McDonald. She didn't have much experience before she shot this picture for me but she's done very nicely. When I plucked her out of documentaries, a lot of people thought I was out of my mind. But she's a real smart little lady, our Miriam.

"Really," he said, "I hardly had to worry at all about the creative side. Miriam looked after most of that and I only had to concern myself with the production end." Howard was the very picture of modesty. She wanted to drive a stake through his heart.

"For what it's worth," Andy said later, "I'd like to say it's a wonderful, sweet, lovely picture. I'm sure they'll screw up the promotion and distribution, and I know you've fucked up Howard's whole strategy, but congratulations, kid, you made a good picture."

Over lunch at the hamburger joint near the Palace building she asked Andy what he meant about Howard's "strategy."

"I'm sorry," Andy said. "I shouldn't have mentioned that. It's . . . something I heard from some business guys I know, and something Solly and I talked about. You know Solly's tight with the dissident element of Palace's stockholders?"

"He said he had friends," she said. "But I can't afford to get involved in boardroom politicking. I didn't know his friends were dissidents. I just want to make pictures."

"You're probably right," Andy said. "Keep your head down and leave business to the businessmen. Anyway, after this picture you can always get into independent production."

She raised her head quickly.

"That's what Solly said, and I didn't appreciate it from him either," she said. "You think major productions are too tough for a woman? It's too much money to risk on a girl? Why should I be shunted off to make 'little pictures' just because this is supposed to be a man's business? Screw you."

He smiled and shook his head.

"Don't be so touchy," he said. "Neither I nor Solly wants to put you in the kitchen. It's just that the studios—Palace in particular—are going through strange times. They're in the hands of money guys, institutions, who don't care about pictures, just profits. They've lost their nerve. Solly and I both think you're on a collision course with Howard Veitch for that reason. He's a gray flannel suit."

"I brought in a picture on time and on budget," she said, still resentful. "That's a damn sight harder than selling shoes or hotel beds. These people may be assholes, but I can handle them."

"Okay," Andy said. "I'm sorry. I didn't mean to say you couldn't. Just be careful, that's all I mean. We don't want you getting screwed after all you've accomplished."

"No one's going to screw me, Andy," she said. "I can handle these people. We're all in the business of making films."

Two days later, Howard called her to his office. He fussed around, actually pulled up a chair for her, and treated her like a real person. She was instantly wary.

"I'm really proud of the way you brought off a most difficult assignment," he began. "And that bunch of deadbeats you had to work with! The way you pulled them all together. The board is just knocked out by your little picture. Of course, you and I know it's not going to do much. Too restricted in its appeal. But as a testimonial to what you can do, it's great. Which is what I want to talk to you about."

He paused, lit a cigar and swung his long legs up on his desk. He was savoring the moment.

"The board and I want to offer you a new position with Palace," he said. "Lately, more and more of my time is being taken up with corporate affairs. I just haven't the time to give to production. So we've decided to take a chance . . . on you. Sure, some of the board members think it's too big a risk but I promised I'd keep myself available to help and advise you at all times. Miriam," he paused for effect, "we want you to be head of production for Palace."

It took her ten seconds to comprehend. For all Howard's patronizing, his hint that she would only be carrying out his directions, it was something she had never even considered. Head of Production for a major studio! To be able to help other filmmakers achieve their best, to encourage talent and nurture established stars, to bring talent together with money!

"Jesus, Howard," she gasped. "I'm a novice. One picture..."

"We think you can do it, Miriam," he said smoothly. "Actually, the fact that you're a woman helps. Makes us look good. Affirmative action and so forth. Good ink." He waved his cigar. "And it will be very good for you. A quarter of a million a year to start, plus the usual bonuses. Complete autonomy, of course, subject only to my veto. I thought we'd put you in the office that resembles this one, a few floors down. I think you and I are going to work very well together, Miriam."

She was stunned. This was all she or anyone else could aspire to.

"I won't let you down, Howard," she said fervently. "You won't be sorry you've gone out on a limb for me."

"I'm sure of that," he said. "Very sure."

Andy didn't trust Howard and said so. "And besides, is this really what you want to do?" he asked. "I thought directing was your passion, being in the front line. Now you're going to be weighed down by the archaic structure of a badly run studio. And under Howard's thumb." Her face hardened and he backed off. "I'm sorry," he said. "You know best. It's you who made it to the top. You'll succeed. We will all be very proud of you."

"All I want, Andy, is to do the best I can by films and by the people who make them. I know Howard isn't the most lovable executive we ever met, but I can cope. They're giving me a chance that's far too big to refuse even if I wanted to."

"Well, you've always known what you wanted and were willing to pay the price," Andy said. "If they give you your head, you'll be a huge success."

Chapter Ten

THE APPOINTMENT GOT HER AND THE STUDIO MORE ink than even Howard had expected. It was the silly summer season and *Time* put her on the cover, representative of the "New Wave" in the American cinema. If she'd been willing to pose in a bikini, Andy said, she'd have made *Sports Illustrated* as well.

She spent the first weeks of her new job just trying to define the job. There was no production infrastructure at Palace: There was the board, there was Howard, and now there was her. After that, you were on your own. Peter Kraft was back in town and she used him as a sounding board.

"I know it's early days yet," she told him over dinner. "But, hell, there's no sense of direction at Palace. There are a few film commitments they don't seem in any hurry to make; a lot of properties they've bought and aren't in a hurry to develop; several films they're in no hurry to release. How in hell does Palace make any money? And what have they hired me to *do?*"

"Now you know why I've got a drug habit," Peter said, spreading a few lines of coke in front of her. "These days, nothing out here works the way it should. Either you run Hollywood like the old studio chiefs did—make the movie as well as you can, believe in it, and spend millions ramming it down the public's throat—or you make pictures for a particular segment of the market, with an appropriate budget. The guys running the studios now don't know which way to go and don't want to have to decide. They just keep balances." He snorted two lines of coke and settled back in his chair. "They're like managers in a lot of businesses; they don't worry about the legacy, just what the annual report's going to say about them. They'll capitalize assets, do bad long-term deals with their workers, sell off stock, just to make them look good for a particular fiscal period."

"Come on Peter, your coke paranoia's working on you," she said. She was getting very tired of everyone's hinting at disaster. "No one deliberately runs down a business, squanders assets, or ignores the potential."

"The ones we're talking about do," he said

firmly. "Their idea of a smart deal is to sell off the studio's film library to television. Sell the back lot for real estate development. Rent out anyone you have under contract to some other outfit that's taking the risk and actually making a movie."

"Okay," she said, "I've got you on the last point. The studio wants me to push ahead with their World War II movie. They've got a hell of a lot of money committed there and they're willing to see it through."

He gazed across the table at her as if she was the sorriest person he'd ever met.

"You mean Howard's trying to unload WW2 on you?" he said. "Jesus, Miriam, don't you know *any*thing? Don't you even read the trades? Palace has been fucking around with that for two years. It's a vehicle for dumping off every writer, director, cameraman, and actor they owe. They ship 'em to Rome and wait until it makes them so crazy they'll tear up their contracts. WW2 is where Howard sends you when he wants to get rid of you."

Miriam said nothing for a few moments. Then she said, "That's very close to what you first told me about the Rio film."

"Yeah, but you pulled that one out of the hat," he said. "What you don't understand is, no one at the studio thought you could do it. It's not going to make you a hero, you know."

"It got me this job, didn't it?" Miriam said.

"They don't promote you for doing something they didn't want done."

"Oh, yes they do, and you've got a hell of a lot to learn, Miriam. That's exactly what they do," he said. "I'm not being smart-ass about it. I owe you. I admit it and I'll always acknowledge it. But until you understand the way studio economics and politics work these days, you'll go on believing all you have to do is bring in a good movie on schedule and on budget."

"What else am I supposed to believe?" she said. Peter shook his head and said no more.

She knew something was very wrong when Howard came down to her office. He was clutching the *New York Times*.

"You've really done it!" he shouted, flinging the paper on her desk. "You and that smart-ass reporter you were fucking in Rio! You just cost me twenty percent of twelve million bucks. The board's going to have your ass for this." He was shaking with fury and Miriam could only sit there, mute, letting his rage roll over her.

"It's sheer treachery," Howard said. "After all I've done for you, you screwed me." He flopped into a chair, glaring at her.

"What's in the *Times*, Howard?" she asked, voice shaking. "Mac's piece?" When he didn't answer, she smoothed out the paper and began to read Mac Hunter's story. It was long, starting on page one and jumping to the second section, but it took her only a moment to get the gist. Mac had done his job well. He had obtained, from Brazil's Federal Reserve Bank, the official film budget the Brazilian investors had been obliged to record. And he had either estimated or gotten from someone the real budget. The official figure lodged with the Federal Reserve was sixteen and one half million dollars. The actual was four and one half million.

"Jesus!" she said. "There's a hell of a difference. What does it mean?"

"It means," said Howard tightly, "if you read right through the story, that my investors have been refused the right to export twelve million dollars. They were going to pay Palace a twenty percent commission for running the money through for them. 'Launder' it, your melodramatic newshound says. On top of that, the investors are going to be fined a fortune."

"But the film *is* paid for? The four and one half million was up front, surely?" Miriam asked.

"Oh, yes, that's all gone," Howard said. "That's got nothing to do with it. We won't make any money off the film. It was the twenty percent deal that was the cream."

"And I thought we were in the film business," she said, not caring about his reaction. "I've got a lot to learn, don't I?"

"You're not going to learn it at Palace," Howard

spat. "I'll see to that. Oh, it will be a big black eye for me, firing you so soon after giving you the job, but that's what I'm going to do."

She looked at him levelly.

"I don't think you are, Howard," she said. "The real budget Mac has printed here didn't come from me—I've never seen the final figures—but I'll damn well use it against you if I have to. Just look at these figures. $225,000 for 'production services' from an outfit called Zetland Inc. We never used them. It wouldn't be hard to discover who Zetland Inc. is. And more figures: $75,000 for the expenses of you and your executive assistant. Howard, you never even came on the set while you were in Rio. If I keep going through this budget I bet I'll find the whole half million we were supposedly over. And I bet almost all of it stuck to your fingers." By then she was angrier than Howard was. "Let's you and me both go before the board and see what their reaction is. I'm real sorry they lost their commission—assuming you were going to cut them in on it. But I figure it would soothe them if they recovered the half million you ripped off."

"The board will back me to the hilt," Howard said. "I've made them a lot of money. And I can justify all the figures."

"Can you, Howard?" she said. "If I were you I wouldn't want to take the risk. Remember, a week before we finished filming you didn't even know where the production office *was*."

"I could win this showdown easily," he insisted. "But I'm not going to. It's a waste of time. I've got a studio to run and I can't be diverted by petty ante crap."

"And I'm head of production," she said. "I'm not going to be railroaded for a deal of yours that came unstuck through no act of mine. So you'll tell the board it was nothing to do with me. Won't you, Howard?"

His face was red. He looked ready to hit her. But she could see his frantic thinking.

"Okay," he said finally. "I'll carry the can on this. I'll save your neck with the board." He stood up. "But I expect total loyalty from you from now on. I put you where you are and I can knock you down again. You just make the pictures and don't try playing office politics."

"That suits me just fine, Howard," she said. "I'm interested in movies, not in making dirty deals."

He strode to the door.

"You left your *Times* behind, Howard," she said. He didn't stop. "Look on the bright side," she called. "Our picture has a big plug on Page One of the *New York Times*. That can't be all bad."

He slammed the door.

The publicity did help *Second Chance*. And the studio, having lost its chance at easy money, hastily came up with a generous promotion and distribution budget. The film got excellent reviews, earning back its budget in six weeks and going on to make a million-and-a-half profit.

No one at Palace Productions ever congratulated Miriam.

Miriam's personal publicity didn't sit well with her. All the stories focused on her being a woman. Hardly anyone bothered to find out whether she was worthy of the job. She hadn't come that far just to be a token woman. And even the symbolism went crooked when the porn movie she'd directed was rereleased by Roger Neil.

"The first hard-core picture from the head of a major studio," was the way it was billed. The gossip columns had a field day with it and her, citing the unlikely alliance of feminists and the Moral Majority.

Howard huffed and puffed about "the scandal" and wanted her to sue. Her mother telephoned, worried. Andy went to see the porn picture when it played on Sunset Boulevard and confessed he hadn't been able to pay much attention to the directorial technique.

Miriam, meanwhile, was bogging down in the nightmare of WW2.

"I should go to Rome and try to unscramble it," she told Claudia. "But I'm afraid of what Howard will do to my own two pictures if I'm not here to protect them."

They were spending a sunny Sunday in the pool that went with Miriam's new little house in Beverly Hills. She had had to take the house: The hotel apartment was just too small.

"Well, Peter Kraft has *The Return* under control," Claudia said. "It's shaping up as a good picture." She was doing the sound on *The Return*, a project Miriam had fought for, for months. "It's too far along for Howard to mess with."

"Howard hates me," Miriam said. "He'd love to find an excuse to scrap my picture. I only got the go-ahead for *The Return* and for the one Marty Leason is doing by agreeing to *WW2* and a couple of other big-budget horrors. People like Howard will never learn. Spin-offs, sequels, something to appeal to kids—they think if you throw enough money at a project you'll pack them in. I get terrified, the millions of dollars they're risking on crap. And when the grosses come in and Palace has laid an egg, I know who gets the blame. Not Howard."

Andy came out with a tray of drinks.

"There won't be any blame," he said cheerfully. "The way the industry works now, no one ever admits to a failure, or not a big-budget failure, anyway. They mumble about foreign rights and television futures and convince themselves they haven't really lost. There'll be no blame until Judgment Day when the studio goes bankrupt or gets taken over. When that happens you'll all be out of a job anyway. So why worry?"

"Thanks, Andy," she said, splashing him with water. "That's just the encouragement I was looking for." She pulled herself out of the pool and took the vodka and tonic.

"I think I'm going to have to go to Rome," she said. "The production reports get worse each month. It's going to end up taking as long and costing as much as the original version, but Howard keeps saying, no expense is to be spared. God, before I even got involved with this disaster they'd wasted a couple of million in preproduction. Now it's rolling without a shooting script, with a dozen of the world's most expensive actors sitting around the set, thousands of extras being paid for doing nothing."

"Sounds just like the original," Andy said. "And why worry about a shooting script? We know how the story turns out."

"I liked you better when you were a shy little boy," Miriam said. "Now you're a tycoon so you have to be a wiseguy."

"What does the line producer say?" Claudia asked.

"If they can just bring Will Benton into line, there's hope," Miriam said. "But he fell off the wagon weeks ago. Some days he's okay, others you can't use him. I'd fire him but Howard says we can't afford to throw out what's already in the can. And Benton's only one of the problems." She sighed. "Isn't it crazy? Normally, anyone would break a leg for a trip to Rome. And I don't want to go. I guess I've got to, though."

"Would you like me to tag along?" Andy asked casually. "I've been thinking about a hotel there and I wouldn't mind giving you some moral support."

"I don't need . . . ," she began hotly. And then she heard herself—bitter, resentful. "I'm sorry, Andy," she said. "Thank you. I'll have to go over there alone, but, hell, if you turn up during filming I'll be awfully pleased to see you."

The day before she flew to Rome Solly and Thelma threw a party for her. The Behns were living in San Fernando, in a fine old house in the middle of an orange grove.

It was a happy day and Miriam managed to put Rome out of her mind for a while. She was among friends, including film friends. There was wine and food and sunshine.

She sat on the terrace with Solly.

"So you're happy with the move out here?" she asked. "And I always thought you were kidding about the oranges. I think of you as a city person, it's a heck of a change."

"It was time for us to make a change," he said. "I've got plenty of bright young folks to run the business. They don't need me and my old-fashioned ideas. Besides, I'm not sure I'd survive another New York winter. I'm getting pretty old, Miriam. I figure I'm entitled to the sunshine."

She looked at him with real love. His hair was sparse but his skin glowed with good health and his eyes were as bright as ever.

"You'll outlast us all, Solly," she said. "Because you're a happy man."

He nodded.

"I won't outlast anyone," he said, "but, yes, I'm happy. And that's what matters. Look at your friends, Claudia and the others from New York. They're all happy out here because they're doing what they care about." He reached out and patted her hand. "Please don't shout at me, Miriam. Don't be angry," he said. "But I don't think you're happy with what you're doing."

"I've got to see it through," she said. "It's a chance to get big things done, to give opportunities to people who might otherwise be shut out of the industry. I think of all the talent and drive among young filmmakers, talent never harnessed because the people who run big studios are too busy to care. I think I can make some changes for those people."

She flew the polar route to London and changed planes at Heathrow. During the journey she thought caustically about dreams and realities. There she was, a top executive in films, jetting across the world to unscramble a multimillion-dollar disaster, when all she really wanted was to make good, small films.

Miles Lee, the producer, met her at Rome airport. He looked like a man who'd just been through the real World War Two. He chainsmoked, and he had a twitch in his right eyelid. He was nothing like the cocky, confident young producer she had known at Palace.

"Come on, Miles," she said as they struggled through the Rome-bound traffic. "It can't be that bad. At least you've got two-thirds of the picture in the can."

"Two-thirds of junk," he said bitterly. "Lots of noise, masses of extras shooting at each other. Your basic B-picture war epic. Christ, we could have pulled all the footage out of the library and no one would have known the difference. But we could still save it if Will Benton gave just half the performance he used to. He should be able to walk through the part. It's even passably well written, considering the number of people who've fucked around with the script." He laughed ghoulishly. "All the effort, the money—twenty-two million and rising, so far—that's what's gone into it! I think I'll get out of this business and go into plumbing."

"Is it just booze with Benton?" she asked. "I always heard he could work bombed almost as well as he does sober."

"The booze is the symptom, not the cause," Miles said. "The man has simply lost his nerve. He drinks to cover that. And he's living in the past. Like, he insisted on staying at the Hotel de la Ville because that was the place they all stayed when Rome was big in the fifties. Benton is trying to re-create those times, when they drank all night and strolled straight onto the set still drunk. Christ, he's an old man now, and he can't get away with that anymore. He doesn't know his lines. He can't even stand up for more than a few minutes at a time. He's too sick and drunk to even make it to the set most of the time, and when he does get there he's worthless."

"Have you slipped further behind schedule?" Miriam asked.

"We were already seven weeks over before we got to Benton," Miles said. "Now we're twelve. I got ten days work out of him in the past six weeks."

"What do the doctors say?"

"He refuses to see a doctor," Miles said. "He won't admit there's any problem." He turned to her. "It's not just the booze, either. He's doing a lot of coke, hoping it'll offset his drinking. And he gets lost."

"What the hell do you *mean*, he gets lost?"

"Lost." Miles shrugged. "He stumbles out in the middle of the night, into the lowest Roman dives. I pay off the police to bring him back when they find him and so far we've gotten away with it. But it's only a matter of time before the paparazzi get onto what he's doing and then there'll be one hell of a scandal. Benton's still a big name here, just like in the US."

"So they'll get pictures of him falling down drunk," she said. "That would fit his image as a hard-drinking womanizer."

"Uh-huh," Miles said. "How about pictures of him falling out of a brothel that employs little boys?"

"You mean the great Will Benton has become a pederast?" She couldn't believe it. Will Benton had carried the mantle laid down by Errol Flynn. He had wooed, and sometimes even married, most of the top Hollywood stars.

"If I were a shrink," Miles said, "I'd say Benton is punishing himself over some great trauma in his life. He's totally self-destructive, but it's his image he's destroying, as if he wants to wipe out everything he stood for."

"Where are you taking me now?" Miriam demanded.

"Check you in at your hotel," Miles said.

"You better drop me at the de la Ville," she said.

"If you'd take my bags on, I'll follow later. I want to see Benton right now."

It was seven PM but Benton wasn't in the bar. She went back downstairs to reception and called his room on the house phone. After six rings, he answered. He sounded awful, the famous voice a parody.

"It's Miriam McDonald, from Palace Productions, Mr. Benton," she said. "I just arrived and I'm down in the lobby. I'd like to see you now."

"Sure, sure," he slurred. "Come right on up."

He answered the door wearing a grubby gray bathrobe. He was unshaven, red eyed, and snuffling.

"I've got this awful cold," he said as he showed her into the suite. "Rome always gives me a cold, the first weeks. Then it passes and I settle down to work."

She looked around the suite. It was big, ornate—and filthy. Empty bottles crowded abandoned coffee cups; picked-over room service meals congealed on silver trays.

"It's a bit of a mess, I suppose," he said, glancing around the suite. "I've been too sick to let the maids come in and clean up."

She studied him carefully. Without makeup or his toupee, Will Benton was a gray-faced old man. The years of drinking had scored deep lines in the famous profile; life in the fast lane had bowed his broad shoulders. In the tatty robe, in the squalor, he looked like a querulous invalid waiting to be taken to the old people's home.

"That punk, the producer, Miles, doesn't listen to me," Benton complained. "No one does. They don't understand how ill I am. If they'd just leave me alone for a little while, let me rest, I'd be fit and ready to give them a performance that would save their dreadful film. But no, they force me onto the set in the worst weather, keep me sitting around in a drafty trailer. I'll get pneumonia if this keeps up." He poured himself a huge brandy and drank it straight down. "Well, I don't have to take it, you know. I can just call my agent and tell him to get me out of this piece of shit."

"I think the movie's too far along for that, Mr. Benton," she said. "The studio has already sunk a fortune in it and without you they wouldn't have a picture."

"Then they'll just have to start treating me better," he said. "I'm the star. What did you say your name was? Miriam? I'm glad you're here. The studios always used to provide me with a secretary. Always a pretty one, like you. Tomorrow, when I'm feeling better, we'll sit out in the sun and I'll go over the script and dictate a few changes. And there are some errands you could do for me. Things I need." He poured another brandy, suffered a coughing fit, and slumped into a big padded chair.

"Why don't I just tidy up now," Miriam said. She moved around the suite quickly, making some order out of the chaos. He stayed seated, drinking and watching her, not moving until she picked up a glass jar from the coffee table.

"Careful!" he snapped. "That's my cocaine. It's very hard to get good coke in Italy. The bastards are too busy moving heroin to the US to deal decent drugs."

She hefted the jar. There must have been half a pound of the white powder. So he really was existing on coke and booze. No wonder he looked so wrecked.

"I wish coke had been there in my early days," Benton said. "All we had was liquor and pot. Coke's great. It gets me up, lets me act my best. I couldn't perform so well without it."

She shot him a glance, then looked away.

"Look, Mr. Benton," she said. "I'm just off the plane and I'm tired and hungry, too tired to go out to eat. Would you mind if I ordered something from room service, up here?"

"Go ahead," he said grandly. "Have anything you like, caviar, truffles, champagne. Spend big. The studio's paying for it."

"I'll just order something for you, too," she said.

"What would you like? Pasta? Or maybe a nice big steak."

"Whatever you like," he said. "I won't eat it, but I'll keep you company."

The meal arrived, accompanied by Miriam's discreetly ordered mineral water. Benton wasn't so far gone he didn't notice, and he shouted at the waiter in fluent Italian, demanding their best champagne. Miriam knew there was no point in arguing with him just then.

She set about flattering and soothing the great actor. When the wine arrived, it encouraged him to eat a little. She lingered over her own dinner, trying to keep him at the table as long as possible.

The pasta brought a little color to his cheeks, or perhaps what did it was having an attentive listener for his stories of past triumphs, the glory days of Hollywood. Even his voice regained a little of the old power that had enthralled theater audiences before Benton took the easy road to riches.

He hardly noticed when she rang room service for hot milk and he did not see her slip a pill into the glass. He drank it, humoring her, and went on talking. Another half hour, though, and he was nodding.

"You may help me to bed now, my dear," he said, and as she turned back the rumpled sheets, he stood up and dropped his robe.

He looked anything but the great lover, standing

there naked, all knees and elbows and ribs. He shuffled over to the bed and lay down with a sigh, and she pulled the covers over him.

"I'm sorry, my dear, but tonight I'm going to have to disappoint you," he said. "A cold plays hell with my libido. Just can't get it up. But tomorrow I'll be fine and we'll work and play together. I'll show you why I'm a legend. Now kiss me and get yourself to bed."

She kissed the cheek he turned to her, feeling a terrible sadness. She had sat for so many hours in dark movie houses watching this man on the screen, romantic, dashing, dramatic. This sick old man. She was so sad that she almost wasn't angry. Almost.

Despite jet lag, Miriam was back at the de la Ville at nine AM the next day. She rang his room and Benton answered sleepily. She ordered coffee and rolls to be sent to his suite and waited a while, so as to arrive with room service.

He was sitting out on the balcony in the sun and she thought he looked a little better after a night's sleep. She tipped the waiter, poured their coffee, and settled across the table from him.

"Will," she said, "there's something we better get straight now. Last night was a slight misunderstanding. I'm not a secretary sent you by Palace. I'm the head of production for the studio."

His hand shook so violently the coffee spilled out

of the cup and into his lap. He tried to stand but his feet got tangled in the chair. His face was red.

"How dare you!" he shouted. "How dare you spy on me like that! I have worked with the greatest producers in the world and never have I experienced anything so underhanded. You, a mere girl, coming here pretending to be a friend and helper and trying to find excuses to fire me from this awful picture. I suppose you've already sent your report back to your cretins in Hollywood. Well, it won't work. I admit I have been taking a drink or two to get over this damned cold, but that's all. Oh, I know what you want. You want me to quit. But I'm not a quitter and you try and fire me, I'll sue you for every penny your despicable studio has." He slumped back in the chair, exhausted by his outburst.

"Will," she said gently, "I'm not here to fire you, or spy on you. We're just concerned because the picture is falling so far behind schedule. Fire you? We need you. You're the star. It's your name that'll bring in all the people."

"You're damn right it is," he said, trying to cover his surprise. "I've carried better movies than this. None worse. The producer's a fool, the script is—"

"Will," she said firmly, "on fifteen of the last twenty-five production days, you have been unfit for work. It's all in the logs."

"Fuck your logs!" he screamed. "And fuck you, too! You god-damned new people, with your accountant mentalities, you don't understand a star. What the hell would you know about the pressure I'm under? And then this damn virus on top of everything."

"Okay," she said firmly. "First we fix the virus. I'll have a doctor here in one hour. If he orders you to rest, that's what you'll do. If he says there's nothing wrong with you, I want you on the set this afternoon."

"Don't you dare speak to me like that, you little bitch. I won't be ordered around by some glorified secretary. I'll call Howard Veitch. I'll have you fired."

She got up and walked into the living room. She found the phone and trailed it out to the balcony.

"Here," she said, shoving the receiver at him. "Call Howard. It was he who sent me. And if you think I'm being harsh, wait till that son-of-a-bitch Veitch is through."

Benton cringed, staring at Miriam, a mute appeal. She gazed back, giving nothing. But then she looked away while, in the bright morning sunshine, the great Will Benton began to sob. Tears flowed over the broken red veins on each side of his nose and down into the gray stubble of beard. She waited until he regained his composure.

"I'm sorry," he finally gasped. "Please forgive

me for the way I spoke to you. I've been confused a lot lately." He nodded thanks as she poured him fresh coffee. "I feel so . . . at sea. Just going onto the set is agony. I feel I've lost the knack. I need . . . time to get it all together."

"I'm sorry, too, Will," she said. "Sorry it has to be me who reads you the riot act. But we can't give you any more time. Either you're sick—in which case we need a doctor's certificate so we can claim insurance for the days we're losing—or you're making yourself sick with drinking. If it's drinking, then you stop right now."

He stood up, angry again but controlled.

"I see you have as little understanding as the rest of them," he said. "I shall have to continue with this farce alone. I do not have a drinking problem, miss. That is the type of insult I would expect from a member of your uncouth generation. Also, I do not need to shelter behind the bogus diagnosis of some Italian quack. I shall be on the set today and will give my best. However, I have one stipulation: You stay away when I am before the cameras. You have attempted to humiliate me. I will not let you disrupt my performance."

"I'll agree to that," she said. She faced him. "Just be aware of one thing, Mr. Benton. My being a woman, and young, may upset you, but don't assume the wrong things. I am a very tough person if anyone gets between me and completing a film.

One more slip from you and I will have your balls." She swept out of the suite then. There was nothing left to say.

She stayed away from the set that afternoon but waited anxiously by the telephone. Miles called just before six PM.

"So far, so good," he said enthusiastically. "The old boy just walked through his lines but at least he was upright and sober. We just broke for a meal and Benton's got a call for nine o'clock tonight. It's one of his bigger scenes so I guess we'll know then whether your therapy worked."

"I hope so, Miles," she said. "I feel so sorry for him. He's so screwed up. But—"

"But we've got a picture to finish," Miles said. "Over twenty million dollars spent already and if Benton collapses again there'll be nothing to show for it. Maybe a documentary on how to spend a hundred thousand a day in Rome?"

"I know, Miles," she said. "I know what's riding on the frail shoulders of Will Benton."

Benton didn't reappear for the night shoot. He wasn't at his hotel or in any of the bars they'd found him in before. At midnight Miriam joined the others in their vigil on the idle set.

"I've bribed the police to look for him," Miles told her. "I guess they'll turn him up in a day or two, as usual. There's nothing we can do now so we might as well pack it in for the night. Shit, I hope they find the bastard floating in the Tiber."

"You can't shoot around him for just a few more days?" Miriam asked.

"I've been shooting around the fucker for weeks," Miles said. "From now on we have to have him on film. Either he comes back or we scrap the film. I've got him walking through most of the early scenes we have shot. There's no chance of replacing him, Miriam, not now. It's far too late for that."

She went back to her room at the Hassler, and at four AM the phone woke her.

"It's Miles," the voice said. "They've found our lost star. Kind of."

"What do you mean, 'kind of'?" she snapped.

"The Red Brigades have him," the producer said. "One of the papers just got a call from some guys who said they snatched Benton outside his hotel last night. They're demanding ransom and some script changes to *WW2*." Miles laughed, near hysteria. "They say our version of *WW2* is ideologically unacceptable. So all we have to do is change the outcome of the war. I hope they hang Benton."

"What do the police say?" Miriam asked.

"We're to sit tight while they search. No statements about whether we'll cooperate or not. Me, I'm going back to bed and sleep all day."

"Okay," Miriam said. "I guess there's nothing

we can do right now. If he's not released in the next two or three days we'll have to shut down production. I'll call Howard in a few hours and see what he wants to do."

She put off the call until she had had coffee in the restaurant and a chance to see the morning papers. They had all gone wild for the Benton story. The reports were that Benton was already far from Rome, being held in a Red Brigades' safe house somewhere in the countryside.

She was paged to the telephone. It was Howard, calling from Hollywood. He sounded jubilant.

"It's leading the radio bulletins here," he told her. "Great publicity, whichever way it turns out. Of course, we're not negotiating with a bunch of terrorists. I've just issued a statement to that effect. No deals."

"For Christ's sake, Howard," she said, "that's exactly what the police told us not to do. They don't want the terrorists to do anything crazy."

"I don't give a shit what the police in Rome want," he said. "They're obviously incapable of protecting anyone, so why expect them to find him?" He dropped his voice. "If Benton turns up dead, we're out of the woods. It's the best thing that could happen. The insurance company has to pay and we escape from this whole mess."

"You're all heart, Howard," she said.

"That old lush hasn't been delivering and he's cost a fortune. I don't want him back."

"But," Miriam said, "I talked with him and got his promise to straighten up."

"That promise and a dollar will get you a cup of espresso," Howard said. "Just remember what the studio position is: no negotiations. And, Miriam, say anything else you can think of to make the terrorists mad. We don't want him returned."

All through that day and the next Miriam refused to talk to the press. She wanted desperately to keep the lid on the situation and save Benton. But Howard's defiant words were splashed all over the local press and there was no way Benton's captors could misinterpret the point.

The waiting was awful. She stayed in the hotel all the time. On the second evening, her room phone rang and she grabbed it.

"Here I am for moral support," Andy said. "I got on the first plane after I heard the news. You must be in terrible shape. Dinner?"

"God, I'm glad you're here!" Miriam said, nearly sobbing with relief. "Where are you?"

"Just one floor below you," he said. "I haven't unpacked yet, but that can wait. How about meeting me in the lounge in five minutes?"

She threw her arms around him and kissed him. Andy ordered her a drink and kept his arm draped around her shoulders. She was so glad to see him.

"I booked us dinner in the hotel restaurant," he said. "I figured you'd want to be where you can be reached."

"Good," she said, taking the drink placed before her. "I've been holed up in the room, waiting and hoping. Thanks for getting me out. But you shouldn't have come."

He looked at her sadly.

"You surely don't think I'd stay away when you're in trouble." He shrugged. "Anyway, as I told you, I'm thinking about a hotel here."

They had more drinks, then went in to dinner. Andy was such a good companion, so witty and intelligent. After dinner they took a brief stroll by the Spanish Steps. He took her arm and led her to the happy bustle of the Piazza Navona, where they had rich ice cream and strong coffee.

"You're starting to relax a little," he said as they strolled back to the Hassler. "This project was such a headache for you anyhow, without a drunken star getting kidnapped."

"Yes, it's been a terrific lesson in how to make a studio go broke," she said. "I can't believe the things that have been allowed to happen on this picture. Even for a moron like Howard, this is downright surrealistic."

"I hate to see you working with idiots like Howard," Andy growled. "For one thing, you shouldn't have to deal with people who really don't belong in the business at all. Guys like him are ruining films. They haven't any of the skill or the flair of the old filmmakers—no heart. And they don't have the vision of the new, independent filmmakers. What you should . . ." He stopped himself in time, without even looking at her face. "Nope. I'm not going to tell you what to do. You just get mad when I do that." He grinned, and what she'd been about to say dissipated.

He walked her to her hotel room and they stood around in the hallway, looking at the walls and trying to act like they knew what came next. When he couldn't stand it anymore, Andy took her key and opened the door. "Am I spending the night?" he asked bluntly, and she nodded, grateful not to have to be in charge.

Neither said anything about their experiment at being "loving friends": She was just as glad to see the arrangement go.

He followed her inside and they undressed swiftly and lay down in the big soft bed. At first they held each other, and Miriam took strength from Andy's warmth. Then slowly, they came together. It felt so good, freeing Miriam from all the tension. This time, she gave all of herself to Andy without wanting to hold back. She wanted him to be satisfied, too, and she was ready when the spasms of release surged through his lean body into her. Holding him tightly, she smiled into the dark.

"Miriam, Miriam," he whispered. "You are so wonderful. Always wonderful. I love you so much."

She put her fingers to his lips, refusing to be drawn into talk. "It's time to sleep," she murmured. As he moved to lie beside her, she snuggled against him.

They left the curtains open to the cool night air and the sunlight woke them early. She felt refreshed and strong, ready for anything. Andy looked so young and gentle lying there. The responsibilities of running his hotel empire had not hardened him or aged him. How did he do it: How could he be so calm and so giving, when most of the people she knew were consumed by fears and ambitions?

The smiling room service waiter moved around quietly, setting up breakfast, and left quickly.

"A beautiful Rome morning," he said, gazing out through the long windows at the city below them. "This is my favorite city, a place for lovers and visionaries. I think I'll live here someday."

"All I see when I look at Rome," she laughed, "is being ripped off for millions on a turkey picture that's permanently stalled." Will's situation came flooding back. "And I see terrorism, a society without any sense of law or decency."

"It's not like that really," Andy said. "You've gotten caught up by the ugly side of Italy. But it's a false picture. Rome is still the world's most beautiful city."

"I guess I've become like a journalist," Miriam said. "I don't *see* places: I cover events in places. Joe used to talk about that, about always being an observer and never a participant. Filming's the same as journalism in that sense. You never look at something or someone for what they are, but for what they will translate into being on the screen."

She sat up and reached for the coffee.

"That's one of the reasons film people make lousy partners. We're totally absorbed in work and not much involved in real life. For an artist, there's not much *to* real life."

"I'll help you change your mind about real life," Andy said, grinning up at her. Why did that grin have the power to reach straight into her heart? As always, she shut the feeling away, and as always, it took all her determination to do so. Did he know how easy it would be for her to let him teach her about real life? Did he have any idea how hard it was for her to keep him at arm's length?

He read her eyes for a while and then sighed. "Look, today there's nothing happening on your film set. I'll get us a car and show you the countryside. Hadrian's Villa is only an hour away. We'll go up into the hills later and have a picnic. You can check in by phone every couple of hours. Please?"

It was a beautiful day. The hotel had packed them a hamper of prosciutto and melon, chicken sandwiches, cheese and grapes. Andy got a cooler with two bottles of crisp Italian white wine. They had lunch under a gnarled old olive tree off a dusty lane in the foothills of Rome. The sound of the fountains of the Villa d'Este were still splashing in her memory. They could see across the green plain to the outskirts of the city.

But after an hour, she was fidgeting. She repacked the hamper and they started the drive back to Rome. There was no word from the police at the hotel and she went up to her room, took a shower and lay down to rest before dinner. Andy was out talking business and she was glad of a little time alone.

The call came at six o'clock.

"They've found him!" Miles yelled. "The police discovered him an hour ago, drugged and incoherent, over in the red light district. They think he'd been driven there and thrown out of the car. He doesn't look wounded, but he's in the hospital. We can talk to him late tonight, after the police have finished with him."

She dressed quickly and went down to the bar. Andy was already there, waiting for her. He ordered champagne to celebrate.

"I don't know what I'm so happy about," Miriam said. "Having Will Benton back means we just go back to all the original problems. Still, maybe the shock of all this will keep Will sober enough to finish the picture." She giggled suddenly. "Howard's going to be livid! He was so sure they'd execute poor old Will. Then Howard could get all his money back from the insurance. Now he's going to have to go through with this doomed picture."

"You mean, *you're* going to have to go through with it," Andy reminded her. "Howard Veitch didn't get where he is by accepting blame for failures. He'll shift it all onto you."

"I know," she said. "I've never had any illusions about this job. If I'm a success it's because of Howard's wise counsel. If I fail, it's because he took a gamble on a young woman and she wasn't good enough." She sighed. "But I don't care, Andy. I'm making pictures, which is what I want. And hell, if I can rescue WW2, everything else will be downhill."

They had dinner together at the dell' Orso.

"Do you want me to come to the hospital with you?" Andy asked.

"No, better not. But thanks. Miles is picking me up. It will be a crazy mob scene at the hospital."

It was. The hospital was under heavy police guard and besieged by reporters. Miles forced their way through and they went up to the top floor suite where Will Benton was sitting propped up in the white hospital bed. He looked old and tired and he looked afraid. Two young nuns fussed over him. He raised a hand in a weary gesture of welcome to Miriam and Miles.

"I'm sorry to have caused you so much trouble, Miles, Ms. McDonald," he said. "It was really stupid of them to think a studio would bargain for the life of an old has-been like me. And of course your studio man was absolutely right—no deals with terrorists. The police are very proud of their work and they believe the incident will convince more people to say no to terrorists' demands."

"How did it happen and what did they do to you?" Miles asked. "And how do you know what Howard Veitch said?"

"It was all so easy for the kidnappers," Benton said. "You know how crowded it is outside the de la Ville? Well, three or four fellows just surrounded me and hustled me into a car. There was no time to shout for help or even react. They put a bag over my head and forced me down on the floor of the car and we drove for a long time. It was pitch black when we got to our destination and they took me inside and locked me up in some kind of cellar or something. They took my hood off. One of them was with me, waving a gun around, all the time.

"After a couple of days they told me they were going to release me. They made me take some pi to knock me out and the next thing I knew I was lying on the street being shaken by a policeman. He thought I was a drunk! You should have seen his eyes light up when I told him who I was. Instant visions of promotion. So there you are. All's well that ends well. And,'' he paused wryly, ''I didn't think Howard Veitch wanted me back anyhow.''

''How do you feel, Will?'' Miriam asked. Of course Will knew he wasn't wanted. Why pursue the subject with the poor old man?

''I need lots of rest, complete peace and quiet,'' he said. ''I'm sorry to inconvenience you, but the doctors think it will be quite some time before I'm ready to resume filming. I thought I might go and convalesce on the Italian Riviera. You can shoot around me, I'm sure.''

''We can't shoot around you,'' Miriam said quickly. ''Miles has been shooting around you for weeks. I'll talk to the doctors in the morning.''

''My, my,'' Benton said, ''you really are a very determined young lady. I suppose that's how you got to be where you are. Talk to the doctors, my dear. I'm sure they'll tell you I'm totally unfit for any work just now. And if you don't accept their word, well, bring in your own doctors and have them check me out. I have been through a most arduous and horrifying experience. And in a moment I must meet the world's press. I would like to be able to tell them Palace Productions is treating me with the utmost sympathy. Think of the glorious publicity I am getting our little picture. Just a brief vacation to recover from my ordeal, that's all I ask."

She and Miles left the suite after wishing Will well and pushed through the reporters jamming the corridor. Miles was despondent.

"That shameless old ham," he said, "is going to milk this as long as he can. It means another couple of weeks lost, but I guess we're stuck with it—and with Will."

"I guess so," Miram said. "You go check with the doctors, though. I'd like to know the truth about his condition. He looked no worse to me than he always looks, and makeup could cover that. I want to talk to the police in charge. I'll see you out front in fifteen minutes."

She found the senior officer preening himself before a band of reporters. He was saying that the police had been aided by the refusal of Mr. Benton's associates to deal with the kidnappers.

"We are confident of early arrests," he told the media. "But even more important, this unfortunate episode will serve a warning on all terrorists that there is nothing to be gained from abducting citizens from our streets."

Miriam cornered him as the media departed for Benton's bedside. She introduced herself and thanked him for the massive police effort to locate her star.

"There's one thing bothering me," she said abruptly. "Are you satisfied with Benton's story? He is a man under a great deal of pressure. You're sure this whole incident was not a hoax?"

He looked her in the eye and did not immediately answer. Then, glancing around to be sure they were not overheard, he spoke.

"You insult our force to suggest we could be hoodwinked, even by a man of the theatrical talent of Mr. Benton," he said. "I am convinced this man has had a lucky escape, but . . . even if I were not convinced, I would never raise any doubts. This case is of inestimable value in our war against the Red Brigades. Frankly, I don't care who kidnapped your man or even if anyone kidnapped him at all."

At ten o'clock the next day, she presented herself at the hospital. She was checking Benton out, she told the medical superintendent. He would be cared for by a private doctor and a staff of nurses. Benton protested but then relaxed when Miriam said she thought he would be happier back in his hotel suite.

"And my convalescence?" he said. "It's all arranged?"

"We'll talk when we're alone, back at the hotel," Miriam said.

She got rid of the reporters and the police and

the awed hotel staff after a struggle and finally had Benton to herself. He was looking quite well but insisted he needed to lie down.

"You lie down, Will," she said, "and just listen to me. First: I know you pulled that stunt and I can prove it. And when I release the story, you will be worse than unemployed, Will. You will be the laughing stock of the entire world. Sure, the police here are happy to go along with your charade. It suits them. But the international media won't give a good goddamn what the Italian authorities want. They'll love this story. I've had private detectives on your case ever since I came to Rome to try and get our movie back on the tracks. I know everything, Will. The drugs, the kinky sex, the drinking I'll see to it that you never work again.

"So, unless you are back on the set tomorrow, prepared to work your ass off . . ." He said nothing, slumping back on the bed in shock.

"The only thing I don't know, Will," she continued, her voice a bit more relaxed, "is why you did it. Why fake a kidnapping? Surely it wasn't just to cover your latest drinking jag? What was the need Will?"

He lay there, tears running down his cheeks. She was not impressed. She hammered on.

"Tell me the whole story," she demanded. " am fed up with you and I'd just as soon call in the media and tell them what I know."

PALACES

He raised a hand, weakly, and struggled into a sitting position.

"Is this room bugged?" he whispered. "They do that kind of thing, the police. And you, having me followed by private detectives."

So her bluff had worked.

"I had to run," Benton said. "I couldn't face work sober and I can't work drunk. I thought if I just got away for a while I'd be able to pull myself together enough to complete the picture. And when I realized you'd fire me if I didn't turn up on the set, I called a newspaper with the Red Brigades story. I'm a very good actor, you know."

A very good actor! Did he have any idea what he'd said? And was she going to stay sane until the picture was finished?

"You're in real trouble," Miriam said. "If I release the story that it was all a hoax, you'll be arrested. You'll be ridiculed in every newspaper in the world. So what do you want to do, Will?"

"I don't know," he said miserably. "Running away didn't help. I'm still terrified of the cameras. Can't you just release me from the picture?" he begged.

"Of course we can't," Miriam said. "I've explained all that to you."

"It will have to be Betty, then," he said, suddenly calmer. "Betty Carson, my ex-wife and constant lover. She's the only one who understands me and who gives me confidence in myself. If Betty were here, on the picture, I could get through it all right. And she's probably flying here now to see if I'm okay. You could write her into the picture easily. It would be great for you: 'Benton and Carson together again.'"

"What the hell," Miriam said. "We've sunk so much already, Betty Carson's fee will hardly matter." She stood up. "If we get her and you still don't toe the line, I'll ruin you," she said. She opened her big handbag. "See this little Sony? I just taped this conversation. I've got you cold. If you let me down, I'll make you a laughing stock and the studio will sue you for false pretences. We'll take everything you've got: the houses, the boats, the cars. You'll end up working dinner theaters in New Jersey and people will come only to see the fallen idol."

He looked about to break into hysteria.

"But if you give me your best," she continued before he could, "all this will be forgotten. You'll be the iron man who escaped the Red Brigades and went straight back to work as if nothing had happened."

"If Betty's here I can do it," he said. "I won't let you down again. Or myself, either. I can't cut it on my own though. Please. Help me."

"I'll speak to her agent now," Miriam said. "In the meantime, if you look out in the corridor you'l see a very large guard. I've hired three of them for around-the-clock duty. And they're on a bonus of a thousand a day each for every day you don't sneak a drink. So I don't think you'll be able to bribe them to smuggle anything in to you." He looked so shamefaced that she relented. "Don't worry. I'll tell people the guards are there to insure nothing more happens to you."

She tracked Betty Carson through the actress's London agent. The agent listened to her proposal and said she'd get right back to Miriam. An hour later, the great star herself called.

"Will's been fucking up, right, and he needs me to nurse him through the picture?" she said without preamble. "Goddamn, he's such a child. And that kidnap business smells to high heaven. Is he going to get away with it?"

"The authorities are completely satisfied with Mr. Benton's version of events," Miriam said sweetly. "More to the point, they're very happy with the way it all turned out. I think we'll let it rest there. But, yes, Will is a mess. He's begging you to come here on a mercy mission. We can write in a nice role for you as his secretary, the girl who loves the general and rides in his jeep as he liberates Rome. Just a couple of weeks filming and we can have this whole damn thing wrapped up."

"Not a bad idea, Betty," said her agent, cutting in on the line. "You fly to your stricken ex-husband. The pair of you together on screen one more time. The press will love it. And you do have the next few weeks free."

"I'll do it," Betty said. "It'll cost you, though. A million bucks for up to four weeks' work, beginning today. Plus the usual expenses, approvals, and my name same size as Will's. Okay?"

Miriam thought for a few seconds. She should call Howard but there wasn't time. It had to be her decision.

"Okay," she said. "Let me know when you're arriving and I'll have Will at the airport to meet you. We'll milk it for every drop of publicity."

It was—even Howard admitted later on—the smartest thing she could have done. Betty Carson swept into Rome and won everyone. She took over the Hassler's biggest suite and moved Benton in with her: "To help him recover from his ordeal," she said, winking her big blue eyes at her hundreds of friends in the Italian press corps.

Benton acted like a grateful old dog. He fetched and carried for her and clearly wanted only her approval. On the set with Betty he was subdued but he knew his lines and some of the enormous talent he possessed began to come through in the rushes.

"I can hold him together long enough to finish your picture," Betty told Miriam. They were in her dressing room, drinking coffee. Betty was spiking hers with brandy. She had made the supreme sacrifice, never drinking when she was with Will.

"Betty," said Miriam, "you've saved all our necks." She had grown to respect and like Betty Carson. Sure, the actress was demanding. The once perfect figure had billowed around the bust and hips, the hair was streaked with gray. But Betty Carson had star quality, the box office kind. It rubbed off on everyone: The crew and cast, who had grown sick of the fiasco movie, now worked with enthusiasm and real hope. Even Miriam was starting to enjoy herself.

"You're paying for it," Betty said. "And you'd better finish soon. I can work my magic on Will for only so long. Then he starts getting confident, jealous of me, and desperate for a drink. It's been the story of our life. We love, honor, and cherish each other for a short while. Then we revert to type. We're both egomaniacs and we're both hot-shit stars."

"But you love each other," Miriam said softly.

"Love? Of course we do." She laughed. "But the ego is stronger than love, always. That son-of-a-bitch, the things he's done to me. Years ago, when it was considered very risqué, he persuaded me to pose nude for his private collection. Then we had a fight over a co-star he thought I was fucking. Come to think of it, I was. Anyway, he got one of the pictures blown up to life size and had it sent to the Vienna Boys Choir with 'Love from your greatest fan, Betty' scrawled across the bottom. It cost the studio a fortune to hush that up. Another time, when we were getting ready for the divorce, I told him it was going to cost him four million dollars. 'Ridiculous,' he said, 'when I can have you killed for ten thousand.' I still don't know if he was bluffing."

She poured more brandy into her coffee cup.

"I did a few things to him, too." She smiled at her memories. "One time we were filming here in Rome and Will took up with some little tart from the production office. He was going through his dress-up period then and he'd spent the whole summer being fitted for thirty-odd silk suits. They were delivered a week before the movie wrapped. He made the mistake of not coming home that night. I sent down to the housekeeper for a pair of shears and I took all those beautiful suits and cut 'em off, every one, at the knees and elbows. He blacked my eye for that and the studio put us both on suspension for six months.

"We were a funny couple," she said. "We never should have married when we did. We didn't need each other enough, so we didn't value what we might have had together. And being in the same racket, of course, was a disaster. If you can just be mature about it, respect each other's need for separate space and time, marriage can be a good thing.

Why, I might even try it again with Will. I *am* a good influence on him. And getting him off the booze, well, he's discovered he can get it up again, at least with me. Maybe we're old and wise enough now to make it work this time. At least neither of us should have any ego problems anymore. We're both just about over the hill. And Hollywood isn't clamoring for our services. This piece of crap you're making, I didn't think they did them anymore." She said it without apology, and Miriam laughed.

"Palace does," Miriam said wryly. "They're trying to make big, big movies to appeal to everybody. They're nuts, of course. It's almost impossible to reach kids with the kind of picture their parents will also sit through. There's no way they could ever make a profit on this picture, but no one seems to care. It's called creative accounting, or something."

"So what's a bright kid like you doing producing Fifties crap?" Betty said abruptly.

"I'm starting to wonder," Miriam said. "I guess it's the challenge of trying to sift something worthwhile out of all the dross."

They finished WW2 in three weeks and everyone was euphoric that it was finally actually over. Most of the cast and crew didn't wait for the wrap party but caught the first plane for New York. Will and

Betty had decided to stay on in Rome for a while, and Miriam went to their hotel to say good-by.

"I've got something for you," Will said, handing her a small gift-wrapped box. He seemed embarrassed, shy. "I hope it will make you remember me a little kindly."

High over the Atlantic, she opened Will's present. It was a solid gold pig strung on a gold chain. "May I never be like this animal again. Love and heartfelt thanks from Will Benton."

Chapter Eleven

MIRIAM STOPPED OFF IN NEW YORK FOR A WEEK. SHE deserved a break. Claudia, who had just finished Miriam's love story on the Coast, arranged to meet her so they could see some new shows and some old friends. Miriam still owned her apartment but it was being sublet and she decided to indulge herself by staying at the Stanhope, where she could just stroll across Fifth Avenue to the Metropolitan Museum. Her first night in town Claudia joined her for drinks in the Stanhope's sidewalk café.

"You don't look any worse for the experience," Claudia said, kissing Miriam and sitting down at the table. Claudia looked pretty and fresh and exuberant. "The way Howard was carrying on, I thought Rome would be a real disaster. And I see you managed to lose another star. First Lisa in Rio, then Will Benton in Rome. Either you'll do anything for publicity or you're accident prone." She laughed.

"Neither," Miriam said. "It's a hazard of international production." The waiter brought their drinks and they toasted each other and looked out at the elegant bustle. The warm late-summer night wrapped itself around them.

"You mentioned Howard," Miriam said. "Does that mean he's been hanging around your set?"

"He turned up a couple of days," Claudia said. "But he made it quite clear *Three Into Three* wasn't his speed. Much too small a project to interest a man of Howard's importance. I think he just came by to make Peter Kraft nervous."

"How's the picture look?" Miriam asked. "I feel like I've been away forever. I hated leaving it for the Rome debacle."

"I've only seen the dailies," Claudia said. "I didn't wait for the rough assemblage, but it's good. We finished only one day over schedule and near enough to budget. Peter was bitching that Howard's loaded on some of the below-the-lines from Rome, but I guess you'll straighten that out. What about *WW2*? Bad?"

"Yes," she said, "but the studio should get out of it without too big a black eye. I figure Howard's done a good deal on European distribution and 'Benton and Carson together again' will help. It'll lose a lot, but it won't be a complete disaster." She signaled the waiter for another round. "The whole thing seems like such a waste of time, energy, and money."

Claudia shook her head and said, "Is Howard still insisting on doing his disco movie?"

"Of course," Miriam said. "He honestly believes it's going to be another *Saturday Night Fever*. I can't convince him it's been six years and disco's passé. Besides, we need a script, terrific music, and some attractive kids. A disco movie could make WW2 look like a triumph of artistic endeavor. Oh, Howard!"

"Yeah. I'll pass on that one, if you were thinking about the sound," Claudia said. "But you will use me on your lifeguard picture, won't you?"

"Of course. When and if I get to do it," Miriam said. "Howard and I have this stand-off. I oversee the pictures he wants the studio to make and, in between, if there's time and if I can pare the budgets right down, he throws me a crumb by letting me make what I want. That's why there's so much riding for me on *Three Into Three*. If I can persuade the studio to give it a chance out there, and if we can make some money from it, I can prove my point."

"It's a good little picture," Claudia said. "We'll all be proud of it and it'll earn back its cost."

"That's the key word—*little* picture," Miriam

said. "The studio is frantically looking for blockbusters; something like *Three* they don't want to know about. But *Disco Madness* they'll lavish twenty million dollars on, then bitch about how fickle the kiddie market is. Anyway, to hell with all that for now. What other news?"

"Well . . . ," Claudia said hesitantly, "Joe called the set from Key West, looking for you. I took the call. He wanted to tell you he's going to be in New York delivering his new book and is there any chance of your getting together. He's arriving the day after tomorrow and he's staying with friends. I've got the number. I didn't tell him you would be here. I wasn't sure you wanted to see him."

"I'd love to see him," Miriam said. "He's a good old friend." She realized she meant it, and she was proud of her maturity.

She called Joe the day after he arrived in New York and they arranged to have dinner at Elaine's. She got there early and was surprised at how many people came over to speak to her. Some of their old friends, of course: She expected that. But also some of the heavy-hitters—directors, producers, stars. It was her first time in the restaurant since she'd been elevated at Palace, of course. She smiled. It was just the way the business worked. She wouldn't take it personally.

PALACES

Joe came hurrying in, casual in jeans and shirt, deeply tanned and looking better than ever. They kissed and settled at the table to talk.

"You're looking wonderful," Joe said. "And I hear you're doing great out there. Jesus, you really did make it right to the top. I'm so happy for you."

"You look good, too," she said. "I guess you were right after all, about getting out of town. It agrees with you. How's your family?"

"All great," he said. "We've got two kids now, another girl in April. It makes work difficult, having them crawling all over you, but it's fun."

"What about the new book?" Miriam asked. "Claudia said you were delivering it."

"I like it and my agent's wild about it," Joe said. He toyed with his drink. "It's kind of about us, the choices people get forced into making. How you long for success without realizing what a change success is going to make in your life. And whether, if you could, you'd go back to the way it was."

"What's the answer to that, Joe?" she asked quietly, watching the face she had known so well for so long.

"Me, I don't know," he said. "All I know is that in the book, they realize they haven't any choice in the matter. You have to keep moving." He drained his beer. "If we'd stayed put in Madison, or a couple of other places along the way, we'd still be married. But we wouldn't be who we are now. More important, you wouldn't be who you are. I'm really proud for you, the way you fought your way through and reached what you wanted. And I'm relaxed with myself, not driven so hard. I'm living and working the way I need to. But I'm sorry the price was so high."

"So am I," she said. "But I think you're right about there being no choice. If I hadn't tried what I did, I would have hated myself and you."

They didn't get around to eating until after eleven. The restaurant was packed, the city just getting over the summer layoff, and there was a constant stream of old friends pulling up a chair at their table. She waited for a lull before bringing up what was on her mind.

"The new book, Joe," she said. "You think it would make a movie? I'm looking for material right now and I like what you've told me about it."

He shrugged. "It's a quiet story," he said. "Not one of your blockbuster films. I think it would make the kind of movie I want to see, but neither the publisher nor my agent thinks Hollywood will be rushing us."

"Would you ask your agent to send it over to me before I leave town?" she asked. "I don't only make mega-budget pictures at Palace. They humor me sometimes and let me do the kind of picture that doesn't play drive-ins."

PALACES

He dropped her off at the Stanhope in a cab. They held hands for a moment.

"I'm glad you're happy," she told him.

"I hope you are, too," he said. He waved to her from the back of the cab as it sped off down Fifth Avenue.

She read Joe's manuscript on the plane to LA. It hurt. It was so close to them, and the message of what might have been ran through it. But that was why it worked and she knew that if she put her side of their experience into the picture, it would be a strong and thoughtful movie.

The next day she spoke with Palace's East Coast acquisitions office and, a while later, they told her they had optioned Joe's book for $75,000. It wasn't a big enough sum to bother Howard about, so she didn't. He and she had enough to wrangle over.

Howard's disco film was shaping up as a major disaster. He had commissioned a score from a group who had made three disco hits and were exhausted of talent. He had signed a put-together group called Urban Dwellers to be in the film. The story was trite. And the "stars" were an Olympic gold medal winner and a very precocious teen-age model.

"It is," she told Howard, "a piece of shit and I refuse to have anything to do with it."

"You'll do as I damn well tell you," Howard

snapped at her. "Right now I'm the only thing standing between you and your getting your ass kicked right out of your job. The board is very unhappy with your work. The rough cut of WW2 is bloody dreadful. We looked at it yesterday. There were tears in the screening room—tears of rage. We're going to have to dump it out fast, pray the influential critics don't get to hear about it, splash it in Europe where they'll accept garbage like this. Thank God for the television deal. It will be on the home screen by January and it's a picture that will improve by having commercials break it up. But even if we're lucky all the way down the line, Palace is looking at a loss of fifteen million dollars, thanks to you."

"You're not going to make me carry the can on that," Miriam said. "You would have lost a hell of a lot more than fifteen if not for me. It was *always* your project and it was *always* going to be a failure."

"It's got your name on it now," Howard said smoothly. "And that's the way this business works: He who gets the credit also has to shoulder the blame. Speaking of blame, we also had a look at the rough cut of *Three Into Three*. Now that one, I'm sure, you are happy to take responsibility for."

"You bet," Miriam said. "It's a damn good picture and it will make us some money with the right distribution and promotion. It even came in o budget, despite the bogus figures I'm discovering in the accounts. I want to talk to you about them, Howard. It's like the Rio scam all over again. Checks to phantom actors and service companies I never heard of, locations we never used."

"The board isn't interested in minor bookkeeping entries," he told her. "What they are concerned about is the picture itself. The unanimous feeling is: It has not one ounce of commercial potential. So we're going to cut our losses. It won't be released in theaters. I'll try and sell it to one of the pay TV systems. They're the only people so desperate for product they might look at it." He leaned back in his chair and smiled at her. It was the smile of a shark.

"So you see, little Miriam, the board is not at all happy with you. Your record is a disaster. You've even made me look bad because I went out on a limb for you. Now they want to fire you. But I'm willing to give you one last chance. The disco movie's a sure-fire hit and I'm willing to trust you with
."

She was not going to sink so easily.

"You can't do that to *Three Into Three*," she said. "It's a good picture. You're talking about destroying it without a chance."

"I'm talking about not throwing good money after bad," Howard said. "And I'm not going to waste any more time talking about it." He stood up. "It's time for my tennis lesson. You think about what I've said and let me have your decision on Monday."

"Damn you, Howard," she shouted. "I'm going to demand to meet with the board and tell them just what's going on."

He turned at the door and looked at her with a chilling grin.

"You really are naïve," he said. "I run this studio. The board listens to me. Only to me. They're not interested in hearing from the hired help, most certainly not when the hired help is a pushy broad out of her depth. You've got till Monday, Miriam."

She left the studio at once and drove home to Beverly Hills, tight with anger, her knuckles white as she gripped the wheel. He couldn't set her up like this. But he had. And he wasn't bluffing about the board. They were just moneymen, and Howard had them in his pocket. They'd see no reason to save *Three Into Three*.

She fixed herself a drink and went out on the deck. She could see the kitschy "HOLLYWOOD" sign over on the hill through the hot afternoon smog. The sign mocked her. Hollywood was supposed to be about dreams, not about tax shelters. Her dream had been to make movies, good ones. Instead she was a pawn in the dubious schemes of Howard Veitch and dreary men like him.

She could have cried but she did not even thin

of it. She still had some fight left in her. Solly had a friend who was a major stockholder in Palace. He would get her message to the board. An end run around Howard, that was the way to go! She called Solly.

"Yes," he said gently, "I heard you were having some problems. I'm not sure there's much to be done about it. Veitch has the board's ear, at least until the day they decide to fire him. Until then they'll back him all the way down the line."

"But Solly," she pleaded, "it's so unfair. I don't care about the job, the embarrassment of being fired, any of that. But he's going to sacrifice my picture to pay TV!"

She ran through her litany of charges against Howard, the swindles he had perpetrated on the studio, the padded bills, the phony checks. Solly listened sympathetically but he wasn't overwhelmed by her story.

"They don't care how much he steals," he said, "just so long as the bottom line looks good."

"But that's the point!" she cried. "The pictures Howard is pushing are all huge losers. How can he produce a good bottom line? They've got to be deeply in the red. You can't make one bomb after another and make any money."

There was a long silence, and then he said, "I'll phone my friend in New York and see if there's anything he can do for you. I'll let you know what he says on Sunday. You haven't forgotten you're coming out here for lunch?"

She had. Solly and his wife had invited her the week before. Just a few friends, from back East. It would be good to be with them all.

"I'll be there, Solly," she said.

She made good time to Solly's place and arrived early. Solly was waiting for her on the sun deck. They kissed. It was a clear sunny day, so far away from the city. The deep green of the orange grove was soothing.

If Solly hadn't looked so somber she might have forgotten Howard and Palace Productions, but one look at his face and she knew something was up.

"Let's go into the study, Miriam," he said quietly. "My friend on Wall Street called me this morning and I have some things to tell you. Nothing good."

After they were settled in Solly's leather-and-mahogany study, where there wasn't a hint of California and where he began looking even more troubled, Solly started to talk, slowly at first and then heatedly. Dear Solly. He always took on her problems as though they were his own.

"Miriam, it's all bad news. You've been caught in what looks like a major financial play. My friend has some Palace stock but not enough that there's a damned thing he can do. Howard and the board are involved in manipulating stocks—hardly ethical, but perfectly legal."

"What does that have to do with me?" she asked. "I'm just a hireling, paid to make movies that'll bring in money."

Solly shook his head.

"Making money is exactly what they don't want you to do. Howard and friends need movies that cost money, turkeys. The more red Howard can show, the faster Palace stock will tumble. Bad movies are very good news when you're manipulating stock."

"Solly, you've lost me," she said.

"Howard and his crowd control a shade more than fifty percent of Palace stock," Solly began again. "The more the stock falls, the more the institutional investors bail out. The way they're going this year, Howard's people will be able to buy up most of the Palace stock at bargain rates, and soon.

"And then," he said, "they're sitting on a gold mine. The studio's film library alone is worth at least two hundred million dollars, sold to television. The building, even in a depressed market, will get them another forty or fifty. There are other parcels of land scattered around worth God knows what. And after they've stripped all Palace's assets, they can become a television production company, churning out crap for the networks, using rented premises. Howard and Company are going to make a fortune."

"But it's immoral!" Miriam cried. "Surely the other investors won't let them run the studio into the ground."

"There's nothing they can do about it," Solly said. "Howard's faction has control, and that means creative control. You know that. You can't prove they're making movies designed to lose money. It looks like a matter of their judgment against the critics' and the audience's. So they make a succession of bombs? That's show biz."

"Why did Howard hire me, then?" Miriam asked. "What was all the fuss about 'new, young talent'?"

Solly looked away. He got the pitcher of Bloody Marys and refilled their glasses.

"Oh, I suddenly see the light," Miriam said bitterly. "Because I was just a woman, Howard figured he could keep me in line. I wouldn't buck his judgment because I'd be so happy with my pretty office, my generous salary, and my name in the papers. I . . . I see." This was dear Solly. She didn't have to pretend, not with him. She felt more embarrassed than she had ever felt.

This, then, was her great success! Her face on *Time* magazine, her ecstatic friends, the talent she had rescued, people like Peter Kraft, her films . . . all a sham. Nothing to her "career" but a puppet's dance, guided by a man whose only interest was money and who knew less about movies than she had when she was twelve. Why, Howard had known all along, had been laughing at her earnestness, had meant all along to scuttle everything she achieved!

Making the moment of her total shame exquisitely painful was the presence of Solly, her friend and mentor, Solly, who had been so proud of her, who had shared her triumphs with such glee. Why had it fallen to *him* to tell her it was all for nothing? Why did he have to be sitting there watching as she turned into nothing?

"You've got to admire Howard's tactics," Solly said hurriedly, trying to cover the terrible moment. "Hiring you looked great. He got all that good publicity about turning production over to the new generation while he kept on pumping out the same old schlock. Now, when the losses come in, he can say it wasn't his fault. He tried to change Palace all he could."

He stopped talking. There was no point in going on. He'd made her see the game. She could fill in the blanks for herself.

After a while she took a deep breath and said, "So what do I do? Walk away? Or stay on salary and make bad movies for Howard until he's gotten the company deep enough in the red?"

"That's something you will have to decide for

yourself," Solly said. "I'd advise you to hang on a while, do the best you can. At least you're in an important job, right at the top of the Hollywood tree. Maybe you'll get the chance to go to another studio." He looked into her eyes. "That is, if you want to go on being an executive."

"I don't know what I want right now," Miriam said desperately. "I hate all the politics of the job, the cheating Howard does, all the waste. But I still think I'm achieving something at Palace. I've got good people working with me and we will succeed with some of our films, no matter what Howard does to sabotage them. Maybe I didn't want this kind of job, Solly, but I've got it and I'm damned if I'll just walk away from it because of Howard and his stocks. Fuck Howard. I'm going to stay and fight."

"Thank God," Solly breathed. "It will be tough but I think you'll be glad you stuck it out. The Howard Veitches of this world eventually get theirs and then you'll come into your own. In the meantime, I'm always here if you need a shoulder to cry on." He lit a cigar and inhaled. "And if you need more contemporary advice," he said casually, "there's Andy East. He's a fine young man. So smart. I think you two make a wonderful couple."

"Cut the matchmaking, Solly," she said, smiling at him to make up for her sharp tone. "I've already used Andy too much. It's been all take and no give on my part."

"That's not the impression I get from him," Solly said gently. "He's very . . . fond of you, Miriam. You should give him a chance. You don't want to live the rest of your life all alone, you know, no matter how independent you are."

He meant well, this kindly old man who had done so much for her. But she was no longer in a listening mood.

"No," she said. "I made my choice a long time ago. And I won't hurt Andy anymore. It's not fair to him and I can't cope with feeling bad about Andy."

"I think you love him, Miriam," Solly said flatly. "And I think you're interpreting the situation all wrong." He raised his hand to stop her protest. "I know, it's none of my business. Come now, it's time for lunch."

He put his cigar in a large silver ashtray and stood up. "Thelma will say I hogged you. She always says that. And she's right: I do." He squeezed her hand and led her to the door.

Chapter Twelve

SHE WAVED TO GUS AT THE EXECUTIVE PARKING LOT gatehouse and waited for him to raise the red barrier. He was slow, and the car waiting behind Miriam's honked at her. Gus clambered down from his seat and moved toward her. She guessed the gate was broken.

"I'm sorry, Ms. McDonald," he said when he reached her red Mustang. He could not meet her eyes. "I've got my orders and there's nothing I can do about this."

There was an angry chorus of auto horns behind her, impatient Palace executives straining to reach their Monday morning problems.

"What's wrong, Gus?" she asked.

He looked wretched. "Mr. Veitch sent an order

down this morning. You're not to be admitted to the studio."

She felt the morning sun hard on her and flushed with anger and humiliation as realization flooded in. Her hands locked on the wheel.

"I'm sorry," he repeated apologetically. "But please, could you move your car out of the line. There's a lot of people waiting."

She backed up, the car behind crowding her. She could feel the other drivers staring at her and she caught some of their expressions: It was as if they had seen this all before.

She drove back to the house, driving very carefully, her mind blank. She could not face what had happened. Was everything she had done up to this point merely a long sick joke leading to this vicious punchline?

She wandered around the house, picking up objects and examining them as a stranger would. The place seemed foreign, and the hot dead air outside seemed threatening.

She stayed in shock for most of the morning, putting off as long as possible the moment when she would have to face herself and her situation. Finally she called the studio.

"I'm sorry," his secretary said. "Mr. Veitch isn't available. But he did leave a message for you. He said for you to look in today's *Hollywood Reporter*."

"I want to speak to Howard," Miriam insisted

"There's been some mistake. They wouldn't let me into the parking lot. I guess that means I've been fired. But I was supposed to talk to Howard this morning and give him my decision. He can't—"

"I can and I have," Howard's voice cut in on the phone. "Our attorneys are drawing up the papers now and we'll have them over to your house this afternoon. I've been quite generous in the settlement and you'll sign a release ending our contract."

"I won't, Howard," she said. "I'll sue you for wrongful dismissal. I'll go to the media. Even in Hollywood you can't just fire someone to cover up your own mistakes." Her anger was rising, surprising her. "It's my good name you're playing with, mine and my pictures and all the people who make them."

"I've given you the message, Miriam," he said. "Read the *Hollywood Reporter* and then think about going public with this."

He hung up. Miriam, no longer buoyed by anger, slumped back in her chair. Something was very wrong. Howard sounded too sure of himself.

She drove to the drugstore and got the *Reporter*. The item was all across page one.

Miriam McDonald had been fired by the board of Palace Productions because she had engineered an option deal with her ex-husband. The deal for his new book included a six-figure amount. It had not been referred to studio head Howard Veitch and could not be defended. Unnamed studio sources were quoted as saying the sweetheart deal, while reprehensible, had gotten the studio off a hook. Miriam's performance as head of production had not been satisfactory and the uncovering of the deal had enabled Palace to cancel her contract. There was more, but the totality of it was that Miriam McDonald had fallen flat on her face and had capped a poor performance by resorting to financial chicanery with her former husband. A tailpiece added that the studio was cutting its losses on her just-completed picture, *Three Into Three,* by selling it to pay TV.

It was as damaging a piece as it could possibly have been. Miriam thought fleetingly of suing the *Reporter,* but she forced herself to read through the story again and saw Howard had used the magazine skillfully. It was no use protesting that Joe's book would have made a fine film: as the *Reporter* noted, there had not been one other bid for the property from any other producer. And she had done the deal without checking with Howard.

Sitting in the drugstore parking lot, drained by the fierce sun, she cried. From the cover of *Time* to page one of the *Reporter* she had gone from golden girl to conniving crook. The dive had taken one year.

When the sun became unbearable, she drove

back to the house and started packing. She had to escape the town as fast as she could.

A messenger from Howard's attorneys arrived during the afternoon and she signed the papers. She was to be paid six months' salary and from that figure was to be deducted the 15 percent downpayment on Joe's book option. Howard, who had squandered so many millions of the studio's money, was twisting the knife over eleven thousand dollars.

The phone rang and rang as Miriam stuffed clothes into whatever came to hand. She tried not to hear the phone but was forced to pick it up at last.

"Tough luck, kid," Peter Kraft said. "Old Howard finally screwed you like he screwed everyone else. I know what you're feeling now and I just wanted to say thanks for all you did for me, and that you're the best I ever worked with. Too good for this town."

She started crying into the phone, feeling stupid and weak but there was no stopping the tears.

"Just hang in there and I'll be right over," Peter said. "I'm not much comfort but I'm better than nothing."

He arrived in fifteen minutes, bearing deli sandwiches and cold champagne, and she fell into his arms and cried some more. He put her down in a chair on the deck, found plates and glasses and made her eat. He waited silently until she was calm.

"So what are you going to do?" he asked, gesturing at the bags on her livingroom floor. "Get out of town?"

She nodded. "I just want to drive, a long way away from here," she said. "I've lost everything. Not the job, so much. I guess it didn't matter, even though this morning I was willing to drop everything to keep it. But I've lost my self-respect. Maybe Howard's right, maybe I don't know how to make commercial movies. It doesn't matter, anyway. I'm ruined in the industry."

He shook his head impatiently. "Nobody believes you were in cahoots with your ex-husband, Miriam. That's a transparent story and nobody'll be fooled by it. Don't worry about that."

"Oh, shit, Peter, I feel like I've been beaten to a pulp. You said he'd screw me. Is this what it means to be a woman?"

He stood up and filled their glasses, then produced a vial of cocaine and offered it to her. She shook her head and he set out four lines for himself. He snorted the coke, drained his glass, and lay back in a canvas chair.

"Miriam," he said wearily, "this has nothing to do with sexism. You've had a colossal crash. But your being a woman had nothing to do with it. You just got caught in a power play. Hell, they flunke me out years ago because I didn't seem as good, as dedicated, as my folks. So should I start a movement to defend the children of famous people?"

"Okay," she said, "I see. But I'm still a public failure, an incompetent, and a thief. What do I do?"

"Finish packing and get out of town," Peter said. "There's nothing here for you now, at least for a while." He looked out into the twilight. "Me, neither. If you like, I'll drive with you for part of the way wherever you're going."

They drove away. The lease on the house was paid for several months, and there was nothing in it she would worry about.

Defeat suited Peter Kraft, she decided during their first three days on the road. He was funny and relaxed, as if all his worst fears had been realized and there was nothing more to fear. She liked being with him, but at the same time she determined she would never be like him. Inside her there still burned a fierce sense of injustice. She could never welcome disaster, as Peter did.

They drove erratically, branching off for silly reasons. They slept in towns Holiday Inn had never heard of, crisscrossing the western states, swinging deep down into Texas, back up into Oklahoma. They always shared a room. Miriam had never figured out Peter's sexuality and now, on the lam, she didn't care. It was enough that she had him there, spaced out, coked out, but *there*. She would watch him drifting through the days and drift with him.

They crossed into Nebraska just after dark on a cold night with a bitter wind howling across the plains. The Mustang had developed a cough and they needed to find a repair shop. The first town they came to was all shut down for the night but a Texaco station on the main street promised a mechanic during business hours. Across from it was a motel-restaurant-bar with a few pickup trucks parked out front.

The check-in was at the bar and Miriam felt the stares of a dozen silent men nursing their drinks. She glanced at Peter. He did look a little weird out here in prairie country. His Rodeo Drive denims were caked with dust, his lank hair was spilling down his back. His eyes, when he pushed up the aviator glasses, were red rimmed and glassy from drugs. The barman took their money, gave them a key, and told them to drive around back to their room. It was a drab, depressing place with a film of dust over everything. But the water in the shower was at least lukewarm and Miriam let it flow over her, flooding away the road dirt and some of the tiredness. When she came out of the shower, a towel around her, she found Peter sprawled on one of the beds drinking from a Beefeater bottle. A small pile of coke was on the table beside him.

"You better take it easy with that stuff, Peter,

she said. "We're in the boonies now and they might think you're a drug-crazed hippie."

"Fuck 'em," he said, grinning. "I'm the nearest thing to the real world they've ever seen. I think I'll put on a show for the natives. Let 'em see what a young Hollywood prince looks like."

There was going to be trouble. She tried to persuade him to stay in the room while she ordered them some food but Peter insisted on going with her. He would not, he said, eat greasy spoon cooking in a flophouse room.

The silence endured as they entered the restaurant-bar again. A grumpy waitress with a boil on her chin took their orders and, a few minutes later, slapped down in front of them plates of charred steak and tired vegetables. Peter cut into his steak. It was gray inside, old and gristly and inedible.

"Oh, shit," he said wearily, beckoning the waitress. She slumped across to their table. The silence in the bar was deafening now.

"Don't make a fuss, Peter," she whispered. "I don't like the look of this place and it's a long way to the next town."

He waited until the woman was hovering over them.

"I ordered a rare steak," he told the waitress. He picked up his steak with his fork and held it up. "I don't even know if this *is* steak. The only thing I'm sure of is, it's dead. Dead a long time. So how about you take this piece of crap back to the kitchen and tell the chef to fix me a nice bit of prime beef, two minutes each side, okay?"

"How about you and your slut get your asses out of here," said the waitress. "We don't need your business." She turned and headed back to the kitchen.

"Forget it, Peter," Miriam implored. "Don't start trouble." She could see the silent men at the bar moving in their seats, lining up on them. "We're outnumbered. Let's just forget dinner and go back to the room. I've got some candy and cookies in my bag."

He didn't hear a word. Slowly, he picked up the offending steak, studied the retreating back of the waitress, and flung it at her. The meat hit her between the shoulder blades, clinging for a moment to her grubby uniform before sliding to the floor.

One of the men at the bar moved across the room to their table. He was huge, even without the cowboy boots and Stetson, and he looked like he was meaning to enjoy this.

"We don't let people treat ladies like that, punk," he said as he towered over Peter. "What you're going to do now is get down on your hands and knees and crawl across the floor and eat that goddamned steak where it's lying. Or else I'm going to break your head."

She looked at Peter, so frail and so wrecked.

was no match. She wondered if there was some way she could summon the sheriff.

"Well, son, start crawling," the cowboy demanded. He reached out, his huge horny hand grasping toward Peter's shirt collar. She heard Peter's mocking laugh and saw him slip out of his chair, duck under the cowboy's arm, and kick him in the groin. The big man doubled over, and as his head came down Peter knocked his hat off and grabbed a hunk of his hair.

Balancing on his toes, he spun the man around and, with his foot against the cowboy's backside, sent him crashing across the room against the bar. Frail Peter!

As the big man lay stunned on the floor two more men advanced on Peter. They were wary now, and came in from opposite sides, but again Peter moved with incredible speed. He shoved his hip into the closest man and flipped him over the table to land on the floor with a crash. He stepped around the second man and took his arm and forced it up his back. With his other hand, Peter removed a long hunting knife from his boot and held it to the man's throat.

"You want your buddy here butchered, just make a move against me," Peter shouted to the spectators. Everyone stayed back, awed by the display of force, scared by the gleaming knife.

Peter called to Miriam, "Throw everything in our bags and bring the car around the front."

She ran, gathered their things, and jumped into the Mustang. She spun up to the front entrance just as Peter came backing out, still pinioning his captive. She leaned across and opened the car door. He kicked the legs from under the man and jumped in beside her.

"Drive back across the border," he said. "They'll have some fat-bellied sheriff out after us. We'll outrun him. I've seen all this in the movies."

The Mustang still coughed but she put the pedal hard down and they got out of town doing one-ten. In fifteen minutes they were out of Nebraska and there were no headlights speeding behind them. She eased up.

Peter had found his bottle of Beefeater and was drinking thirstily, between throwing back his head and laughing into the night sky.

"You could have gotten us both killed," she yelled. "What the hell were you playing at?"

He drank some more and waved ahead to where a dull glow indicated a town in the distance. Soon they were on quiet streets. It was still only ten thirty. She turned into the town's main street and saw a couple of motel signs and a fast-food sign, all still lit. She pulled up outside the red shack.

"This is the last place we'll find open tonight, so don't send back your chicken, okay?"

He started laughing. At first she was angry. Then the mood caught her and she found herself near hysteria, the two of them shouting laughter into the night on a deserted street in an anonymous town.

They bought a take-out basket, checked into a motel, and, still giggling, sat on the beds to eat their chicken and drink warm gin.

"So tell me," Miriam said, "how did a meek and mild producer suddenly turn into Captain America? I'm *most* impressed."

"It finally paid off," Peter said. "Ten years of paying for every unarmed combat course ever offered in Los Angeles. I got black belts from all of them but until tonight I never got a chance to do anything with any of it. It was a combination of a lot of things—the courage of cocaine, just being pissed at the whole world. And I made myself believe all those bums at the bar were Howard Veitch." He started laughing again. "Hey, it was hairy for a few minutes but, hell, wasn't it fun?"

Just before she fell asleep, Miriam understood what Peter meant. It had been a catharsis. She almost felt like herself again. It was time to end their crazy journey.

They headed for Chicago the next morning. It suited Peter to head for a major city because his dope supply was running out. Miriam figured they could split in Chicago and she would drive down to Madison.

They spent their night in Chicago at the Whitehall, feeling they were due a touch of luxury after all the grimy days on the road. Peter bought a day-old copy of *Variety* at the hotel newstand and crashed on the bed with it, reading her items about people they knew and adding his own comments. He was funny and cutting but Miriam wasn't comfortable with industry gossip. Then she heard him whistle.

"Listen to this!" he said. "There's this new in-house video system set up for hotels and they're buying up big. They just did a deal with Palace for a bunch of old movies. Plus one unreleased picture *Three Into Three.* So there goes our little epic. Not even cable tv! Fucking hotel television, where a bunch of tired traveling salesmen will see it."

"It's what Howard said he was going to do," Miriam said. "He wants our film dead and buried."

"Wait," Peter said, still reading *Variety*. "Wait till you hear who owns the hotel video outfit. It's a new company, just put together by Andy East. Did you know about it?"

"Oh, shit, no," she said, surprised.

"I can't blame him for picking it up," she said. "I guess I owe Andy a few. And he does run a nice chain of hotels. But I didn't think he'd do some thing like that to me. Oh, hell, Peter, isn't there anyone you can rely on anymore?"

He swung his legs down from the bed and moved to her. He put his arm around her shoulders and hugged her.

"Only unreliable people like me, kid," he said. "I'm sorry."

She cried a little as she steered the Mustang out of Madison after a short visit and pointed it toward New York. She hadn't spent even two whole days in Madison. There'd been a day with Deborah, all children talk and analyzing the past. Miriam had decided before calling her sister that there was no way Deborah could understand what had happened to Miriam. If she brought it up, what could there be but endless questions, her sister trying like mad to comprehend something alien? No. It would hurt less, she knew, to tell only what she had to and change the subject.

Madison was Madison. It was nice to see something familiar, but it was not home, hadn't been for ten years. She was just as glad to head for the East Coast.

It was near dark when she drove into New York. She drove straight to the Stanhope, her apartment still unavailable. At least she had no immediate worries about money. The settlement would see her through a year or more if she were careful.

The Stanhope manager greeted her warmly, and soon she stood at the window of her pretty suite, looking down at the evening strollers on Fifth Avenue. It seemed as if she had been away from New York forever and she wondered how she would again find a place for herself in the city.

Miriam sank into a deep hot bath and felt the water revive her. She should have been tired, but the thought of New York ticking away just outside excited her. She dressed and left, taking a cab to Elaine's.

A friend spotted her at the door and came sweeping down on her, arms wide to embrace Miriam.

"I hope you're home for good," she said squeezing her. "You've been away too long, out there with those crazies. Everyone missed you. Come sit with me. We'll have champagne."

It was a happy evening and Miriam was thankful for Ellen's vivacity. She could pretend for a while she had never been away. It was the same crowd, big names who hadn't forgotten what it was like to be struggling. The talk was of films and books and theater and Miriam felt right at home. Failing in Los Angeles was a badge of honor among New York chauvinists.

Phil Ashton came in late and sat at the table with Miriam and Ellen. He said he was trying to put a new film together. If he got the money, and if she didn't have anything better to do, would she like to direct? He didn't know when he'd be ready, though; the New York film scene was very depressed just then, and nobody was spending money.

"I can wait," Miriam said. "I don't figure there's going to be a rush to employ me. It's kind of hard to see where I can go now."

"Well," Phil said. "You are hard to pigeonhole. It's okay for me—we've worked together before—but a lot of people are going to feel awkward about offering you a job after you've been right at the top."

"Will I be able to overcome the prejudice, Phil?" she asked. "Can I go back to just doing what I like?"

"I don't know," he said. At least he was leveling with her. "I know a few people who've tried and failed. But you're young enough. And good enough. They'll forget about Palace in time. Just hang in, Miriam."

"It's so unfair," she protested hotly. "I mean, I paid my dues. Why should I have to start all over again just because I lucked into a top job and then fell out of it? And being unable to get along with a creep like Howard Veitch should work in my favor, don't you think?"

"People don't like to be associated with anyone who's crashed," Phil said gently. "They fear the scent of failure will rub off on them. Or they'll offend someone powerful by working with you. Or they're just plain envious because you've been right to the top. Whatever, there's nothing you can do about it."

She wished he didn't have to be quite so honest. Late that night, back in her plush hotel, she thought it all through again. She was virtually unemployable, thanks to Veitch. If only she'd never won that Oscar, never gone to Hollywood. She had been so happy struggling to make good little films on tiny budgets. She thought of the fun they had all had together in those days and compared it with the year of hell she'd just lived through. She was still putting the pieces together when night became dawn.

Miriam got her apartment back and tried to get work. But there was nothing for her: plenty of promises for the future, many good wishes, but no job. The apartment began to feel small and cramped and she felt her self-esteem ebbing away. Had all the gains she had made been lost? She was worse off than a beginner.

She called Joe in Key West one dreary night. He was kind.

"You've just got to hang in," he said. "I know how tough it must be for you, but things will pick up. You're too good to stay unemployed. But you have to live with this a while."

"I'm sorry about the book option, Joe," she said.

PALACES

"I really wanted to do that picture. It could have been something damned good."

"I'm only sorry the option caused you so much embarrassment," he said. "At least I got the fifteen percent from Palace. It bought us a new boat."

She didn't tell him the option money had been deducted from her own severance.

"Anyway," Joe said, "when you get to working again, if you still want to do something with the book, consider it yours. I figure I owe you one for having faith. By the way," he added, "where are you calling from? Your friend Sol Behn called me a week or so ago trying to find you. Said it was urgent."

"I moved back into the apartment last week," Miriam said. "Hardly anyone knows I'm back, apart from the low-budget producers I've been pestering. What did Solly say?"

"He needed to talk to you badly."

When she reached him, Solly sounded relieved.

"Miriam!" he said, "I've been chasing you everywhere. What were you thinking of, running out on all of us like that!"

"I'm sorry, Solly," she said. "I just couldn't face Hollywood after all the scandal. I hit the road and drove for a while. Now I'm back in New York, trying to find work."

"Miriam," Solly said. "One of the reasons I had to talk to you is, something big is happening at Palace. My friend who has the Palace shares? H[e] called me on behalf of some of the board. The[y] want to talk with you. I don't know what about but it must be in your favor. Anyway, call m[y] friend and he'll arrange everything. They'll giv[e] you a first-class ticket, suite at the Beverly Hills limo, the lot. Just to come out and talk with them Please do it. I want to see you and you might a[s] well make the trip on someone else's money. An[d] Andy wants to see you, too. He has something t[o] explain to you."

Three members of Palace Productions boar[d] were waiting for her when she checked into th[e] hotel. They wanted to talk in her suite but Miria[m] insisted on meeting in the Polo Lounge. The mor[e] public the place the better. If they were seen an[d] the trades printed something it could only help he[r] shattered reputation. She unpacked in the sui[te] and let the board members wait a little.

They were nervous and impatient when she f[i]nally joined them in the booth.

"This is all very confidential," said Lars Sande[r]son. "John and Eric," he added, nodding to th[e] other two, "and I trust you won't tell anyone abo[ut] this conversation, no matter what you decide to d[o] after you've listened to us."

"No promises, gentlemen," Miriam said. "[I] found promises aren't worth a damn when you'[re] dealing with Palace. Just tell me what's bothering you so much you had to fly me back here."

"All right," Sanderson said. "We'll have to risk it." He lowered his voice and leaned across the table.

"Howard Veitch has gone too far," he said. "We want to be rid of him and you can help us."

"It took you long enough," Miriam said. She was enjoying herself. "Howard is the worst moviemaker in the industry."

"We don't give a fuck about the movies he makes," Sanderson said. "They are the least of our problems. No, Howard's been robbing us blind. He's been letting out millions of dollars, interest free, to some of his associates. All kinds of enterprises, high-risk stuff. He's been taking a share of these loans in return for being so generous with our funds. It all came out when one of his cronies was destroyed in some funny oil deal and killed himself. If the market gets to hear about it, we'll look very bad. So Howard has to be publicly spanked."

"What do you need me for?" Miriam asked. "Why don't you just sue him for stealing from you?"

Sanderson coughed and studied his hands.

"That's the problem," he said. "Howard's terms of employment are rather vague. In fact, the contract is so badly drawn, it actually gives him the discretion to do as he likes with the company's money. We might not be able to prosecute him over these scams. We can't even actually fire him. And that's where you come in. We heard you had the facts and figures on Howard ripping off budgets. Phony invoices, ghost actors, bogus production facilities. Now, that kind of thing isn't covered by Howard's contract. With the evidence, we can call in the D.A. and fix Howard."

"What's in it for me?" Miriam asked.

"You can have your old job back, bigger salary," Sanderson said. "And no interference, I promise. As soon as we're rid of Howard, we're getting Jimmy Woodruff in as president of the studio. You'll get along fine with him."

"Jimmy Woodruff?" She laughed. "He's a bigger crook than Howard. And he knows even less about making pictures, if such a thing is possible."

"You leave the business side of it to us," Sanderson said. "Woodruff did a wonderful job running the talent agency. He doubled their gross in three years. As for all those rumors, that's all they were. He was cleared in the kickback case. It was sheer professional jealousy. Anyway, will you help us nail Howard? I figure you must want revenge."

"I do, gentlemen," she said calmly. "If you were firing Howard because he's a talentless fool, I'd testify anywhere you want me to. But you're only knifing him because it's expedient. You people make me sick. You shouldn't be in the movie business. You should be trading pork bellies. Or loan sharking." She stood up. "No, I'm not going to help you. I think you deserve Howard."

She went straight to her suite and called Solly.

"Have you got a room for me out there at the ranch?" she said. "I figure I'd better be out of here in the morning. After what I just did, I can't see Palace picking up the tab for this expensive suite." She explained quickly. He seemed pleased at the outcome.

"I told you it couldn't do any harm to talk to them," he said. "And it served its purpose. It got you out here. Sure, come out in the morning and stay for as long as you can. We're looking forward to seeing you."

She checked out early and had the Palace limo drive her all the way to Solly's, musing that a tiny revenge was better than none.

As the car climbed up Solly's long driveway, she was dismayed to see Andy's Mercedes. Andy! She couldn't see him now; there was too much to talk to Solly about, too much going on. But she would have to see him, and she couldn't quite suppress the feeling of happy anticipation coursing through her, try though she did.

Solly was at the door as she got to it. She kissed him and carefully eyed Andy as he came up behind Solly.

"Andy." She gave him her hand, establishing immediately a certain formality between them. As he took her hand she gave him a smile. This relaxed him a little.

Watching them carefully, Solly said, "Bloody Marys on the deck, you two?" Without waiting for a reply, he led them to the sun deck. Miriam and Andy followed along, both silent.

After the three were seated, drinks in hands, Solly said, "I took the liberty of telling Andy about your dealings with the Palace board. He's happy you turned them down."

"Yes," Andy said. "Once the story gets around it will do you a great deal of good out here."

"Good for what?" she said curtly. "I'm washed up in pictures and you both know it. You particularly, Andy. I heard you got my picture from Howard in his last garage sale."

"You know then?" he said happily. "It's a lovely picture, Miriam. I virtually stole *Three Into Three* from Howard. But, as you say, he doesn't know a thing about movies. I got it for four hundred thousand dollars for in-hotel screening, plus anything else I want to do with it. A very smart deal." He grinned again, so proud, and she snapped.

"You bastard!" she said. "You're as bad as the rest of them. I trusted you, and all you cared about was some cheap footage for your lousy TV system." She turned on Solly. "I suppose you think Andy's pulled a fast deal, too. I guess you're in on it with him. My two friends, my wise counselors. Okay, I've learned my lesson. I'll never trust anyone again."

She jumped up from the table, spilling her drink. It formed an ugly red pool on the white cloth. She almost fell as she ran through the house and down the steps, eyes blinded with tears of anger. She stopped when she reached the driveway. She had no car. She was stranded. She moved to Andy's convertible and saw keys in the ignition. She got in, but before she could start the car, Andy's hand had grabbed hers.

"Steal my car if you like," he said, "but listen to me first." He was still smiling. "I'm sorry," he said, "but I always forget how straight you are. Don't you see what I've done? With Solly's help, we've screwed Howard beautifully. You're going to come out of this a big winner." He gently tugged her from the car.

"Just walk back to the house with me and I'll explain it all to you," he said.

She was suspicious, resentful, but listening intently.

Back on the deck Mrs. Behn was changing the tablecloth. She gave Miriam a nervous smile and scuttled back inside the house. Miriam felt like two cents. Solly took her other hand and he and Andy led her to her seat.

The pair of them were still acting as if something was the greatest joke they'd ever heard. It was fine for them, she thought bitterly. Fine they had screwed Howard, fine they had bought her picture at bargain-basement rates. But they were just businessmen and couldn't be expected to understand what she and her people had put into the film, how much it would have meant to sit in a darkened theater and watch the title roll.

Solly squeezed her hand.

"I guess you don't understand what we're trying to tell you," he said. "And after what you've been through, I wouldn't expect you to. Andy, tell the girl what's happening."

Andy looked deep into her eyes and said, "This is what we've done and this is why we've been trying to find you all over the country. Howard was so eager to dump your picture he ended up giving me *all* rights to it, not just in-house TV. He said I could do anything I damn well pleased with it." He paused for effect.

"So now I'll tell you what I'm going to do. I've lined up deals in every major city in the nation. Within the next couple of weeks I'll have market researchers all across the country telling us where to exhibit the picture. There'll be a TV and print advertising campaign aimed at the real market for the picture—three million dollars' worth in the first two weeks.

"Miriam, six hundred prints are going into six hundred theaters, which is a bigger launch than most of the major films ever get. *Three Into Three* is going to get the promotion and distribution it deserves and I figure it will make back ten million bucks in the first month. The picture will have cost us three and a half million in all, while bringing in ten million. Howard Veitch is going to look like the dumbest guy who ever rode a casting couch."

She listened, not sure she understood. Were they really talking about her despised "little picture"?

"It's okay, Miriam," Solly said gently. "We may be novices about film, but we do know business. Andy and I have been studying the independent distribution market for six months. All we needed was the right product to prove our theories. We'd decided even before your disaster that your picture was it."

"But that's crazy," Miriam said. "You hadn't even seen *Three Into Three*. I haven't seen a final print and I bet you haven't either."

"It didn't matter," Andy said. "Solly and I knew if you'd made the picture it was the kind of product we needed for proving our theory. If Howard hadn't canned you we were prepared to go to him and offer to buy *Three Into Three* for what it cost to make plus ten percent of the gross. So he saved us a hell of a lot of money. And by firing you he also saved us the hassle of trying to steal you from Palace. See, Solly and I are only businessmen who can put this system together: You're the one we need to make the films."

"Yes," said Solly. "The papers have been drawn up. Simply, what we're proposing is a three-way partnership. Andy and I will put up twelve million seed money plus plow back the profits from *Three Into Three*. You and Andy and I are equal partners and there's no one else involved. You make the pictures you want to, with the people you need. Andy and I will market them. A couple of pictures a year, is what we were thinking of."

"I couldn't go into a deal like that," Miriam said. "You're putting up all the money and I'm putting in nothing but time. And may I remind you, my time isn't exactly valuable these days."

"Stop it, Miriam," Andy said sharply. "The kind of movies you make—'little' pictures on real budgets, the stuff the big studios are too overcapitalized to do—is going to be the wave of the future. Tom Laughlin showed the way with *Billy Jack*. No, if you join us *we'll* have the easy ride. Once we've got this releasing system running, it fuels itself. Solly and I can sit back and watch the money roll in while you do the work."

"The creative decisions are all yours, Miriam," Solly said. "We'll just be the business end. But if you were looking for your next production, Andy and I would be very happy if you picked up a new option on Joe's book. It would be a nice final kick in the gut for Howard if the property he fired you over came in a winner."

"So what say, Miriam?" Andy asked. "Will you join us? We need you to make this go. And I think we'd all work well together. We all love each other . . . in our funny little ways."

She couldn't speak. Something was choking her. She was trapped, trapped between the two people who loved her most, who had given so much, always freely. Solly was sitting in front of her, leaning forward, begging not to be misunderstood. Andy stood to her left, gazing hard at her. How many times had she disappeared on them, and how many times had they waited for her to come back? It would be so easy to say yes, but all she could think of was frantic escape.

Grabbing her bag, she fled down the corridor to the bathroom and locked herself in, leaning against the door. She stared across the room through the window that bordered blue sky; one of those endlessly cheerful, empty, California days. She stayed there a long time, staring into the sky.

Andy had turned away from the door, and as she entered all she could see was his back. Solly was looking at her anxiously. He rose and went to her, putting his arms around her, hugging her tightly. Andy turned, saw her face, and reached them in three strides. He wrapped his long arms around them, the old man and the woman, and grinned down at her, watching as the tears coursed down her face.

Andy wasn't far off in his projections. *Three Into Three* grossed only eight million its first month but it did nine in the second and looked to have the legs to go on making money for a long time. It played strongly in the college towns where their market research had pointed it and had record grosses at carefully selected art houses in major cities. If the picture had been a typical studio production with a bottom line of twelve or fourteen million, it would not have been anything to get excited about. But the picture had cost them, all told, only three and a half million, so it was a bonanza. They were committed to making pictures for three or four million dollars at most, and they could repeat this success over and over.

The film of Joe's book was in preproduction and Miriam was looking at two other properties which suited her. The artistic decisions were all hers but she enjoyed bouncing ideas off Solly and Andy and she respected their keen business sense. Andy particularly. She had worked with him closely in the three months since their partnership began. Their relationship had become deeper and warmer, more mature, because of that.

PALACES

Early one evening, her doorbell rang. She was on the phone with Peter Kraft, and she waved Andy inside and went back to talking with her producer. Half an hour later Andy quietly placed a gin and tonic in front of her and she realized how long he'd been there.

"I'm sorry, Peter," she said. "Andy's here and we've got a dinner date. Come up in the morning and we'll go through all this stuff and settle it, okay? Thanks."

She found him in the living room, his long body sprawled on the couch. He seemed perfectly content, but she was disturbed: How could she accept so much from him and give so little? She sat down beside him and they watched the red and gold sunset across the room, the lights blinking on in the canyon below. The comfortable silence that had become a steady part of their being together took hold of her, making her blurt, "It's just not fair, Andy, the time you spend waiting for me to clear up some problem or other. It's not, is it? You must think the film business is all that matters to me."

"Most of the time that's true," he said. "If it bothered me too much, I wouldn't still be here."

He got up and walked to the window, then turned to face her. "Speaking of business, I'm going to have to start paying more attention to my own. The hotels run themselves just so long. So, next month I'm going to start a swing around the whole chain—three or four months in the field, at least. You don't need me here. Solly's always available."

The thought of their being apart that long threw her. She couldn't tell why, exactly, but she was panicked by the thought of his absence. Before, it had always been her leaving him. This time, she was the one being left behind. She rose from the couch and went to him, taking hold of his arm.

"Andy," she began, then couldn't think what she wanted to say.

"Do you have to go?" she asked at last. "I don't know if I can get along without you."

"You don't need any help from me, Miriam," he said.

"It's not just . . . help, Andy," she said softly. "I guess I . . . I like very much having you here."

"And I very much like being here with you, Miriam," he said briskly. "In fact, I love you. I always have. When you've finally made good on your ambitions, when you believe you're a success, I hope you'll make time to love me. Then you'll learn it's possible to love somebody and still be free. One person doesn't have to take over the other's life, Miriam.

"You see, I love you the way you are, and that includes your crazy schedule and your preoccupation and your tensions and your living most of the time in your own world. I love you . . . *that way*, as you are. Now, why do you suppose I'd want to take you away from all the things you are?"

She was too surprised to say anything, but at the same time, she really wasn't surprised at all. She stood there gazing up at him, loving the lean, boyish face, content not to say a word. In the dusk, she took his hand and he squeezed it, saying, "You'll understand it all someday, and someday you'll trust me. Someday."

She leaned against the familiar, strong, warm shoulder as they moved toward the bedroom. He undressed her slowly and they made love with the curtains open.

The last rays of sun were falling on the Hollywood sign. It looked magical again.

MONTHS ON NATIONAL BESTSELLER LIS

The powerful and sexy novel about a woman's rise
the heights of success and wealth in the world
international real estate.

Castles

NEAL TRAVIS

Mitzi quietly plays second fiddle in her marriage t
handsome—and unfaithful—plastic surgeon a
caters to two demanding children. Her illusions
living happily ever after and her dreams of be
someone in her own right seem shattered.

But when her ambitious husband decides to move
family to Los Angeles, Mitzi reaches for her drea
She takes a real estate course and soon lands a
with Castles, the prestigious agency on Rodeo Dr
run by impressive and worldly Jay Pressler.

Suddenly, Mitzi's life begins to change. Her new
takes her from Hollywood to London and to Te
where she deals with ruthless billionaires, pow
brokers and socialites in exclusive cliques vying
power and prestige. And her heart takes her to
who teaches her about passion and living.

An AVON Paperback   79913-8/$3

Neal Travis is also the author of Avon's
PALACES   (84517-2/$3.95)

Buy these books at your local bookstore or use this coupon for ordering:

Avon Books, Dept BP, Box 767, Rte 2, Dresden, TN 38225
Please send me the book(s) I have checked above. I am enclosing $_____
(please add $1.00 to cover postage and handling for each book ordered to a maxima
three dollars). *Send check or money order*—no cash or C.O.D.'s please. Prices and nu
are subject to change without notice. Please allow six to eight weeks for delivery.

Name _____

Address _____

City _____ State/Zip _____